Take a Byte Out of Murder

Millie Mack

ISBN: 1517223601
ISBN 13: 9781517223601
Library of Congress Control Number: 2015914741
CreateSpace Independent Publishing Platform
North Charleston, South Carolina

Other Books by Millie Mack

Take a Dive for Murder (Book 1 in the Faraday Murder Series)

Take Stock in Murder (Book 2 in the Faraday Murder Series)

DEDICATION

This book is for my sister-in-law, Val, and all the
other health professionals who have spent
their careers helping others feel better.

ACKNOWLEDGMENTS

As always there are good people to thank for their help and support. I want to thank Pam from Mia Sorelle Nail Salon for providing the steps to make sure Carrie's french manicure was performed correctly.

There are several people to thank for their assistance with the development of the fictional Kingwood Medical Intel System developed for the plot of this book. Ann of Farrell Associates, LLC, thank you for your valuable advice on combining the different elements of medical programs into one system. Also for helping me find materials on the latest developments in medical software. Thanks, Dan, for your suggestion of adding a hardware component to the medical system. And thank you, Dr. Stephanie Linder, for being a wonderful doctor and pointing me in the right direction for finding resources on current medical developments.

I also want to thank Mark and Jason for maintaining and improving my website www.darkandstormynightmysteries.com.

And last but not least, thank you to Stacy, whose friendship and support always helps me get through the writing and editing of each book. Thanks for your first read of the manuscript. Your advice is always on target and of course was adopted.

1

"Happy New Year, darling." Charles Faraday bent down to kiss his wife, Carrie, and almost missed her lips. "Whoops." He straightened his six-foot-two-inch frame and pushed a tuft of silver hair from his forehead. "Have I told you, my s'marvelous Carrie, how s'marvelous you've been all these years of marriage? More than any man could ask."

"Exactly how many is 'all these years'?" Carrie asked mischievously.

"Oh no, you're not catching me on that one. I wrote it right here on this piece of paper."

Carrie watched Charles remove an imaginary piece of paper from his pocket and pretend to turn it from side to side.

"Yup, here it is. More than a lifetime, less than eternity, but all s'marvelous."

"Very cute. But should it ever come up again, it's been four wonderful years. I've got another tough question for you. How much alcohol have you had tonight?"

"I've had only one drink. After that one drink, I've had nothing but champagne, and that doesn't count," Charles said.

"It'll count tomorrow when your brain tries to remember how much you drank tonight." Carrie took her husband's arm and directed him toward the food buffet. "Perhaps we should get you a little food to go along with that one drink."

Carrie's parents' house was blessed with a very large dining room that was parallel to the living room. Both rooms ran the length of the house and were perfect for entertaining. Carrie noticed the food spread was more lavish than her parents had ever served at previous parties. Her mother had placed the extra leaves in the dining room table, and the caterer had filled the table from end to end with food. Carrie was sure this magnificent spread had more to do with her younger brother Norton's upcoming marriage to Ginny Ellwood than the celebration of the New Year. Ginny, her mother, and her father were honored guests at tonight's affair. The Ellwoods, in addition to becoming in-laws, were in the process of becoming business partners. While the wedding was important for the families, the merger affected the lives of all the people who worked for the two firms. For her parents, this party needed to be a success.

"With all the excitement of the party, I haven't had a chance to wish you both a Happy New Year!" Carrie's mother, Caroline, kissed both of them. Carrie spotted that her mother merely smiled at the dumb look on Charles's face as she wiped her lipstick smudge from his cheek.

Carrie's mother was a slim woman in her midsixties, with short curly hair like her daughter's. However, unlike her daughter she had allowed a certain amount of gray and silver to mix with the brown, which gave her hair a highlighted look.

Carrie's parents lived year-round at Pear Cove seaside resort, about seventy-five miles from Tri-City, where Carrie and Charles lived. A few decades earlier, her father had had the chance to purchase a software company. It was the beginning of the computer explosion, and her father's decision proved to be a profitable one. Her brother, Norton, was a software developer and was an integral part of the company's success.

It was important to Pear Cove not to lose one of their year-round employers. Carrie's father, mother, and brother made the decision to move here, rather than move the company to Tri-City. It was a good choice. Employees were loyal, and the company prospered. Cost of living was lower, and her parents were able to purchase a house right on the water.

Her father's new business partner, Randolph Ellwood, had also relocated his computer hardware company to Pear Cove from Tri-City. Now the two firms would merge, and Carrie knew both men could look toward comfortable full retirement, with their two sons managing the combined companies. Norton was fully involved in the business and Randolph's son, Fred, would join the new firm after he finished his military service.

"Are you two enjoying your vacation at your beach house? Not that we didn't enjoy having you stay with us when you came down for a day or two," Caroline added quickly. "But it's so nice to have a place of your own."

"We are. Pear Cove in the off-season is quite nice. And there's no reason for us to close the house Labor Day. Our house is heated, and the beach and the ocean views are very different from the summer months," Carrie said.

"I like that you can get around in your car. No pesky little traffic jams. And I can park anywhere I want," Charles said.

Caroline laughed and said, "Well, there are a few parking restrictions even in winter."

Carrie was helping Charles fill his plate. He was having trouble moving the food from the serving dish onto his plate. "Mom, everything looks absolutely delicious. You outdid yourself this year."

"Actually, I did very little. I simply decided what I wanted to serve, and Nick did all the work."

Carrie knew her mother was referring to Nick Pender, co-owner of the Barn Restaurant and Catering Company. Although her mother was a good cook, she had done the smart thing and let Nick handle all the food for this party.

"Nick brings one of his chefs to the house to prep everything on site. Then he makes sure his serving staff handles everything after the chef is finished. All I have to do is concentrate on the guests. It's a great way to have a party," Caroline said.

"Well, all the food looks delish," Carrie said.

"Be sure to give Charles some of the London broil with the sauce. The sauce is delicious. Oh, and give him a large spoonful of the pasta salad; it's filled with lobster, shrimp, and crab." Caroline stopped speaking and directed an apprehensive gaze around the room. "Everyone seems to be having a good time, don't you think?"

"Caroline, this is a swell party, and I can't wait to dig into this food." Charles took a forkful of the pasta salad. "Carrie and I are very glad we got to come here for New Year's. With Mother taking my nephew, Christopher, and one of his friends on a cruise during semester break, our annual holiday visit with them was cut short," he said through a mouthful of food.

"As you can see, Charles is having the time of his life, and I think everyone else is too. It seems to be a very congenial group," Carrie said.

A small burst of laughter emerged from the other side of the room. Carrie turned toward the source of the sound. It was Randolph and Helen Ellwood at the center of the laughter.

"The Ellwoods seem to be having a swell time," Charles said.

"Yes, they do. They really are very nice people," Caroline agreed.

"Mom, I haven't seen Dad or the other half of our newly engaged couple. Where's Norty?" Carrie asked.

She moved closer to her mother as Caroline lowered her voice. "Your father and your brother were going at it earlier. I know your father pulled him into his study for a chat. Be nice to him when you see him."

"Which one," Charles interrupted. "Harry or Norton?"

"What? Well, be nice to both of them, of course," Caroline said.

"I wish those two would stop 'going at it.' They really have more in common than either one realizes," Carrie said.

"It seems to me, the going at it has gotten worse since all this wedding stuff started." Charles received a sharp elbow from Carrie for his comment.

"Charles, you may be closer to the truth than your wife wants you to say. Norton told me just yesterday that he wasn't sure Ginny wanted to get married. Maybe it's just cold feet, but it's not making life any easier between Norton and your father. Well, I'd better mingle. If Charles needs some coffee, it's over there on the table in the corner."

"This bickering must be taking its toll," Carrie said as she watched her mother wander away. She had always seemed ageless. She kept her figure trim through tennis and swimming, and she always knew how to buy the right clothing for her age. But now for the first time she seemed older to Carrie.

"You don't really think the deal will go down the tubes if the kids don't marry?" Charles asked.

"Probably not. The merger talks between Dad and Randolph were taking place before Norton and Ginny announced their engagement. Although once the kids became engaged, business talks and the personal relationship seemed to also merge," Carrie said.

"Well, it's never good to mix business with personal relationships. Look at the situation with the Barringtons," Charles said.

Charles was referring to the murder case they had recently solved. The Barrington's family business had become entwined with the personal relationships of the sons, and that led to murder.

"Please don't remind me," Carrie said. "Being charged with the murder was not exactly pleasant."

"I know it wasn't pleasant for you. But we did solve the murder, and everything ended for the best. Anyway, now we have a normal life without crime."

"You sound like you miss not having a murder to solve. Fortunately, there's very little crime in Pear Cove," Carrie said.

"It was exciting, but this situation isn't anything like the intrigue of the Barrington murder. We're talking about a little spat, maybe some cold feet. It will all end happily without a murder." Charles ended his sentence with his best slightly inebriated Boris Karloff impression of the word *murder*.

Carrie finished filling their plates, and they began to circulate the room. They spent a few minutes with Helen and Randolph Ellwood. Carrie wondered if the Ellwoods had given any thought to why both Ginny and Norton were absent from the party. When they reached Hugh Simpson and his wife, Mary, the conversation quickly turned to Norton and his engagement to Ginny.

"Hey, where's that handsome brother of yours and his lovely bride to be?" Hugh asked.

Carrie had first met Hugh Simpson when she came back to Tri-City to solve the murder of Charles's brother, Jamie. Simpson had been the Faraday family lawyer for over thirty years. But he was more than a lawyer; he was a family friend. And now he was the lawyer for her family too.

"Oh, Hugh, those kids probably have a lot more exciting places to be on New Year's Eve than with their parents and the friends of their parents. We should be feeling lucky that we got half the young people in the family with Carrie and Charles," Mary said.

Hugh's wife, Mary, was slightly overweight, but Carrie noticed she never got any heavier. However, she never lost those few extra pounds, either. She was a positive person and always had a pleasant word for everyone. Her personality was a perfect match for Hugh, who dealt with so many serious problems.

"Mother said Dad and Norton were in his study. Perhaps one of us should ask them to join the party," Carrie said.

"No need, here's Harry now," Hugh said.

2

Carrie turned as her father emerged from his study. However, it wasn't Norton who was with him, but a man Carrie didn't recognize. Her initial thought was that this man was very gray. Dress for the party was casual, so most of the men wore sport coats with turtle necks or shirts with sweaters, like Charles. This gentleman was dressed in an expensive gray suit, with vest and tie. But it wasn't just his suit that was gray. He was balding with gray hair, and his glasses were platinum gray. His skin was pale, as was the color of his eyes. In fact, the only color the man displayed was the bright red of his bow tie. Carrie thought the tie must be his contribution to the holiday spirit.

"Hello, everyone. Carrie, you look marvelous as always," Harry said as he leaned over and kissed his daughter on the cheek. Harry extended his hand to Charles.

"Hello, Harry. Happy New Year," Charles said.

"I know Hugh and Mary met you earlier, so let me introduce you to my daughter, Carrie, and her husband, Charles Faraday. Children, this is Dr. Steven Bessinger."

Charles shook hands with the doctor. However, Carrie stood frozen for a moment, wondering why her father was consulting with a doctor. Carrie's look revealed concern.

"Don't worry dear. I'm not ill. The good doctor is a consultant on a little software program we're working on," her father said.

"Harry, I'm not sure—"

"Hugh, you're right. I know I shouldn't discuss business at a party, especially one of my wife's parties. But Dr. Bessinger raised some interesting thoughts that you and I should discuss from a legal perspective. Perhaps we could spend a moment while these folks chat."

"Of course," Hugh said.

"Dad, wasn't Norton with you?" Carrie asked.

"Norton? No, he left my study more than an hour ago. I assume he's out here somewhere."

Carrie watched as Hugh Simpson and her father returned to his study. Carrie, Mary, Charles, and Dr. Bessinger stood together for an awkward moment, not knowing what to say.

Then Carrie broke the silence. "Dr. Bessinger, do you specialize in a particular field of medicine?"

"Please call me Steven. And yes, my field is genetic and biometric testing."

"I'm afraid I'm not up with all the medical terminology. Although I've recently been hearing these terms," Carrie said.

"With biometric testing I mostly work as a consultant with employers—and of course the medical profession—to set up employee testing. Many employers have discovered that offering wellness programs is a benefit to both their workers and their bottom line. The testing screens employees for things like diabetes, heart disease, hypertension, cholesterol, and the basics, like weight and body mass. Employees like the benefit."

"Sounds excellent. You and I should talk about adding this for my employees," Charles said.

"I would be happy to discuss it with you," Steven said as he handed Charles his business card. "It's really a nice benefit. If something is discovered, employees can get treatment before it becomes a medical problem. For the employer, healthy employees don't miss work. And all the tests are confidential," Steven said.

"And the genetic testing?" Charles asked.

"This is one of the new exciting fields in medicine. Scientists are looking at the genetic structure of diseases and then testing the patients for these same genes," Steven said.

"There's been much in the news lately about gene testing," Mary said excitedly. "Scientists are discovering the genes related to particular diseases. Then the weak gene can be altered prior to the disease materializing. Or if the disease is present, doctors can isolate and treat only the weak gene causing the problem."

Carrie was impressed with Mary's knowledge and wondered if she had done the research because it was something personal.

"Unfortunately, the news is getting ahead of the science. This area is still very much in its infancy. On the other hand, some great advances have been made with cancer diagnoses, especially with breast and lung cancer cases. It's all about predicting, diagnosing, treating, and preventing," Steven added.

"And how are you consulting with Dad?" Carrie asked.

"Well, of course I can't speak for your father. Perhaps you should ask him about the specifics of the work I'm doing."

Carrie noticed that Steven's eyes were darting about as if he was looking for someone or perhaps something to interrupt the conversation.

"Folks, it's been a pleasure meeting you. But if you'll excuse me I really would like to get some of this wonderful food I see everyone enjoying."

Carrie, Charles, and Mary watched as the doctor headed to the buffet table. The three exchanged small talk for a few more moments, and then Mary moved away to chat with another couple. Carrie looked at Charles, who seemed to be recovering from his alcohol overindulgence now that he had some food.

"Did you notice how quickly Dr. Bessinger escaped when I asked what Dad was developing? And what was so important that Dad had to pull Hugh away from the party?" Carrie asked.

"It was obvious that Dr. Bessinger felt he shouldn't be the one to discuss your father's work," Charles said. "If we want to find out, I'm afraid we'll have to ask your dad."

Charles and Carrie continued to mingle with the guests until around one thirty. Charles was about to pour another glass of champagne.

"Oh no, you don't. No more champagne. Let's get our coats and blow this joint."

"But darling, I'm not driving, and all that food made me thirsty."

"You'll be driving tomorrow—driving right to the drug-store to get headache medicine." Charles made a face, but

Carrie continued, "I'll get our coats while you say good-bye to my folks and let them know we're leaving. Tell Mom I'll call her tomorrow."

"Why aren't you saying good-bye to your parents?"

"I don't want to get drafted for the cleanup crew. It's New Year's, and the night is still young." She made a clicking sound and winked at Charles as she went to get their coats.

3

A few minutes later Carrie and Charles were walking along the beach headed back to their house. Carrie was completely bundled up in her new cashmere coat, a Christmas present from Charles. She wore a hooded scarf and tennis shoes. She carried her dress shoes in a cloth bag and held it tightly against her rib cage. Charles held her free hand.

"You know it's the shoes that make the outfit," Charles said. "You're the height of fashion in those sneakers." He started tugging at her shoe bag.

"Will you stop fooling around? I'm going to drop this bag," Carrie said as she ran slightly ahead in the sand.

"You're protecting that bag of shoes like it's a brick of gold." Charles started to run after her.

Charles found that winter sand was easier to walk on than the hot soft summer sand, which seeped in around your feet. In the winter if you walked near the water the ground was as solid as a road.

Charles was quite content walking home via the beach. By this route they lived a little more than a mile from Carrie's parents. It was several miles if he drove the car. The main road went inland to the village before it came back out to the shoreline.

They had nearly reached their home when Charles caught up with his wife and turned her toward him.

"You know, I do love you, darling, more than I can express in words. Have I wished you a Happy New Year?" He hugged and kissed her and then pulled back abruptly. "Golly, what do you have on under that coat? It felt like I was holding a suit of armor."

Carrie unbuttoned her coat, took out a plastic bag, and removed a large bottle of champagne. She held the bottle up and said, "For us!"

Charles took the champagne bottle and removed the foil. Then Charles watched as Carrie removed an oversize beach towel from the bag. She spread the beach towel on the sand and took two slightly crumpled paper cups from her pockets.

"Where shall I shoot the cork?" Charles asked as he looked around the beach.

"I know," Carrie said as she pointed to the moon above them.

Charles aimed the bottle and watched the cork head straight for the moon above them. "Bull's-eye."

Charles helped Carrie sit down and then poured the champagne. They sat huddled together on the beach towel.

"I propose a toast to the most wonderful woman. I love her dearly. And I will visit her faithfully every Sunday while she's in jail serving time for stealing champagne."

"And to my husband, whom I love so much that I'd even steal for him," she said as they gently slapped cups together.

Charles pulled Carrie close to him as they drank the champagne. Then he felt Carrie suddenly pull away and lean forward. She was staring down the beach.

"What is it, darling?" Charles asked.

"Someone is walking toward us. It looks like a man."

"Well, it's a public beach. And since it's New Year's, people are out and about."

"Wait a minute! He's stopped. Look—he's found something on the beach. He's stooping over it," Carrie said.

"I see it—that large dark object. Maybe it's a beached shark. Or maybe it's Jonah's original whale visiting our shore."

"Really, I think it looks a little too small for a whale. Charles, look! He's collapsed in the sand. Is he trying to gather the object in his arms?"

"It looked like it, but now he's up. He must be drunk. See how he's weaving as he tries to run?"

"Wait he's turning. He's coming back to the object. He's checking it over a second time. Can you see what time it is?" Carrie asked.

Charles hit the button that illuminated his watch. "It's almost three. Two fifty-three, to be exact." Then Charles looked up. "Hey, where did he go?"

"Look at our house. Follow the light by the steps down to the beach and then along the dune about fifty feet. Looks like he's trying to run, but the sand must be holding him back."

Charles followed along the dune with his eyes. "Okay, I see him. Look, he's turned. He's running up the steps to our house. Come on, let's go."

"Go? I don't particularly want to run into him."

"You've run into him many times before," Charles said.

"What are you talking about?"

"Carrie, I'm pretty sure that man is Norton. Norton has a certain walk, and I got a brief glimpse when he moved under the light on the steps."

"I thought the guy looked familiar. Why is he running?"

"He was probably frightened by two dark shadows moving on the beach. But the real question is what Norton was doing on the beach. And where's Ginny?" Charles said.

"Maybe he was clearing his head after the skirmish with Dad. Come on, Charles. As lovely as drinking champagne with you on the beach under the moon may be, I'm starting to get cold."

"Cold, my foot! You want to go over and find out what the object is that Norton was examining."

They gathered up their towel and quickly threw the other items back into the plastic bag. The cold sea air had a sobering effect, and they walked quickly toward the dark object on the beach. At twenty-five feet, Charles laid the plastic bag on the ground. "Wait here. It might only be a washed-up sea creature, but let me check."

Charles was surprised when Carrie raised no objections to not accompanying him. Maybe she was concerned about what he might find as he moved closer to examine the object. Charles returned to Carrie within a few seconds.

Carrie almost whispered, "Is it a sea creature?"

"It's certainly a creature of sorts. We need to get to the house and call the police."

"Charles, what's wrong?"

"It's a dead body."

"A dead body…" Carrie's last word trailed away. Then she recovered and asked, "Did you recognize who it is?"

"Oh yes, I recognized the body. It's hard not to recognize that blond hair. It's Ginny Ellwood."

4

"Oh my heavens. Are you sure she's dead?" Carrie said tentatively.

"I don't think there's any doubt. There's a scarf tightly wrapped around her neck. Look, are you okay to go up to the house and call the police? I'll stay here with the body."

"Yes, I'll make the call. Hopefully, if that was Norty, I can catch up with him and find out what's going on."

Carrie turned and started toward the house, but Charles reached out and grabbed her arm. "You know, I've changed my mind. We'll go together, and then I'll come back down and wait for the police."

"Don't be silly. I'm not afraid of Norton." She paused. "But just in case it wasn't Norton, I'd like your company. Should we call Mom and Dad?"

"For right now, I don't think we should call anyone other than the police."

Charles picked up their bundle and took Carrie's hand, and they headed to the house. They tried to hurry, but it was difficult. The sand nearer the house hadn't been packed down by the waves. When they reached the house, Charles saw no sign of Norton or anyone else.

Charles called the police. In the few minutes before the police arrived, Carrie and Charles changed into jeans. While they were changing, Charles noticed that Carrie was wiping her eyes and then applying fresh makeup to cover the redness.

"Are you okay?" Charles asked.

"I just can't believe that Ginny is dead. It's bad enough to die young, but murdered! Who would want to kill Ginny?"

Charles took Carrie in his arms and held her tight. He didn't have time to answer Carrie's question as he heard the sound of approaching sirens.

"Should we tell the police we saw my brother?" Carrie asked quickly.

"Let's say we saw a man but not volunteer our suspicion that it was Norton. After all, you didn't think it was Norton until I mentioned the possibility."

~

"I'm sorry, sir. We would prefer that you stay inside." This statement was made by a very young police officer who barely seemed to fit into his uniform. He made it clear that Charles wasn't needed or wanted on the beach.

"I was going to show you where the body is," Charles said. "Plus, I'm sure one of your superiors will want to question me."

"I'm sure we'll find the body, sir. You said it was to the left of your property near the water's edge. You see, we want to preserve the crime area without additional people tramping around. However, if you could turn on any additional outside lights, we would appreciate that help. One of the detectives will be in shortly to interview you and your wife." And with that the young officer left to join the investigation.

Charles was annoyed as he flipped the electric switches for the back floodlights. He then strolled to the front of the house to view the scene.

Charles and Carrie's house was off Shore Pike to the north of the town of Pear Cove. At the point the pike took a turn to the left toward the village, a sharp right brought the traveler down a side road. This side road continued along the beach for two miles until it ended at the water's edge. On both sides of the road were houses. Midway down the road was a small general store that sold gas and a combination of food items and seashore supplies, including bait. At the very end of the road was the Barn restaurant and marina.

Things were pretty quiet in the small town of Pear Cove, especially in the off-season. When Charles called about a murder, it seemed every squad car in the area responded. The police cars lined the road for as far as the eye could see.

Charles noticed that with all the commotion, the police were still allowing cars to go to and from the Barn. The Barn was the only restaurant of quality to announce it would be open all night on New Year's Eve.

Thank heavens, they're letting the cars pass through, Charles thought. *I wouldn't want to deal with the wrath of Otto Kolvik if he lost business tonight.* Charles watched as every car slowed down to a crawl, carefully navigating between all of the police cars. Several cars came to full stops as they attempted to get information from the policemen directing traffic.

Charles returned to the kitchen and fixed himself another cup of coffee. He sipped his coffee standing at the open door, looking out at the beach. "Preserve the crime area, my foot. There are hundreds of them out there. Fortunately for us, most of our neighbors aren't in Pear Cove for the holiday. They're missing this circus."

Many of the houses were only used in the summer months because they lacked central heating. When Charles had their house remodeled he added the heating system plus several fireplaces to provide added warmth from the cold winter winds. He also redesigned the rooms to allow maximum views of the ocean. The kitchen, with a large open dining area, was at the back of the house, with a marvelous view of the water. The kitchen sliding door opened onto a deck that wound around past the master bedroom and den. The living room was located at the front of the house along with an open stairway that led to the second floor, where there were three more bedrooms with ocean views. Charles and Carrie didn't need all this space, but it came in handy when their nephew Christopher, Charles's mom, or other guests joined them during the summer months.

"Come in, darling. It's cold with that door open. I know you're feeling left out because you want to be part of the investigation. But you can see just as much with the door closed," Carrie said.

"I don't feel left out. I don't want to be part of that group. I just don't like the way we're being treated."

"We're being treated the way anyone would be treated at a crime scene. They want to keep the public, the witnesses, and even amateur sleuths at a distance until they finish gathering the evidence." Carrie was busy transferring more coffee from the smaller kitchen pot into a large urn that the couple used for parties. Lots of police meant lots of coffee.

"We're on a dead-end road. There's no need for all those police cars to have their flashing lights running. They don't want people tramping through the area, and yet they're doing everything to attract attention. And they have those special beach patrol vehicles with the big wheels running all over the sand."

"It looks like those vehicles are providing light and moving equipment into place. Try not to be too mad at the police when they come to question us. I don't want them to treat us as adversaries. Here's the aspirin you wanted." Carrie shook two tablets into Charles's hand.

Charles took the aspirin with a gulp of coffee. "How can we be adversaries when you're providing all this coffee for them?" His annoyance was interrupted by someone knocking on the sliding door. "Is that additional coffee ready? I'm sure they're ready for more refills."

Charles opened the door. There were two plainclothesmen standing there. "The coffee is over there on the kitchen counter. Help yourself." And he started to walk away.

"Mr. Faraday?"

Charles stopped and turned.

"I'm Detective Hilton. Could we come in and talk with you and your wife about the discovery of the body?" He presented a badge in a leather case.

"Oh, yes, of course. Come in. Darling, the detectives are here."

Detective Hilton spent several seconds trying to wipe sand off his tan suede boots on the kitchen doormat. He was slightly overweight, and his brown suit jacket stuck out below his short green hooded jacket. The other detective was much larger. He was almost as tall as Charles, but with more weight. Charles noticed as he entered the room that, unlike the crumpled Hilton, this man was wearing a very expensive overcoat covering a tuxedo. His shoes weren't soft suede boots but quality polished-leather shoes. The duo was certainly an odd couple.

Carrie came out from behind the kitchen counter wiping her hands on a dish towel. Charles saw a look of surprise on her face as she approached the two men.

"Chief Engler! We certainly didn't expect the chief of police to be here. Charles, this is Chief Engler."

"You can't be a chief if you don't know what's happening on your streets," Engler replied.

He had an affable face and a very pleasant smile, but Charles wasn't fooled. Engler was the type that would smile, give you a good slap on the back, and then sell you twenty tickets to the policemen's gala.

Charles and the chief shook hands. "Carrie, this is Detective Hilton."

"Would either of you like some coffee?" Carrie asked.

"That would be very nice, ma'am. It's mighty cold out there tonight. But don't you bother, ma'am. I see you have everything right here on the counter," Detective Hilton said.

Charles watched as Chief Engler took off his overcoat, folded it neatly, and carefully draped it over the back of the kitchen chair. He had no sooner placed it on the chair when Baxter, the Faradays' long-haired orange-and-white cat, jumped onto the chair. He started sniffing the coat. Charles didn't scold the cat. After all, it was Baxter's chair.

"Baxter, get down," Carrie said as she lifted the cat off the chair and dropped him carefully to the floor. Carrie apologized to Chief Engler for Baxter's behavior, but the chief didn't appear pleased. Baxter swung his tail high into the air as he headed for the living room.

Carrie waited while Engler shook out his overcoat and replaced it on the chair. He then proceeded to fix a cup of coffee. Engler put extra sugar in his coffee, but Hilton took his black. Carrie showed them into the living room, where Charles was already seated on the sofa with Baxter curled up on his lap. Carrie realized she should have taken Hilton's coat when they were in the kitchen. He placed his coffee on the table, removed his coat, and dropped it in a pile next to his feet. Carrie started to pick up the coat.

"Don't bother, Mrs. Faraday. This coat doesn't deserve a hook, especially after being out on the beach."

"Hilton, if we could get started. I'm sure these folks would like to get us out of here, so they can get to bed," Engler suggested.

Carrie watched as Hilton pulled out a retractable pen and a small spiral notebook.

"If we could start with you two reviewing exactly what happened leading up to the discovery of the body," Detective Hilton said.

Charles and Carrie looked at each other, and Carrie nodded to Charles.

"My wife and I were returning from a New Year's Eve party. We stopped on the beach to drink a toast to the New Year."

Hilton interrupted Charles. "Was your toast champagne by any chance?"

"Why yes, it was, but how…" Carrie hesitated and then smiled. "Of course, you found the cork."

Hilton nodded and turned back to Charles. "You were saying that you were walking home from a party. You really mean you drove home and then went for a walk on the beach?"

"No, we walked home. The party was hosted by Mrs. Faraday's parents. Using the beach is quicker and shorter than going through the village when coming from their house. And on a clear night like this…well, it's a little more romantic." Carrie had the feeling that Charles was beginning to ramble. She knew he was definitely feeling uncomfortable.

"I see. What time would you have left your parents' home, Mrs. Faraday?"

"I believe it was a little after two o'clock," Carrie said.

"And you walked straight home, Mr. Faraday?"

Carrie felt they were in a tennis match. Hilton was throwing a question to one side and then back to the other. It was obvious he was using this method to try to fluster the couple and look for holes in their story. She couldn't help but wonder where they were going with all this.

"No, we already told you. We stopped to open the champagne and toast the New Year. While we were drinking the champagne we saw a figure coming down the beach. The figure stopped and bent over a dark object on the beach. We watched for a few minutes. Then the figure turned, walked past the dunes, and—I assume—went up to the road."

Carrie waited to see if there were any additional questions before adding, "My husband went over to see what the object was on the beach. We discovered the body and came up to the house to call the police. I believe we called a little after three."

"Actually, you called at 3:11 a.m." Hilton consulted his notebook. Then he looked up from his writing. "Is there anything else?"

"No, that's about all there is," Charles said.

"Do you have anything additional to add, Mrs. Faraday?"

"It's just as my husband said. There wasn't much to it. It all happened pretty fast."

They all sat silently for a minute. Then the chief broke the silence. "You don't mind if I ask a few additional questions. Many times people really see more than they think they have."

"We don't mind. Ask all the questions you want," Carrie responded.

"Was the person you saw a man or a woman, Mrs. Faraday?" Engler asked.

"Well, let me think. When we first saw the figure it could have been either. However, when the figure moved past the dune and up the steps, I believed it was a man."

"You didn't recognize the man?"

"We weren't close enough to see who it was, Chief Engler," Carrie answered quickly. After all, as Charles had pointed out, she hadn't recognized the man as Norty.

"How about when he passed under the light near the steps. Couldn't you see who it was?" Hilton asked.

"The light? The light over the steps isn't very bright. We didn't have the search lights on, as we do now. Plus, it was a split second."

"Neither of you thought to call out?" Hilton continued.

"Good grief, no. Why would we call out to a stranger?" Carrie asked trying to sound sincere.

"I see." Again there was a pause while Detective Hilton took his time making notes. Then he had another sip of coffee. "And did you think it was a body, Mr. Faraday, when you saw this stranger go up to it?"

"No, actually, we thought it was some sort of a beached sea creature."

"You said you went over and examined the body, Mr. Faraday."

"I really didn't examine the body. I simply checked to see what it was," Charles said.

"And you didn't think it was important to tell us that you knew the victim. That you knew the dead body on the beach was Ginny Ellwood."

"I didn't tell you in my account of the events because I knew you would do your official identification of the body," Charles said.

"Actually, we prefer that you tell us everything you know and not rely on what you think we may or may not discover. To clarify, you did recognize the body was Ginny Ellwood?"

"Yes, of course I did," Charles said.

The chief rose and walked back to the coffeepot. As he was pouring himself another cup of coffee, he asked, "Mr. Faraday, did you or your wife call anyone to tell them of your discovery?"

"No. The only call we placed was to the police. We felt it wasn't our place to notify others, especially since it was a devastating discovery," Charles said.

"Not even Mrs. Faraday's parents—or her brother, to let him know that his fiancée had been murdered?" Engler asked.

Carrie looked at Charles but said nothing.

"You see, I keep up with what happens socially in Pear Cove. I'm fully aware that your brother Barton is engaged to the murder victim, Mrs. Faraday."

"My brother-in-law's name is Norton. Exactly what's your point, Chief Engler?" Charles asked.

"My point is simply this. I believe you saw the murder. As the murderer ran to escape, you recognized him as Mrs. Faraday's brother. You called out to him, and then the three of you concocted this story to help protect him and give him a chance to get away. Before calling the police, you probably called a lawyer and Mrs. Faraday's parents."

"This is pure supposition on your part, Chief Engler. And you're wrong. Our phone records will show that the only call made from this house was to the police. We didn't confront the man on the beach. It happened exactly as we stated," Charles said.

"Well, this isn't supposition." From his coat pocket he removed a small plastic evidence bag that had a man's ring in it. "The ring is inscribed, "All my love G. E." Have either of you seen this ring before?"

Carrie felt that if Chief Engler had been a dragon, the sentence would have ended with a flame coming from his nostril. She took the bag from Chief Engler and handed it to Charles.

"I've never seen it before," Charles said and passed the bag back to Carrie.

Carrie turned the bag in her hand. She was pretty sure this was a very expensive ring. It looked to be solid gold and was very heavy. "This is the first I've seen this ring. Where did you find this?"

"We found it on the beach under Ginny's, the victim's, body. You see, we believe Norton and Ginny were on the beach. She told him their relationship was over. He took the ring off to give back to her when his anger got the better of him. He may have killed her in a moment of passion, but it's still murder. The rumors on the street say this was more than a marriage. It was a business merger. It would be a major disappointment financially to your family if the marriage didn't occur. After all, your family seems to do very well when choosing marriage partners, Mrs. Faraday."

Charles stood up so quickly he practically dumped Baxter on the floor. "That's enough, Engler. You have no way of knowing when or if my brother-in-law gave that ring back—or even if it was his ring. You're not only making wild accusations, but you're insulting."

Carrie felt the ring was Engler's trump card. He had played it well. Certainly she and Charles were surprised by its existence. That's when she knew the interview was over.

Detective Hilton stood and in a calm voice asked, "Do either of you wish to change anything in the statement you have given?"

"Yes, I'd like to add something. I'd like to remind you, Chief Engler, that—"

Carrie stood and touched Charles's arm. "We have nothing to change in our statement. And if you have nothing more to ask, it has been a very long night."

Hilton looked at Chief Engler, who gave a slight nod. "No, we're finished for now. Needless to say we would like both of you remain available if the need arises for additional information. If you go back to the city for any reason, please let us know," Hilton said.

Engler put on his coat and then asked, "Do either of you know where your brother is right now?"

"Sorry, Engler, we've no idea where my brother is." Carrie too had dropped the formal title when addressing the police chief.

"Not to worry, we'll catch up with him. Oh, and by the way, I know you two have been involved with the police solving two other murders. I want to make this clear! While those police departments may have indulged your little interferences, we at the Pear Cove Police Department don't need or want the help of amateurs. Do you understand?"

"Good night, Engler. Good night, Detective Hilton."

As soon as the two men had cleared the kitchen slider, Charles flipped off the deck's light.

After the interview, Carrie and Charles were both exhausted. They had done little to protect Norton from police theories and, in fact, may have hurt him. Carrie thought of calling Norton but knew that the phone records would be checked. Any phone call would only add fire to the police theory of Norton's involvement and their conspiracy to protect him.

Charles's last act was to turn out the beach floodlights and lock the doors. "Let them use their own light and buy their own coffee," he said.

Carrie unplugged the coffeepot and turned the lights out in the kitchen. Within minutes, they were both in their bed and sound asleep.

6

Charles all too early discovered that Chief Engler was true to his word. During the early morning hours while Charles and Carrie slept, Engler and Detective Hilton acted on their theory that Norton had committed the murder.

At nine the next morning, Charles awoke to the sound of a ringing phone. The phone was on Carrie's side of the bed because most of the time the calls were for her. But on this morning Charles reached over Carrie to answer the phone.

"Charles. Oh good, I'm glad I got you. You and Carrie need to get over here right away!" Charles sat straight up in bed as Carrie stirred next to him.

"Caroline, calm down! If you're calling about Ginny, we all ready know. I discovered the body."

"Yes, I know. I can't believe that darling girl, our little Ginny…" Caroline caught her breath. "I'm not calling about last night's awful news—and by the way, why didn't you call us last night?" Before Charles could answer, Caroline continued, "But never mind that now. We'll discuss that later. Here's the latest update. Early this morning, the police arrested Norton for Ginny's murder. They arrested him right here in our driveway. We never knew they had him until he called us from the police station. Your father called Simpson, and they both went over to the station to find out what's happening."

Charles was having trouble waking up and catching everything Caroline said as she raced through the information.

"Now calm yourself, Caroline. Make some coffee. We'll be right over."

Charles hung up the phone and turned to Carrie. "Carrie! Carrie, wake up! We need to get to your mother. That big idiot arrested Norton."

Carrie moaned as Charles gently shook her. "Come on, upsy-daisy." Charles pushed his wife toward the edge of the bed. "I'll get you a glass of tomato juice and grab a couple more aspirin for my head."

∾

Charles and Carrie dressed quickly and were in the car in a matter of minutes. Carrie wanted Charles to turn in the direction of the country store for some coffee. But Charles reminded her that Caroline would have fresh-brewed coffee ready for them, and he hoped there might be some leftover pastries from last night's party.

When they reached the end of their street, Charles noticed there was still a police car parked on the grass at the intersection.

He turned right onto the highway and watched in the rearview mirror. The car stayed in place, but it looked like the policeman inside the car was calling in a report. There was very little traffic on New Year's morning, and Charles pulled the car into the Kingsfords' driveway in record time.

Everyone entered the Kingsford house through the back door. The front door faced the water and was located on the opposite side of the driveway. As Charles reached for the kitchen door handle, the door swung open.

"Come in, come in." Caroline took her daughter's hand and led the way to the kitchen. "I'm so glad to see you two. Neither Harry nor Hugh has called. I've no idea what's happening."

Charles went over to the coffee maker. He fixed cups for himself and Carrie and replenished Caroline's cup. Upon taking his seat at the kitchen table, he discovered happily that there was a plate of miniature pastries waiting for him. He winked at Carrie.

"What time did all this police action with Norty occur? I don't think the police left our house until after six this morning," Carrie said.

"I only got a few pieces of information from your father before he flew out of here. When Norton arrived at his apartment he saw the police waiting for him. He decided to come here to get his father's advice, but the police were apparently watching our home, too. When he arrived here a little after six o'clock, the police nabbed him. He was taken into custody and allowed his one phone call. That's when he called us, and we learned that Ginny was found dead on the beach. Your father called Hugh and then left for the police station. When it got to be nine o'clock and I hadn't heard anything, I called you two."

Caroline took a drink of coffee and then said, "What do you mean the police left your house around six o'clock? You said you found the body. How come I seem to be the only one who doesn't know what's going on?"

Charles was about to answer Caroline's questions when the phone rang. Charles shrugged and took another pastry as Caroline left the kitchen to take the call in the living room.

"I can't believe Chief Engler arrested my brother. While his men were still gathering evidence on the beach, he decided to arrest Norty."

"Actually, now that I've had time to think about it, I doubt if Engler arrested Norton. I don't think he has enough evidence. However, Norton would be on the top of Engler's list for questioning."

"I hope you're right," Carrie said. "Mom sure is worried."

"Simpson is a fine lawyer. He won't let Engler get away with anything. I'm sure once the questioning is complete, Simpson will get your brother out of there," Charles declared.

Caroline returned to the kitchen. "That was your father. Simpson is wrapping a few things up with the police, but they're getting ready to leave. Norton is free to go." Caroline sat down in her chair, wiped her eyes, and began to wring her handkerchief. "I'm sorry, I guess I overreacted. The news of your brother being taken to the police station and learning that Ginny was murdered was a shock. She was murdered, wasn't she?"

"There seems to be little doubt that it was murder," Charles said.

Charles took the next few minutes to tell Caroline how he and Carrie had discovered the body. Although he left out the gory details about the method of murder, Caroline continuously wiped her eyes with her handkerchief during his explanation. He ended by telling Caroline why they decided not to call any of the family at the time of discovery: for fear it would work against Norton.

"I never thought of the police checking phone calls when I called you two this morning. But I wouldn't have cared. My only concern was to get help for Norton. Especially since you two have already solved two murders," Caroline said. "But since he's free, I guess we won't need your help. Now we need to give our support to the Ellwoods during this sad time."

"Caroline." Charles pulled his chair over next to hers and took her hands. "I think Norton is still going to need our help. Simpson may have convinced the police to release him for now. But I'm sure he's still the prime suspect. While we've a quiet moment, let me ask a couple of questions. Maybe we can get a timeline for the events leading up to Ginny's death. Did Norton drive Ginny to the party last night?"

"No. The Ellwoods were attending a christening earlier in the afternoon, and Ginny came with her parents."

"Mom, how was Norton? I mean, did he seem upset or nervous yesterday?"

"Actually, I was surprised when he showed up early for our party. You know how boys are. They usually don't hang around the kitchen when there's a party in the making. But here he was, sampling the food. Then he started kidding with the catering staff, and he even greeted the guests as they arrived."

"You told Carrie and me last night that Harry and Norton were going at it. When did that occur?" Charles asked.

"I'm not quite sure. I know guests were already arriving. Everything seemed to be going along just fine. It was nearly ten when I noticed neither one of them was around. He must have called Norty in after his cigar with Randolph."

"Were the Ellwoods here at that time?" Carrie asked.

Charles looked at Carrie. He always found it somewhat amazing that they were able to get inside each other's minds. That was the very question he was about to ask.

"Oh, yes, they arrived around nine. Your father had received his monthly cigar club selection earlier in the day. Soon after Randolph arrived, those two went off to your father's study to partake of the latest installment."

"Has Norty said anything about the relationship between him and Ginny? Maybe they were having a few issues. You know, a few little spats, a little bit of cold feet," Charles asked.

Caroline took a deep breath and began to smooth out her damp handkerchief on her lap. "Not in so many words, but a mother knows. Like that christening the Ellwoods attended. If you're engaged, you take you fiancé with you, don't you? Then there were a couple of Friday and Saturday nights where Norton popped in for dinner. Once Norty was engaged, I figured I'd never see him again for a meal."

"He never said anything specifically about their relationship?" Carrie asked.

"No, not a word. I figured they would work it out."

"Caroline, I have to ask this next question. I expect Carrie will give me a kick under the table, but we need to know everything if we're going to help. What about the business deal between Harry and Randolph? If the kids decided not to get married, was the merger deal off?"

The tension was so great in the room that none of them heard the kitchen door open.

7

"My business deals don't revolve around the escapades of two young people in love. They're founded in sound business judgment," Carrie's father announced as he entered the kitchen with Hugh and Norton.

Charles felt this statement was made for Norton's benefit as much as it was for the other people in the kitchen.

Harry kissed Caroline on the cheek. "Is there more of that coffee for us?"

"None for me, Mom. I'm going to go up to my old bedroom. I'm exhausted, physically and emotionally," Norton said.

Charles could see the exhaustion in Norton's face as he left them in the kitchen.

"Don't forget, Norton. You need to stay in Pear Cove and let your father know where you are at all times. If you leave the area, even for business, you need to let the police know. And finally, please keep in touch with me, especially if you think of anything additional." As Hugh turned to leave he added, "Or tell Charles or Carrie. They have a way of helping with these types of situations."

"Wait a minute, Hugh. Was Norton charged with anything?" Charles asked.

"No, they really didn't have any evidence to charge him. But they did get sticky over the fact Norton couldn't leave the area. We solved the issue by saying his father would be responsible for him. We also promised that Norton would be available for any additional questioning. And as you heard me remind him, he can't leave Pear Cove without notifying the police. It seemed like a small compromise in order to get out of the police station."

"How is Norty doing?" Carrie asked her father.

"He's putting on a brave face, but I know inside he is devastated. When I arrived at the police station he practically collapsed in my arms. I held him until the tears stopped and he regained his composure. I know he really loved Ginny. Then there's the other matter," her father answered.

"What other matter?" Carrie asked.

"Survivor's guilt. He's thinking if he had been with her, he could have prevented what happened. He's going over and over the events of the evening trying to figure out why Ginny left without him. He thinks if he'd had been a little quicker catching up with her he could have stopped—"

"I feel so sad about what happened to our darling Ginny. But now I'm speaking as a mother. I'm glad Norton wasn't with Ginny. I don't want to even think what could have happened to Norton if he had been there too," Caroline said.

Harry patted Caroline's hand and continued, "Then of course he's trying to deal with his grief and has to deal with the police. That Chief Eagle is a pompous ass."

"Dad, his name is Engler. Does anyone know if Engler is from Pear Cove?" Carrie asked.

"Yes. In fact, his family goes back several hundred years. They were part of the original fishing village along the peninsula. They turned a boat into a couple of boats, then into a fleet. They added a processing plant and a packaging plant, and now their seafood supplies most of the restaurants in the Tri-County area and along the coast," Hugh said.

"I've never heard of Eggler seafood," Harry said, ignoring his daughter's previous name correction.

"No, but I bet you have all heard of Mediterranean Seafood. That's the family business name."

Charles and everyone else at the table nodded in recognition of a well-known name.

"From what I understand, the business pretty much runs itself, so Engler decided to try his hands at politics. I think this is the cause of our problem. Being chief of police in a small resort town is just the start of wanting to go after bigger political jobs. Visibility from a nicely solved murder case is always good for a politician. That's why I think we have Mr. Engler personally handling this case," Hugh said.

"Great, so my brother becomes a suspect in a murder case because of this guy's political ambitions. What happens next?" Carrie asked.

"They really don't have anything more than some circumstantial timing," Hugh said.

"You mean circumstantial evidence," Caroline corrected.

"No. I mean timing. They don't really have any evidence. That's why I was able to convince Engler not to look foolish by sending a premature case to the district attorney."

"Then we'd better start working right away to figure out this case. Harry, we need to understand what happened last night. What did you and Norton argue about? Did it have to do with the engagement?" Charles asked.

"Look, folks, I really need to leave. Mary has her relatives coming over for a brunch, and I don't want to start the New Year in the doghouse," Hugh said.

"Are you sure you're not afraid of hearing damaging evidence?" Harry asked with a grin.

"No, Harry, I'm not. Besides, knowing the talents of Carrie and Charles, I'm sure by the end of the week they'll have this whole thing solved. I'll be in touch." Hugh grabbed his jacket, kissed Caroline on the cheek, and left.

"Okay, Dad, you're up. Tell us what happened last night. And don't give us the executive-summary version. Give us all the details and when they occurred," Carrie said.

Harry hesitated for a moment. "I'm not much for discussing things, but if you two think this will help, here goes. I was mingling with the guests, when Randolph, Caroline, and Ginny arrived. When the ladies started chatting with friends, Randolph asked if we could talk. That was fine with me, because I had received the latest installment from the cigar club. We went into my study to have a smoke and a talk. This was shortly after nine."

Harry stopped talking while he removed his brown-tweed sport coat and poured another cup of coffee. "I got out the cigars and poured us each a brandy. After a few minutes of small talk, Randolph asked me if I was aware the kids were having problems. He didn't think it was anything too serious. Just that they had decided to give each other a little more space. Randolph used the example of the family christening that had occurred earlier in the day. Ginny said Norton had backed out. She went to the christening with her parents and then left early. Randolph felt she left the christening party early because she was embarrassed that Norton wasn't with her. She returned home in time to change for our party."

"Did you and Randolph specifically discuss changes in the merger based on any changes in the kids' relationship?"

"Charles, I've always thought your ability to cut to the chase a fine quality. However, I must admit it's more uncomfortable when I'm on the receiving end of the question."

Charles felt a little uncomfortable being called out by Harry, but he knew his question was important.

"We both agreed that Norton was getting a mild touch of cold feet. But let me state this clearly. The merger deal was complete, regardless of what Ginny and Norton decided to do. Then we finished our cigars and brandy talking about our joint project."

"Well, I don't how the others feel, but that sounds pretty mild. In fact, that's exactly what I told Carrie and Charles. They're taking a little time to think about the commitment and its importance. Every couple does that," Caroline said.

"Dad, what happened when you and Norton talked?"

"Well, it's not as you might think. I didn't call him in to tell him, how do you young people say? 'Get it together.' We may have had problems communicating when he was a teenager. But I've been mighty proud of Norton and the work he has done at the company. I wanted to offer him support. Tell him we all go through this doubting phase when we take a big step like marriage."

Charles looked at Carrie. He pointed to himself and shook his head no. He received a gentle punch from her.

She turned back to her father. "Dad, I always knew you were a softy, but Mom said she heard shouting."

"It was the strangest thing. Here I'm ready to offer support. Norton says that it isn't him—it's Ginny who wants time and space. I tell him there's no reason to feel embarrassed, and he gets upset. He says he didn't refuse to go with Ginny to the christening; he wasn't invited. Then he stamped out of the room. It was a short and one-sided conversation."

"What happened next?" Charles asked.

"I returned to the party. Later I ran into Dr. Bessinger, who asked for a few minutes of my time. By the time we finished talking it was the New Year. As you know, when Dr. Bessinger and I returned to the party we ran into you two. When I looked around both Ginny and Norton were gone. I assumed they went off together."

"Harry, have you given any of this information to the police?" Charles asked.

"The police didn't ask me any questions. And I certainly didn't volunteer any information."

"Look, Harry, I guarantee the police will be following up on the movements of both Norton and Ginny. If you get questioned, tell them the truth, but avoid assumptions. Since you didn't see Ginny and Norton leave together, don't suggest they did. Also, avoid using words like 'stamped' out of the study. In fact, unless the police specifically ask about your discussion with Norton, don't volunteer you met with your son," Charles said.

"Ah, I see what you mean. Any other advice?" Harry asked.

"Problems occur when people add their own interpretations to events or add things the police didn't know anything about in the first place. We don't want to give the police anything else to add to a circumstantial case."

"Well, on that profound note, my brilliant hubby and I should head home," Carrie said.

"You two look like you could use a little more sleep," said Caroline. "I'm sorry I woke you up, but I feel so much better with you involved. Be sure you keep in touch. We want to know what progress you're making."

"We will. But remember to keep our involvement quiet. Your favorite police chief made it quite clear that we're to stay out of his investigation," Charles said. He looked back and saw Harry holding Caroline's hand. Ginny may not have been a family member yet, but her death had deeply affected both of them.

"What do we do now? We have only a very short time to figure this out before Norton may have to answer more questions," Carrie asked as the couple got into their car.

"Whatever we decide to do, let's start with a nap." Charles leaned his head back against the seat.

"I've got a better idea. Let's start with the Barn," she said.

"I don't think they'll let us sleep there. They prefer to serve food rather than cots."

"Unlike some people I know, I didn't stuff my face with pastries. I'm hungry." Carrie made a face. "Besides, a little food combined with a little conversation will get us back on track."

"Are you sure, Carrie? Anyone who came to Pear Cove for the New Year's holiday and wasn't at the Barn last night will be there this morning having brunch. When we walk in, we'll be the center of the attention. I'm sure the gossip grapevine has been rampant."

"That's why I want to go there. In this sleepy off-season beach resort, the Barn is the center of gossip. Please note the key word is gossip. Hopefully, somewhere in that gossip will be some actual facts. And don't forget, Nick was also the caterer last night at Mom's party," Carrie said through a yawn. She leaned her head back against the headrest and dozed for a few minutes until they reached the restaurant.

"Come on, sleepyhead, your big breakfast awaits you," Charles said as he pulled their car into the parking lot.

The Barn restaurant was housed in the former Coast Guard building. It was a sturdy building with a beautiful stone front to protect it from the elements. It had two floors, with boats and equipment housed on the first floor in a huge open room and dorms for the men on the second floor. When the beach community expanded, the fishing piers were rebuilt on the other side of town. The Coast Guard found itself too far away from the action in an outdated building with facilities only for men. A new modern building was built on the opposite side of the town for them with all the updated requirements.

Nick and his partner, Otto, purchased the building for pennies, considering resort prices, then had borrowed a fortune to renovate the building into a fine restaurant. Together they did a great job of managing the restaurant. Nick had been trained traditionally at one of the well-known culinary colleges. It was rumored that Otto was a chef at a top restaurant in a Soviet bloc country. He immigrated to America once travel restrictions were lifted.

They added a marina, and the catering business allowed them to expand their eatery beyond the boundaries of the building. It also helped them to cut down on waste. Catering overruns, planned and unplanned, could be used at the Saturday and Sunday breakfast buffets. With little competition, especially in the off-season, the Barn did a fantastic business.

The restaurant was one of Carrie's favorite places. She liked the coziness of the building with its high ceilings held up by aged wooden beams and the large stone fireplace that had been restored in the center of the room. Nick and Otto sectioned the room with stone half walls to provide privacy for the diners. The individual sections and the stones also provided natural soundproofing for table conversations.

When the couple arrived, Nick was at the front desk to greet them. He took Carrie's hand and kissed her on the cheek.

"You're about the last two people I expected to see this morning." Nick was small in build. He was only about five foot seven with very thick straight black hair that had a way of always covering his intense dark eyes. "I thought after all the excitement last night, you two would definitely be sleeping in."

"I take it you've heard about Ginny," Charles said.

"Oh, please, Charles, of course I know. First, Chief Engler was here with a party of friends when he received the call about a body being discovered on the beach. Then there was a brief time when the road in front of your house was blocked by all the police cars. Of course Otto went down and spoke to the chief personally about making sure the road stayed open so our customers could come and go. I must say the chief was very helpful keeping the road open to traffic."

"It's nice to know the chief is helpful to some people," Carrie said.

Nick arched an eyebrow. "Otto checked to make sure you two were okay. Then the chief revealed that the body was Ginny Ellwood. He said he might have to question some of our staff to see if anyone had seen her. So to answer your question. Yes, I heard about the murder."

"Is it the topic of discussion this morning?" Carrie looked around the restaurant. Their presence didn't seem to be causing a stir.

"Of course it is. After all, the New Year's bells had barely tolled when one of our own was found dead. Besides, what else is there to talk about in this sleepy town? But don't worry. No one seems to be pointing fingers. It's terrible to say, but I think they're just thrilled to have something discuss other than 'isn't it cold' or 'will it rain today' as a topic of conversation. However, if you want to sit away from the crowd—"

"Carrie is very hungry. She would like to sit right next to the buffet table. However, we would also like to chat with you about last night. Perhaps a secluded table right by the buffet."

"Am I considered a suspect?" Nick said as he walked them to their table.

Carrie looked over both shoulders to make sure no one was listening. "No, we're looking for you to be our personal snitch. You know, let us pick your brain until we stumble on a piece of information. The one piece you didn't know you had that leads to the solution of the case."

"Ooh, this will require a special table," Nick said.

He seated them up the steps in a section that had been closed. Carrie lingered over the buffet to gaze at the food selections before taking her seat.

"If you're interested in breakfast foods go and fill your plates quickly. We're about to start the switchover for the lunch buffet. I have to get the changeover started. Then I'll come and sit with you."

~

"You know, for someone who had four pastries, that belgian waffle with all those bacon strips went down awfully easy," Carrie popped the last piece of toast in her mouth.

"Well, my little omelet queen, you were able to put away a small feast yourself."

"Yes, sir, and I enjoyed every bite." Carrie rubbed her tummy. "What's our plan with Nick?"

"I'm hoping Nick or one of his people might be able to tell us a little more about Ginny's activities last night. According to Norton, Ginny slipped out of the party without him. Why come to a party at her fiancé's parents' house if she didn't plan on being with him? But more important, what caused her to suddenly leave? Unless things were—"

"Unless things were worse than we've been led to believe by Norton." Charles finished her sentence.

Carrie reached out and touched Charles's hand. "For the moment, let's believe everything we're hearing is one hundred percent the truth. If we approach the facts this way, the discrepancies will become apparent."

"Here's Nick, so maybe we'll hear our first discrepancy," Charles said.

"How was the breakfast? Never mind, I can tell by your empty plates that you hated everything," Nick said.

"It was delish. It hit the spot for two tired people who were up late and out early," Carrie said.

"Soo, what's the scoop? Did you find the body? Was it murder? Is it true Norton's been arrested? Was the body nude? Are the police questioning anyone else? Are you working the case?" The questions flew from Nick's mouth like a barrage of bullets.

"Good grief! Are these your only questions?" Carrie said.

"They're the highlights. Of course, I never bother with the lowlights," Nick replied.

"Let me see. Yes, yes, no, no, maybe, and of course." Charles smiled.

"Being cute, huh," Nick said.

"All right, Nick, I'll level with you. But in return I want some answers from you. Deal?" Charles said.

"Of course I agree. Now tell all." Nick pulled out one of the extra chairs at the table and sat down.

"Carrie and I found the body on the beach when we were walking back from her parents' party. It appears to be murder. From the little bit I could see in the dark, I believe she was strangled with her own scarf."

"That makes it sound like it wasn't premeditated. I mean, if the murderer used Ginny's scarf, he didn't bring a weapon with him. Crime of passion?" Nick suggested.

Carrie ignored Nick's supposition. "As her fiancé, Norton was questioned. He hasn't been arrested. In fact, he's at our parents' home, sleeping. The body was not nude. I've no idea if the police are questioning anyone else. I'm not privy to their process. However, if Chief Engler could get publicity from it, I'm sure he would question the street sweepers. And just so you know, the police have told us to stay away from the case and not interfere. Since Norton is family, of course we're making a few discreet inquiries."

"Nicely done, you two. You answered my questions honestly and to the point. Now it's my turn. What can I tell you? Although I'll admit, most of what I know is probably more gossip than fact."

"Within the gossip may be the truth. Did you like that answer? A big breakfast makes me feel profound. Let's start with your thoughts on Engler," Carrie said.

"You're exactly right to think he may be a publicity seeker. He's from one of the wealthiest families of the original shore people. He really enjoys playing cop, in between his golf games and running the family business. He's particularly a hardnose when it comes to crime committed by the elite. He doesn't want the rest of the voting population to think he's letting his friends get away with the crime."

"Hey, my family is not elite and certainly not one of Engler's friends," Carrie said defensively.

"I know, darling," Nick said, patting her hand, "but unfortunately, that handsome publisher you married is considered one of the 'swells' of Tri-County. And with your dad and Randolph Ellwood owning their own businesses, they're at the top of the elite pile here in Pear Cove. I'm sure within seconds of receiving the call, Engler made the connections between all the players and their asset sheets."

"You said Engler was here when he received the call about the body," Charles said.

"That's true. He booked a table for a breakfast party starting at one thirty. It was for eight. I assume three couples plus him and his wife. He was here when I returned from catering the various parties."

Carrie looked around the room and noticed that most of the late brunch people were lingering. Nick must have noticed the same thing.

"Don't worry, if they don't start to clear out soon, I'll just blink the lights," Nick said.

"Nick, any gems you can add to what you saw at Mom's party last night? Did you see Ginny?" Carrie asked.

"Well, I wasn't at your mother's house that long. As you can imagine, New Year's Eve is very busy. Otto stayed here at the restaurant. I was out with the catering crews, going from party to party. Let me think back. I saw Ginny when she first arrived with her parents. Norton came and greeted her, and they went off to another part of the room."

"Did Ginny and Norton seem friendly?" Charles asked

"They were fine. They acted just like engaged people do, or I should say all the engaged people I've met. There could have been a hundred people in the room, but they were only concerned with each other. In fact, I heard Ginny giggle once during their conversation. Then I ran up the street to check another party. When I came back they were still together, visiting with people. Then your father called Norton into his study. That left Ginny wandering among the guests."

"Isn't there anything else you can remember?" Carrie's tone showed her disappointment.

"Of course there is. I saved the good part for the last." Nick smiled.

9

"She got a phone call. Just before midnight," Nick said.

"Mom never mentioned a phone call this morning when I talked with her," Carrie said.

"She may not have known there was a call. I didn't personally pick up the call, but one of my staff did. It's part of our service when we cater a party. The host and hostesses are busy entertaining, so we always answer the phone for them."

Before Charles could ask more questions, he saw Nick gaze about the room.

"It looks like everyone is running up a huge coffee bill watching us, and there's no profit in coffee refills. Let's go upstairs. Tom is setting up one of the dining rooms for a private party. Tom Gaston is the one who took the call for Ginny."

Charles walked with Carrie and Nick out of the room. He nodded at several people they knew but avoided any conversations. When Charles stopped to pay their bill at the desk, Nick snapped the check from his hand.

"No, you're providing me with a diversion from the mundane world of cooking and catering. Brunch is my treat."

They followed Nick upstairs. The staircase was on the far left of the restaurant and hidden behind a stone column. Up the stairs and to the right were several private dining rooms. To the left was a small suite of offices where Nick and Otto ran the operations for their business. Nick opened the office door and ushered Carrie and Charles past an empty secretarial cube into the administrative offices. Their arrival caused Otto to come and look out his office door.

Otto was the opposite of Nick. He was over six feet, muscular, with thinning blond hair. It was hard to tell his exact age because of his boyish good looks of his Eastern European heritage.

"Ah, good morning to the Faradays. I'm sorry to hear of the family's loss of Miss Ginny. Please extend my sympathies to your brother, mother, and father." With this formal statement, Otto bowed slightly and returned to his desk.

Carrie and Charles went into Nick's office. At the back wall, Nick had a computer that was turned off. There were piles of orders and other paper work on the desk, with a checkbook sitting on top. Nick went over to an espresso machine and fixed cappuccinos for them. As Charles was sipping his sixth cup of coffee of the morning, Nick left the office. He was back in just a few seconds with a young man.

"Tom, this is Mr. and Mrs. Faraday. Mrs. Faraday's mother hosted the party you worked last night. Tom works for us during the summer and also holidays when he's not in school."

Before Charles had the opportunity to acknowledge the greeting, Tom jumped right in. "Hey, I'm really sorry about Ginny."

"Thanks, Tom. I'll extend your thoughts to my family and hers," Carrie said.

Tom was a lanky local high school kid who relied on the beach town each year to earn a little money and get a suntan. His brown hair was still highlighted from the sun. His black slacks and white shirt, the uniform for the waitstaff, hung loosely on his thin frame.

"Tom, we understand that you took a phone call for Ginny last night at the party," Charles said.

"I did. I was passing by the phone in the hallway between the kitchen and the living room when it rang. I waited a couple of rings to see if anyone picked up, then I answered it." He stopped.

"Well, man, don't leave us hanging. Go on." Nick reached over and nudged his shoulder gently.

"There isn't much more. It was a man. He asked if Ginny Ellwood could come to the phone. I went and found Ginny and told her she had a phone call."

"Did you know Ginny Ellwood?" Carrie asked.

He grinned, as if he expected the question. "Sure, I know—I mean knew—Ginny. You see, there aren't that many young people in Pear Cove who aren't part of the tourist crowd. We all know one another. Even though Ginny and Norton are older, I'd occasionally see them at parties, plus they came in here all the time to eat."

"You called Ginny to the phone," Carrie prompted.

"Yup, she came right over. Almost like she was expecting the call, I'd say."

"Did you recognize who was calling?" Charles asked.

"It's funny about that. For a brief moment, I thought I recognized the voice, but then it was gone. Looking back, I think the person was deliberately attempting to disguise his voice."

"Did you hear any of the conversation after Ginny answered?"

"Not the actual conversation, but I heard her laugh. I naturally turned to look at her. She saw me looking and turned her back and lowered her voice. I went back to filling the buffet table. I didn't see her again after that call."

"And what time did the phone ring?" Charles asked.

"I don't know exactly, but it was soon after midnight. I heard everyone celebrating. I figured with all the noise, that's why no one heard the phone ring."

"Did you see Norton and Ginny after the call?" Carrie asked.

"Not really. I got busy filling the food buffet. People were really wolfing down the food."

"Thanks, Tom." Nick quickly dismissed him.

As soon as Tom left, Nick said, "I did."

"You did what?" Carrie asked.

"I saw Ginny after her phone call."

"Holding out on us, are you, my dear Nick?" Carrie said.

"Not at all. I'm creating a story," he said with an impish grin. "I was coming from the kitchen just as she was hanging up the phone. She rejoined the party. I saw her in a corner giving Norton a kiss. Then she spent some time visiting with people. I saw her talking to Sally Watford, Mary Simpson, and your mother."

"Did you hear any of the conversation between the women?" Carrie asked.

"Of course. After all, I'm like a piece of furniture."

"A piece of furniture." Carrie giggled.

"Yes, a piece of furniture. I'm not part of the party, so people don't have to acknowledge me. People don't see me as an intrusion when I'm in the room, just like a piece of furniture. Anyway, Ginny chatted with Sally about how mild the winter had been. Then after a few minutes I saw Ginny in the kitchen with your mom, saying what a great party it was and thanking her for inviting her. She also made a funny statement about hoping your mother wouldn't be disappointed if she left. The next time I saw her she had her coat on and was slipping quietly out the back door. And before you ask, she was by herself."

"My mother never mentioned the conversation."

"I don't think your mother interpreted Ginny's words the way we're interpreting them," Nick said.

"By all means, continue. I can honestly say I don't have a single piece of furniture that has told me this much," Charles said.

"People understand information based on their own frame of reference," Nick said. "Your mother was one hundred percent focused on the party. She took Ginny's comments as they related to the party."

"How did you interpret the comments?" Carrie asked.

"It sounded to me like a farewell. As if Ginny was saying good-bye. She was thanking your mother, not so much for the party, but for having been nice to her in general. In hindsight, I think Ginny knew it was over between her and Norton. She knew she might not have another chance to thank your mother."

10

Charles and Carrie returned to their house after the visit to the Barn and were asleep the minute their heads hit the pillow. Baxter knew it was quiet time, even if it was the middle of the day. He could always use a cat-nap. He curled in a little ball at the bottom of their bed and fell asleep too.

It was Baxter who first awoke to the sound of light tapping. Baxter climbed onto Charles's chest and nuzzled his face with his cold nose against Charles's chin. Charles at first attempted to push Baxter off him. Then he heard the light tapping at the sliding door in the kitchen. He put Baxter on the floor and slipped quietly from the bed. He grabbed his robe as Baxter led the way down the hallway.

Charles quietly addressed Baxter. "I think the next trick I teach you will be how to tell people knocking at the door to go away. Maybe you could hold up a small sign with your paws. Or better yet activate a voice recording that tells people to go away." As Charles came into the kitchen, he saw Norton standing at the sliding door.

"Hello, Norton. Come in," he said as he slid the door open. "But be quiet. Carrie is still sleeping."

"Gosh, are you guys still in bed?"

"After last night's party, over to your parents' this morning, then out to brunch, we discovered the only thing we were missing in this day was sleep."

"Gee, I'm sorry. I'll come back later," Norton offered.

"Don't be ridiculous. You're here now. Let me wake your sister. Then I'll get us something to drink."

"No, don't wake her! I mean, I'd rather talk to you alone. I need an objective opinion. Carrie sees me as her brother who can do no wrong."

"And have you done something wrong?" Charles asked.

Norton looked straight at his brother-in-law. "I've made some stupid mistakes in handling this situation. But if you're asking did I kill Ginny, the answer is absolutely not."

There was a moment of silence between the two men. "What can I get you to drink?" Charles asked.

"Nothing fancy, maybe just a Coke."

While Charles got the Cokes, Norton moved outside and stood by the deck railing, looking out at the spot where Ginny's body was found. Charles said nothing. He saw Norton's shoulders heave up and down, and Charles was sure he was crying. Charles deliberately made a noise, and he saw Norton quickly wipe his eyes.

Charles handed him a napkin. "The wind and the salt from the seawater plays havoc with your eyes." He placed the sodas on the table.

A moment later, Norton joined him at the table. "That tastes good. My mouth has been so dry. I'm sure it's related to pure nerves and the amount of alcohol I consumed last night. Charles, I didn't kill Ginny. But I need someone to believe me."

"I think everyone in the family believes you."

"I'm not so sure. I think they're supporting me because I'm their son or their brother. But sometimes when I look into their eyes...I see more sympathy than belief, more emotion than conviction of innocence. I know, I know, you're family, too, but you're different. You're not emotionally involved, and I can count on you for clear thinking. I need someone who can look at the evidence and use it prove my innocence. I know that you solved those other two murder cases. You're good at this stuff."

"We didn't solve them on our own. We had the local police helping. Unfortunately, the local police, particularly Engler, have told us to not to interfere with this case. You need to understand we might actually hurt your chances if we annoy the police," Charles said.

"I'm not worried about the police. I need your help," Norton said.

"I'm worried about the police. Especially Engler's apparent rush to judgment concerning you."

"See, that's exactly what I'm afraid of. The local police will use whatever circumstantial evidence they have and go for a conviction. And for Engler, a quick solution would provide the best political results. That doesn't leave me with a warm fuzzy feeling about my chances. Won't you help?"

"I didn't say I wouldn't investigate," Charles said. "I just want you to be aware of the potential issues with our friend Engler. We can't draw attention to the fact that we're helping."

"When you find the clues that clear me and solve the case, Engler will have to accept the help," Norton said.

"Believe me, nothing would give me greater pleasure than to bring Engler down a notch by finding Ginny's murderer. We just can't tip our hand until we have solid evidence," Charles said.

Norton took another sip of soda. "You know, I've run into him at a couple of parties. I never really hit it off with him, but he was very fond of Ginny. He's probably not too happy that Ginny's gone and I'm the one left. These feelings will also push him toward a quick conviction of me."

"Carrie and I are very glad you're the one left," Charles said. When he finished the statement it seemed a little awkward. There was that pause where neither man knew what to say. He continued, "Norton, as I mentioned, I'm willing to help you, but I've a couple of rules. Regardless of what you tell others or what you have told the police, you have to tell me the truth. Not part of the truth, or half the truth, but the entire truth. If I find you haven't told me the truth, I can't help you."

"I agree," Norton responded. "What's your second rule?"

"You have to think out of the box. Go beyond just the facts. Tell me what others were thinking. How others were behaving? Tell me about all those little incidents that may seem minor. Can you agree to these two conditions?"

"I can," Norton said. "Will you tell Carrie what I say?"

"Oh yes, I'll tell her. One reason our relationship is so strong is that we tell each other everything—no secrets. Don't worry, she wants to help, too. And it's to your advantage to have her involved. The murders you alluded to that I solved—we solved together. They were solved through a joint effort with both of us working the clues. Let me get a note pad. I want to record what we discuss." Charles noticed Norton's empty glass. "I'll also get more soda."

As Charles entered the kitchen he saw that Norton had moved his chair so he wasn't facing the spot where he had found Ginny. Once inside, Charles grabbed his note pad and pen plus a couple more cans of Coke and ice from the refrigerator and then returned to Norton.

"If you're ready, let's start with one of the last events first. Why were you wandering on the beach at that hour of the morning?"

"It was New Year's Eve. I wanted to spend the time with Ginny. No wait. You said I had to be honest."

Charles was glad Norton had listened and comprehended the requirements.

"Ginny and I…something had happened. It wasn't the same between us. Not being invited to the christening was sort of the last straw. It was obvious she didn't want to be with me. I decided I was going to ask her if she wanted to break off the engagement."

"And did she?" Charles asked.

"I never got a chance to ask her. We were being polite, saying Happy New Year to people at Mom's party. You know, putting up a good front of being the happily engaged couple for the guests. Then Ginny got a phone call and left the room. I said hello to a few more people and then got sidetracked by Dr. Bessinger.

He was coming in from the outside. He smokes a pipe and was afraid he would disturb people if he smoked inside."

"Who told you she had left?" Charles asked.

"Dr. Bessinger did. He mentioned at the end of our conversation that he'd seen Ginny when he was outside smoking. She had her coat on and was heading to where the cars were parked."

"What did you do?"

"I decided she wanted to get away from the party. Maybe find some of our crowd. There are a couple of places Ginny goes—the bar at the country club, the Seafood Cottage restaurant, and the Barn. I eliminated the country club because they were having a big party, and I knew our crowd wouldn't be there. I went out to the Seafood Cottage first. I found out she had stopped in but had left. Then I headed to the Barn. I stopped here to see if you guys were home. When I discovered you weren't home, I decided to walk over to the Barn. But Ginny wasn't at the Barn."

"We saw you, but it was when you were returning from the Barn."

"You did? Where were you guys? I was here twice and didn't see you."

"We were on the beach up by the bend, drinking champagne. We saw you stoop over Ginny's body. Of course we didn't know it was Ginny until later. In fact, we weren't sure it was you. But when you passed in front of the light on the steps leading to the house, I recognized you. Why didn't you call the police from our house?"

"I would have, if you'd been home. I panicked when you guys weren't here. I wasn't sure what to do so I got into my car and drove. I was really shaken up finding Ginny like that. Finally, I stopped at a convenience store out on Route 216. The store still had a pay phone, and I made an anonymous call to the police."

"Didn't the police ask for your name?"

"The operator told me the police were already on the scene. I hung up before she could ask me any questions."

"I went to another bar out on the point. I think the realization of what had happened was catching up with me. I left the bar and sat in my car. I'm afraid my emotions and the alcohol caught up with me. I eventually fell asleep. The next thing I knew, it was after five. I drove to my place. Saw the cops camped out. Drove over to Mom and Dad's. That's when the police took me into custody."

"Did you tell the police all this information? More important, did you tell them about a possible break-up between you and Ginny?" Charles asked.

"No way! Simpson told me to give minimal answers to the questions. I only told them about the two places I visited looking for Ginny. I didn't tell them about parking in your driveway or that I had found the body on the beach."

"I assume when you visited the two restaurants you asked people if Ginny had been there."

"At the Seafood Cottage I asked Pete, the bartender, if he had seen Ginny. At the Barn I first asked Otto. Then I went into the bar and asked Josh. He was one of the bartenders on duty. I sat at the bar and ordered a beer, thinking she might show up."

"Good. This gives us a couple of places to start to verify your timeline."

"You know, verifying the time won't really give me an alibi. I was at the Seafood Cottage before Ginny died. My timing at the Barn is so close to her death, the police will say I went inside to establish an alibi after I killed her."

"That may be true. But by following your trail we may just learn about someone else who was around at the same time. Let's go back to the beach for a moment. You obviously parked your car in our driveway. Did you walk to the Barn by the road or by the beach?"

"The road. That way I could watch incoming cars in case Ginny passed me. When I returned I wanted to think. I decided to walk back along the beach rather than the road. Not to mention the fact that your road was a pretty dangerous walk with no sidewalks and drivers who had been drinking heading for the Barn."

"Do you remember anything unusual about your walk to the restaurant, other than the dangerous road?"

"No, nothing I can think of." And then Norton stopped midsentence. "Wait! Now that I think about it, there's something else."

"What's that?" Charles prodded.

"After I knocked on your door, I walked to the end of your deck and looked out at the ocean. The moon wasn't covered by the clouds as it was later when I was walking back. I'm positive that Ginny's body wasn't on the beach at that time. The body was so obvious when I was walking back I'm sure I'd have seen it from your deck."

"Then it's even more important we narrow the time down. What time did you get to the Barn?"

"I'd guess it was just about one fifty-five."

"Was it one fifty-five when you reached our place or when you reached the Barn?"

"I was here at one forty-five, and I'm allowing ten minutes for knocking on your door, looking at the beach, and walking to the restaurant. The first person I saw was Otto. He asked if Mom's party was over, and we both looked at the clock."

"We had a couple of minutes of conversation about the party and whether everyone was pleased with the catering. Then I asked him if he had seen Ginny. He said he had been upstairs until the restaurant started getting busy with early morning breakfast arrivals. Ginny could have been in and left. Or for all he knew, she might have been sitting in the bar or the dining room. I looked in the dining room, and then I went to the bar," Norton said.

"No Ginny, but did you see anyone else?"

"I saw the Buckleys. I just waved at them. Then I saw Jeff and Jennifer Hanson."

Charles shook his head.

"Oh right, you wouldn't know them. Jeff and I went to college together. He met his wife at college, and they returned to Pear Cove after school. We're the same age, so we often attend the same parties. He and Jennifer are also year-rounders. Jeff's family owns the Hanson funeral establishment. They'll probably handle Ginny's burial," Norton said. He paused for a moment and took a deep breath. "Anyway, I spent a couple of minutes with them. They had been a few places but hadn't seen Ginny. Oh by the way, Chief Engler was there. I saw him when my attention was drawn to a rather loud party up in the loft."

"Then I headed to the bar. I said hello to Sally Watford. She was returning to a table in the bar. She had been table-hopping, greeting some of the other folks who were there. She returned to her table because she said she was expecting the Silvas, who were joining them for breakfast."

"Was she on her own?"

"No, John was there, but he had gone to the men's room. I left Sally sitting at her table alone. I wanted to check with the bartender, and the bar was really getting busy. I spoke to Josh and ordered a beer. As I finished my beer, John Watford was walking down the hallway from the men's room. I just waved at him and left. I walked back along the beach, met no one, and... well, you know the rest."

"Carrie and I called the police at 3:11 a.m., according to the police. Prior to the call we'd been sitting on the beach about ten to fifteen minutes, another five as we watched you approach. The killer had about twenty to thirty minutes max to meet and kill Ginny."

"Probably even less. You have to remember I didn't see anyone walking back along the beach, and neither did you."

"Interesting point because that means the killer had an even smaller window to commit murder and get away. Speaking of getting away, he would have had to return to the street or walk along the beach to get to his car. This means he parked his car at one of the houses along the street or in the Barn parking lot."

"Would he take a chance parking at someone else's house?" asked Norton.

"If he parked at a house, he would be closer to the beach. With so many of the owners not down for the holiday, it probably wasn't that big a chance. Aside from us, the only other people here for the holiday are the Cranstons and the Habers. Mr. Cranston is in his seventies and recovering from a heart attack. They were probably already in bed and asleep at that hour. The Habers are on the opposite side of the road from the beach."

"The Habers were having a party. People were leaving as I was walking by. Both Habers were at their front door waving good-bye. I don't think he would have had time to slip away from his wife, go down to the beach, and get back to a party that was breaking up."

"No, but maybe one of the Habers' guests could slip down to the beach. What about cars? See any cars out of place?"

"Not really. Of course, there were cars parked along the roadway from the Habers' party, and quite a few cars passed me coming to or from the Barn. The Barn has a huge parking lot. The murderer's car could have been parked on that lot. With all that traffic, no one would notice one more car passing or one more car on the parking lot. I didn't," Norton said.

"Timing is tight. Ginny and the killer were probably on the beach at the same time you were walking along the road."

"But why didn't I meet him on my way back along the beach?" asked Norton.

"The beach is pretty wide along that stretch, and there are the dunes and plenty of shrubbery along the way. All he had to do was hide behind a dune or one of the closed homes until you passed," Charles said.

"Why didn't he hide her body behind one of the dunes? Why leave her body out by the water?"

"I'm sure she was left there on purpose. He probably hoped the incoming tide would carry her away. By the time the body washed back in and was discovered, the time and location of her murder would be compromised. By the way, did you see Ginny's car on the road or in the Barn parking lot?" Charles asked.

"You know, come to think of it, I didn't see her car at all."

"Maybe the police found it and had it towed to the impound lot," Charles said.

"But if they didn't, how did she get here? Where's her car?"

11

"Where's whose car?" Carrie asked, as she tied the sash on her woolly robe and joined the guys on the deck. She reached over and took a sip of Charles's Coke. "Mmm. Tastes good."

"We were reviewing last night's events. I take it you would like a Coke," Charles said.

Carrie took another long sip of his soda and nodded her head yes.

"Do you want me to also bring you a coat or a blanket?"

"A blanket would be nice for around my legs. If you two are discussing the case, why didn't you call me?" she called after Charles. She went over and kissed Norton on the forehead. She saw the redness around his eyes. "How are you, Norty?"

"I'm okay."

"Sure you are. I can tell you've had plenty of sleep."

Carrie reached out and took the blanket from Charles and wrapped it around her legs. Then she took a sip of the Coke he brought her. She handed Charles back his almost empty glass.

"Did you guys figure this case out yet?" Carrie asked.

She saw the look on their faces. "I'll assume the expression on your faces indicates a no. I'm sure Charles will fill me in later on what you discussed. But I've a few questions. Hopefully I won't be asking the same questions you've already discussed." Carrie smiled lovingly at both men. "All right, Norton, I want the scoop on you and Ginny. Straight out—was it over between you?" Carrie saw the shocked looks on their faces. "Look, guys, this is serious. I'm not going to pull any punches—we don't have the time."

"Sis, I don't know the real answer to that question. We had started to experience some problems. At first, I thought our feelings were being affected by the merger deal. Maybe we had lost sight of the fact we had fallen in love first, before the merger. On the other hand, regardless of the merger, it seemed Ginny just didn't want to spend time with me. As I told Charles, I was about to ask her if she wanted to break the engagement."

"Are you saying you think there was someone else?" Charles asked.

"I don't know," he responded.

"Norty, when a woman is interested in someone else she behaves differently. For instance, she tells you she's too tired to go out with you. Or wants to cut short your time together and go home early. She says she needs to be at family events, and you're not invited. In other words, she's not available for you. When in reality she should always be available for you."

Carrie was aware Norton was staring at her. He said nothing but just stared.

Carrie nodded. "When did her behavior start to change?"

"I guess it started at the beginning of summer," Norton said.

"Did she modify her behavior when the summer was over?" Carrie asked.

"Not completely, but she did seem to focus on me a little more."

"Paying attention on weekdays, but losing her on certain weekends?" Carrie asked.

"Gosh, it seems so obvious when you say it. How come I didn't see it?"

"Because, my dear Norty, you were in love. When you're in love you're the last person to see the obvious."

"I want to know how you're so familiar with the symptoms of wandering females," Charles said. "I want you to know I'm taking copious notes on this subject for future reference."

Carrie winked and said, "We'll talk later, darling. All right, Norty, I know you haven't had time to think this through. But I want you to concentrate on anyone who showed an interest in her. I'd bet the man is married. He's probably a summer settler like us, who comes down on occasional weekends or holidays. This would explain her lack of interest in Norty during the summer months but improving somewhat as the season ended."

"I might point out this guy could still be a year-rounder. Even the year-rounder tends to be out and about more in the summer when there are plenty of parties to attend. In the winter months the regulars concentrate on business," Charles suggested. "Plus, with the summer crowds gone there's a greater likelihood of being spotted by someone."

"I agree that's a possibility," Carrie said.

"Good grief, sis, how have you come to all these conclusions in such a short time? I mean, I'm hearing for the first time an explanation of why Ginny might have been acting the way she was."

"Yes, I'd like to know, too. When did you come to these conclusions, darling?" Charles asked.

"Oh stop it, you two. I thought about it before I went to bed last night. Believe me, it's not that hard. I started with the simple premise that Norton isn't guilty. Then I tried to think what the other possibilities might be."

"This sounds like something from Sherlock Holmes. Eliminate the obvious and the other possibilities emerge," Charles said.

"Correct. If it wasn't Norton, then it was someone else. I think this someone called Ginny at the party and asked her to meet him. Why else would she leave the party and Norty? He asks her to meet him on a lonely section of the beach. Why? Did he plan in advance to murder her? Did he want to meet her on a section of beach near our home to throw suspicion on Norty? Or did he want a lonely section of the beach away from the boardwalk. Why? So people wouldn't see them. Why? He would be recognized. Why doesn't he want to be recognized? Regardless of what he may have been telling Ginny he was not ready to have this affair known. Probably he didn't want his wife to know about it," Carrie said.

"Definite possibilities. But we still don't know who 'he' is, do we? That didn't happen to come to you while you were sleeping?" Charles asked.

"Sorry. No such revelation."

"I must say, sis, somehow I feel a little better. I know you two are just starting on this case. But at least you have shown that someone else could have committed the murder. I have faith that you will find the guilty person."

"Good. I'm glad you're feeling better. You're also right about just getting started. Norty, I'm serious when I say I want you to think about possible candidates. In fact I want you to write them down," Carrie said.

"How many do you think there might be?" Norty asked.

"More than one if you really take this seriously. Don't try to put an entire relationship together. In fact, don't think about whether the guy fits all the criteria—married, single, knows her from a party, knew her before you two got serious, summer settler or year-rounder, etc. Just write down the names of anyone who might have shown an interest in Ginny. That's your assignment. Can you have the list ready by the funeral?"

"Ah, the funeral. We need to get through that next," Norty said.

Carrie noticed as quickly as she had lifted Norty's spirits, his sadness had returned with the mention of the funeral.

"Perhaps this little assignment will give you something else to focus your mind on," Charles said.

"Perhaps. I guess I'd better get back. Thanks, Charles. Thanks, sis. I'll talk to you both later." Norton stood and downed his remaining soda.

"Norton, remember. Don't let it be known to anyone outside the family that your sister and I are helping on this case," Charles said.

"I understand. I won't tell anyone." He turned to leave.

"Wait, Norton! I've one more question. The police showed us a ring last night that they found near Ginny's body. When did you give the ring back to Ginny?" Charles asked.

"The police showed me the ring and asked the same question. I'll tell you the same thing I told them. There was nothing to return. I never had the ring. Maybe Ginny bought it and had planned on giving it to me. But at the time of her death I wasn't the owner. Besides, they wouldn't let me touch the ring, but it looked awfully big to me." Norton held up his ring hand. "See, I have very thin fingers. Probably all the computer typing I do keeps them trim."

Norton left Carrie and Charles on the deck and climbed the short flight of steps up to the driveway where he had parked.

Charles waited until he heard the car start and pull out of the driveway. "You know, maybe the ring was a present for the other man."

"That's an interesting thought, but here's another. Was the ring being given by Ginny, or was it being given back to her? Another possibility for us to explore," Carrie said.

"Well, at least you cheered your brother up," Charles said.

"It was more than cheering Norty up. I believe what I said is a workable hypothesis. The problem is I haven't a clue where to start."

"Well, I do. We need to work on a timeline of New Year's Eve and the morning. We need to interview the people who saw Norton the night of the murder. We might as well start with a friendly face. Tomorrow, let's go visit Sally and John Watford. Maybe they saw our mystery man."

12

Sally and John Watford were year-rounders. This meant they stayed in Pear Cove the majority of the year, unlike the summer settlers who came like clockwork on Memorial Day and packed up and went home within two weeks after Labor Day. Settlers might return for an occasional fall weekend but were rarely seen in winter.

There was also a social distinction between the two groups, except at the Pear Cove Country Club. Settlers asked for a limited-membership option, but the country club held fast to the rule that dues were for an entire year. No reduction in dues was provided for summer settlers.

The Watfords' house was one of the older homes located near the boardwalk in the central Pear Cove tourist area. John and Sally purchased the home at an estate sale for a fraction of its potential value. The house may have been purchased at a good price, but it required massive renovations to bring both the interior and exterior up to modern standards.

The outside was finished with natural wood that had begun to turn seaside gray from the harsh winter sea weather. Winters could also be cold, and the house was centrally heated and had working fireplaces in most rooms. Sally had performed miracles with the house, and now it was one of the most beautiful in Pear Cove.

Parking was so tight on the streets during the summer months that most settlers had turned their backyards into asphalt. If space permitted, the homeowner would have a grassy section for the grill and picnicking, but the rest of the yard was for parking. Carrie and Charles didn't have to use the Watfords' backyard for parking. They found a spot on the street and took the front steps up to the wraparound porch.

Carrie and Charles were dressed in the typical beach attire—khaki pants, polo shirts, sweaters, and loafers with tassels known as kilties. In summer months socks were not worn, but in winter, socks were added to the outfit. Carrie left her winter jacket in the car, because the temperatures had suddenly soared into the upper fifties. It certainly didn't seem like the day after New Year's when she and Charles knocked on the door of the Watford home.

"Oh my…well, hello, I didn't expect—" Sally had trouble hiding her surprise at seeing Carrie and Charles on her doorstep.

Carrie knew Sally was one of the leaders in year-rounder fashion. Today she had on the traditional khakis with a light-peach polo and a cardigan in a darker peach with flowers down the left side.

"I hope you don't mind. Charles and I decided to take a New Year's walk on the boards and thought we would take a chance and stop by."

Carrie's reference to the "boards" was the local term for the boardwalk. She also knew it would be very natural for people down over the holiday to take a walk on the boards.

"Oh no, not at all. Actually, I'm glad for the visit. My daughter, Junie, went off on a ski trip with college friends, and I'm feeling a bit lonely. It's not like summertime when people drop by every day. The winter really is a much lonelier time. There have been times after the season ends when I've been here in the house and haven't seen a single person for days. There's a core group of year-rounders, and sometimes we get together for cards or lunch. Maybe I should organize a regular card group," Sally said.

Carrie knew that Sally had a way of rambling on about every topic. She could certainly see her table-hopping at the Barn on New Year's morning. But she was glad when Charles jumped in on today's conversation.

"Carrie and I couldn't agree with you more. We were getting a bit of cabin fever. That's why we decided to go for a walk."

"Maybe John and I'll do that as soon as he gets back. Why don't we go into the sunroom? It's so nice at this time of day."

Sally led them down a hallway past the living room toward the back of the house. Just before the kitchen they turned into a room that was surrounded by windows on three sides. It was bright and sunny and filled with plants and oversize wicker furniture.

"I was just having some lemonade. Would you like some? I like lemonade even in the winter."

"No thank you, we really can't stay long. Did John go to Tri-City?" Carrie asked.

"Tri-City? Oh no. Since we moved down here permanently over a decade ago, we rarely go into the city. Although we still maintain a condo in the city for those occasions when we go shopping or to the theatre or when the children come to visit. But neither of my two older girls and their families was able to fly east this year. With the exception of some Christmas shopping we haven't made many trips to the city this year."

"You were telling us where John is," prompted Charles.

"I was. Oh yes. I was, wasn't I. He's over at the country club. He swims for exercise. Of course, in the winter he has to use the indoor pool." Sally took a sip of her lemonade. "Carrie, I'll drop your mom a note, but in the meantime you must tell your mother what a wonderful party she hosted. It really was one of the best. Her parties are always so cozy. She brings such a congenial group together, with everyone chatting and enjoying one another's company. I much prefer that type of party to the larger country-club-style parties. I'm just sorry the evening ended so dismally for your family. You know, with the death of Ginny and all."

Carrie wondered if the "and all" referred to Norty's involvement. *Was public opinion already turning against Norton?*

"Actually, that's the other reason we stopped in to see you. We heard you and John were at the Barn after Mom's party. Since Ginny's death occurred on the beach near the Barn, we wanted to check with the people who were in the area. You know, to see if you and John saw anyone or anything unusual," Charles said.

"Are you two working the case? I thought you might be helping out. Wasn't your brother murdered, Charles?" Sally paused and then added, "And here's another family member murdered—well, almost a family member. What's the world coming to?"

"Unfortunately, we have had some experience working on murder cases, but for right now our working on the case is pretty much a...well, let's just say it's a bit of a secret. Certainly the police would prefer for us not to be involved, if you know what I mean," Charles said, lowering his voice.

"I completely understand. Knowing Chief Engler, he wants to get the credit for solving the case without any outside help. How can I help?"

"What time did you and John arrive at the Barn?" Charles continued.

"We left your mother's party just before one o'clock. I really didn't want to leave," she said apologetically, "but we had promised the Tanners that we would stop by their party, just down the street from your mother's. We must have spent about forty-five minutes to an hour at the Tanners'. We left there about one forty-five. We had been drinking at the Tanners' but hadn't a thing to eat. It seems at the holidays we're constantly hungry. It's probably because we expand our stomachs with all the overeating. We had read that the Barn would be open the entire night and was serving breakfast starting at midnight. We had arranged to meet the Silvas there at two," Sally said.

"You and John didn't happen to see Ginny while you were there?" Carrie asked.

Sally suddenly clapped her hand over her mouth.

Carrie looked at Charles, wondering if Sally's lemonade was having an effect.

Then Sally recovered. "You know, I didn't realize until just now. John and I were sitting in the Barn, warm and cozy, having something to eat with the Silvas at the very time that terrible person was…well, you know…killing poor Ginny. Excuse me. I need to refill my lemonade." Sally left the room.

Carrie whispered, "Do you think that's really lemonade?"

"Oh, it's lemonade, but I bet it's got a little gin or vodka mixed in."

Charles barely finished his comment before Carrie heard Sally returning to the sitting room.

"I'm sorry. Sometimes your ears hear something, but your brain hasn't fully processed the information. It finally hit me that I wouldn't see and talk to Ginny again. I think it's even harder to accept her death having just seen and talked with her at your parents' party."

"You spoke to Ginny at the Kingsfords'?" Charles asked.

"Oh yes. John and I greeted her and her parents when they arrived. You know, just small talk. How the winter wasn't too cold, did they have a nice Christmas, wasn't it a lovely party. Nothing too intense."

"How did Ginny appear?" Carrie asked.

"She looked lovely. She had on a black dress, plain but very stylish." Sally took another sip of lemonade. "Oh, but you want to know did she seem upset or worried. No, nothing visible.

She looked perfectly fine other than she was rather quiet. You know how young people are when they meet friends of their parents. She did glance around the room a few times. I figured she was looking for Norton."

"Did you speak to her again?" Charles continued the questions.

"No, that was the only time," Sally said.

"Did you see her again?" Carrie asked.

"Actually, John and I did see her again. One of the servers from the caterers spoke to Ginny, and she left the room with him. That was the last that I saw her." Sally paused.

"Is there something else, Sally?" prodded Charles.

"You were asking me if I saw Ginny at the Barn. I was just thinking that the last time I saw her, she was talking to one of the servers from the Barn. Do you think there's a connection?"

"That's wonderful, Sally. This is why Charles and I are talking to different people. Everyone sees some little piece of the puzzle."

"As you said, we also saw Norton," Sally said. "The Barn was packed with people. We couldn't get a table right away, so I was sitting in the bar, and Norton was there."

"Did my brother say anything?"

"Only that he and Ginny had gotten separated earlier in the evening. He was trying to catch up with her. He seemed fine. I mean, he wasn't angry or anxious. I figured he had stayed a little longer at your parents' party to be polite. Ginny had gone ahead to another party, and they missed their rendezvous point. He was pleasant and polite and then went up to the bar."

"Did John say anything when he saw Norton?" Charles asked.

"Oh, he wasn't there. I mean he was there, but he had gone into the men's room. I think his cold was beginning to hit his stomach, if you know what I mean. Norton was leaving the bar when John got back to our table. Harold and Jenny Silva joined us, and we began to talk. I don't know if John even spoke to Norton, but I'll ask him when he gets back."

"Is there anything else, Sally?" Charles asked.

"I don't think so. We were fully engaged with the Silvas. Then Otto told us our table was ready. We moved to the dining room to have breakfast. How is Norton doing? This must be very difficult for him. I mean not only the loss, but the questioning by the police."

"He's doing as well as can be expected. How did you hear about Ginny's death?"

"We had just been seated in the main dining room when our waitress told us the road was partially blocked by police cars. There was an investigation in progress because a body had been discovered on the beach. We saw the police cars when we left, but wasn't until we listened to the television New Year's morning we learned the body was identified as Ginny's. The television also mentioned that Norton had been brought in for questioning."

Carrie realized in all the excitement and running around, they had missed the television announcements about the murder.

"I mean, if Norton is a suspect, I'll be glad to tell the police what time we had our conversation," Sally offered.

"Norton hasn't been charged!" Carrie said defensively. She realized they didn't want to leave Sally with the impression that Norton was a suspect. "The police obviously wanted to question him about what he and Ginny were doing. But he wasn't detained by the police, and he's at my parents' house."

"See, that's not right. The television station is reporting that he was brought in for questioning, implying he's a suspect. They never once mentioned that he had been released," Sally said.

"We're all so busy we want only sound bites, instead of full news coverage. However, it means we're not getting the whole picture," Charles said.

"That's an honest assessment, especially from someone in the media business. At least in your magazines, Charles, you can provide a full picture. John and I do enjoy your publications, especially the *Tri-County Monthly*."

"That's very kind, Sally. And Carrie and I appreciate that you're taking the time to talk with us."

"Glad to help. After all, our families will be seeing a lot more of each other. I mean, with John getting the contract to do the advertising and marketing for the new software your father's company is developing. Oooh—" Sally covered her mouth with her hand. "I forgot I'm not supposed to say anything."

"What do you know about this new product?" Charles asked.

"Actually, I know very little. Except that it is some sort of a medical program that will solve lots of paper-work problems for the medical profession. But I guess you two know much more than I do."

"Yes, we were chatting with Dr. Bessinger just last night at the party." Carrie covered their lack of knowledge by mentioning the good doctor. "Thanks again, Sally," Carrie added as she and Charles stood.

"I'll be sure to check with John, but I doubt seriously he saw anything different from what I told you. I'm sure Nick and Otto can provide you with names of other people who were in the Barn at that hour." Sally escorted them back to the front room. "I do hope you'll stop by again for a visit. Or maybe we can have everyone over for dinner as we get closer to the software rollout."

"Sounds like a wonderful idea," Charles said. As they were leaving, Charles turned and asked politely, "How is John feeling today?"

"He seems to be much better, but that's why he wanted to go to the club. He claims a quick swim in the warm pool and then an hour in the steam room clears his head."

Carrie felt Charles take her hand as they returned to their car. Once inside the car she asked, "What do you think?"

"Well, we now know why the good doctor was consulting with your father. There's a medical software program in the works," Charles said.

"Yes, that's very interesting, but what about the case?"

"The good news is Sally pretty much verified the times that Norton gave us. The bad news—she's another witness who puts Norton near the scene of the crime at the right time. The police can say Norton went to the Barn to establish an alibi."

"Charles, I think we made a big mistake. By not telling the police we saw Norton, we've hurt his case. We could have testified that he leaned over a body that was already dead on the beach. Instead we've got a roomful of people at the Barn who can testify he was there at the right time. What are we going to do now?"

"Something very important. We're going to take a walk on the boards and look out at the ocean. Things never seem as bad when you see the vastness of the sea."

Carrie snuggled against him. Despite their problems, she felt good about the day.

13

It was now two days after New Year's Day, and Carrie was relaxing with Charles and Baxter on their deck. It had been a dark and stormy morning, but the clouds had cleared. Carrie was enjoying what turned into a beautiful winter day. It was chilly enough to require a winter jacket to stay warm, but not so cold that they couldn't sit outside. And of course she needed hot coffee to ward off the chill that rolled in with each wave.

Neither Charles nor Carrie spoke. Carrie had been working on writing a mystery book for several years. Today she had tried to do some editing on pages she had previously written but had put the sheets aside to just sit and watch the waves. Even Baxter's constant batting of his stuffed mouse across the deck did nothing to break the silence of her deep thoughts.

Then Baxter, perhaps on purpose, pounced on his mouse so that it sailed in the air and hit Carrie in the shin. Carrie left her thoughts and retrieved Baxter's toy.

"I'm glad someone is enjoying his holiday at the beach. Here's your mouse." Carrie tossed it back to him, and Baxter sprang into action.

Carrie watched Baxter's antics for a few more moments. Then her attention was drawn to the beach. There were only a couple of remnants of yellow police tape flapping in the wind to mark Ginny's final spot. Thank heavens it was winter and off-season, which limited the number of gawkers wanting to visit the scene of the murder.

Carrie had no sooner thought about the lack of beach traffic than she spotted a man. She missed him the first time she looked because he was kneeling in the sand.

"Charles, Charles, wake up," Carrie said as she pulled on his sleeve.

"I'm not asleep. I'm just thinking," he replied.

"Look at that man on the beach," she said.

"Probably just another gawker," Charles said as he followed where Carrie was pointing with her finger.

"Charles, I think it's Ginny's father." Carrie watched, and when the man finally stood, she knew it was Randolph Ellwood. "Should we leave him to his private thoughts or invite him to join us?"

"We should leave him to his thoughts," Charles said as he stood and headed for the stairs.

"I thought you said we should leave him alone."

"There's a difference between what we should do and what we need to do to solve this case. We need to talk with Randolph about his daughter," Charles said.

Carrie watched as Charles cut across the beach. Randolph was now standing looking out at the ocean. In all the years

Carrie had known Randolph he was always animated. Now as Charles approached him he looked small and lifeless. Perhaps it was because Charles was tall, or perhaps everyone looked small against the backdrop of the ocean. She adopted a positive attitude as the two men climbed the steps to the deck.

"Hello, Randolph." Carrie kissed him on the cheek. "I'm glad you're joining us. Do you want to continue sitting out here, or would you prefer to come inside where it's warmer?"

"If you two are okay, I would prefer to sit out here," Randolph said as his eyes drifted back to the area with the police tape.

"We're fine out here. However, let me refill the coffeepot. I'll be right back."

When Carrie returned, the men were sitting quietly. She had the feeling nothing had been said while she was gone. She placed the tray with the coffee items on the table. She took a mug and filled it with coffee. She pushed the plate of pastries and the cream and sugar toward Randolph.

"Randolph, Charles and I want you to know how very, very sorry we are about Ginny. More important, what can we do to help?"

For a moment he said nothing and only stared at the coffee in the mug. Then he looked up at Carrie and asked softly, "Could you tell me about finding my Ginny?"

"Randolph, I'm not sure recounting those details will help you," Charles said.

"It's all right, Charles, I understand."

"I'll tell you what we saw." Carrie very slowly gave Randolph every detail of what they discovered, but with some modifications. As with the story they gave the police, she left out the part about seeing Norty. However, she emphasized other elements that the police weren't interested in hearing. "It was a beautiful night, with a full moon. The water was calm and silvery, and the waves caught the light from the moon. The only sound was the gentle slapping of the waves as they came to the shore. When Charles went over to Ginny, he thought that she was simply sleeping. It was an incredibly quiet morning."

Baxter had remained quiet at Carrie's feet the entire time she was speaking. Carrie finished her narrative without breaking down and crying. However, Randolph took out a handkerchief and wiped his eyes.

"Thank you, Carrie, I needed to hear that," Randolph said. He took a moment and then added, "I know that you two have some experience in solving murders. Charles, I'm sure you had some of the same emotions I'm experiencing after your brother's murder. Including the resolve to find out what happened."

"Yes, I do understand what you're feeling," Charles said.

"Carrie, you asked how you could help. I want you two to find out who killed my little girl."

Carrie looked at Charles and then lowered her voice, even though no one was around to hear. "Between you and me, we're working on the case. However, we're doing it quietly so as not to annoy Chief Engler."

"Ah yes, Chief Engler. He wants the case solved for his personal political purposes. He'll opt for the quickest solution. He won't search to find out what really happened. Just so you know, I don't believe for a moment Norton had anything to do with Ginny's death."

"Now that you mention Norton—" Charles said.

Carrie nodded that she agreed with what Charles was about to say.

"You see, we know that Norton didn't do it. But because we didn't say anything to the police at the time, we're trapped into keeping quiet."

Carrie listened while Charles told Randolph the part about Norty that she'd left out.

"Because Norton discovered the body moments before we did, we know he didn't kill Ginny. In fact, Norton made a call to the police to report the murder," Charles said.

"Unfortunately, we wanted to talk to Norty about we saw before we said anything to the police. Now it's too late," Carrie added.

"I see what you mean. Trust me, I won't say anything. I know the kids were having some issues, but I know Norty was truly in love with Ginny. He would never have hurt her," Randolph said.

"Did you notice a specific change between Ginny and Norton?" Carrie asked.

"I did. It was the laughter," Randolph answered.

"The laughter?" Charles asked.

"Yes, the laughter. You see, Ginny and Norton were always happy. They were always giggling and laughing. Telling little private jokes and laughing at the comments each of them made. Experiencing the true joy of being with each other and being in love."

"When they stopped laughing, were they fighting?" Carrie asked.

"No, it was as if they had simply gone silent around each other. I know that sounds strange when I say they went silent. But it summarizes not wanting to be with each other."

"It isn't strange. Mom mentioned something similar. Something about a family christening that Ginny attended without Norty," Carrie said.

"Exactly, just another example of what I mean. Instead of wanting to be with each other twenty-four hours a day, they started making excuses not to be together."

"Randolph, do you think the pressure from the merger was affecting the kids?" Charles asked.

Carrie knew Charles was asking what many other people were thinking, including her.

"You and everyone else are wrong if you think the merger could be responsible for my little girl's death!"

14

"The merger was the best thing that could have happened to the kids. All the kids. By kids I'm including you, Carrie, and my son, Fred, too. The new company, which is called Kingwood, combines the knowledge and development capabilities of both companies. It means a much larger and expanded business for our families."

"Are you sure it had no effect? I mean, the merger is announced, and suddenly Norty and Ginny are having problems," Carrie said.

"I'm positive. The merger talks were started over a year ago and were pretty much completed before the kids got serious about marriage. It's just that with all the legal paper work required, it wasn't finalized until August. That's why the announcement to the public was just made in September. It appears that the merger and the marriage plans were at the same time, but it's simply not true."

"Randolph, can you tell us more about the merger? We were just visiting with Sally Watford, and she mentioned there's a new piece of medical software being developed," Charles said.

"And what did Sally tell you?" Randolph looked concerned.

"Believe me, she didn't know any details about the program. She only knew that John would be handling the advertising and marketing once the new company was ready to launch," Carrie said.

"That's because the details of what we're developing are secret."

"Secret?" Carrie asked. She noticed that some life had returned to Randolph's eyes.

"Yes, you see, what your father, Norton, and I are working on will have an impact on the medical community. Before I continue I need your promise that what we discuss here will not be repeated or discussed with anyone else."

Carrie looked at Charles. At first she thought Mr. Ellwood was kidding, but the stern look on his face indicated he didn't consider it a joke.

"Of course we promise," Charles said, and Carrie nodded in agreement.

"Have you heard of EHRs?"

Carrie shook her head no.

"It stands for electronic health records. Every doctor, medical practice, and hospital in the country is required to track patient care because of all the health-care reforms."

"Aren't there multiple programs already available that do this?" Charles asked.

"Yes, but there's also a general consensus that the existing systems are poorly designed, cumbersome, and take too much time for staff members to learn and manage them. However, at the same time no one wants to return to the old days of managing paper charts and files."

"So that's what you and Dad have been doing. Designing a program to manage patient medical visits," Carrie said.

"Yes, but it's so much more than a program for managing a medical visit. It's true some programs track your doctor visits; other programs analyze symptoms and suggest a diagnosis. Others suggest medications based on the diagnosis. There's a program to track lab work and another to track prescriptions."

"Our pharmacy has that program. It tracks our prescriptions to make sure that the drugs don't interact adversely with one another," Carrie said.

"That's good. But what happens if you change pharmacies? Pharmacy programs don't talk to one another. You see what I'm saying. There are lots of programs out there that only do one thing. And most of them don't talk to one another. We're developing an entire medical-management system."

"Ah, that explains one thing," Charles said. "We met Dr. Bessinger at the New Year's Eve party. I assume the development of this system is why he was hired as a consultant."

"Yes, Steven is our expert on genetics and biometrics in addition to his knowledge as a practicing doctor. This is really the cutting edge in patient diagnosis and recommending targeted treatments. For instance, there have been great advancements in identifying the BRCA genes responsible for hereditary breast and ovarian cancers. But there are new frontiers, such as finding the right treatment for PTSD."

"You mean posttraumatic stress disorder?" Charles asked.

"Yes. And this one is near and dear to my heart. As a family, we've been very lucky with Fred's military service. Because his expertise is computers, his work has been mostly behind the scenes. However, many of his military friends haven't been so lucky. They were affected by their battlefield experience and returned home needing medical help. Now, by mapping their genetic histories, we can help the doctors determine the best treatment for these brave soldiers."

"Wow, I have to admit this sounds very exciting."

"Now you know why there's such secrecy surrounding the development. Because this program does so much we're calling it the Kingwood Medical Intel System. We just finished securing all the copyrights and branding, so we've got a lock on the name. This is one system where the first company in the market will have the upper hand."

"Randolph, I've another question for you. I always understood from Dad that you weren't really competitors. Dad's company concentrates on software, and your company is more adept with hardware. I was wondering—"

"You want to know what I'm contributing," Randolph interrupted.

"I'm sorry. I didn't mean for my question to sound impertinent," Carrie said.

"Not at all. It's a good question. My company was designing a tablet computer that allows either the patients or the medical persons to input data. It's designed to be very easy to use. If the patients are filling out the information, they can use a stylus or the keypad. The data entered on the tablet interfaces with all PCs, so the information is easily uploaded. And once the data is in our system, it can be transferred to a hospital or another doctor. We're designing the portion of the program concentrating on the hardware interfaces. We are protecting patient information while making it easy for those who need it to access it."

"That makes perfect sense for your company," Charles said. "Since you concentrate on hardware and Harry on software, how did you two end up working together?"

"Your father and I are members of the Chamber of Commerce. At one of their luncheons we were seated at the same table. We started talking about all the changes in health-care requirements. Then we found ourselves sharing what each of us was doing to solve health-care problems. Within a couple of minutes we realized we should be working together."

Carrie refilled everyone's coffee cups. She also moved the pastries away from Charles and over toward Randolph.

"However, I should add that my company also does software development. Hardware needs software to operate. I have some terrific programmers working for me. You know my Ginny is...was...a good programmer."

"I didn't realize Ginny was a programmer," Carrie said.

"Yes, both Ginny and Fred have degrees in computer programming. Of course Fred will join the new company when he finishes his current tour of duty. Ginny had no interest in being directly involved with this current project. However, she attended a few meetings and knew what we were developing. And I'm sure she and Norton discussed the project and the programming. On the business side, everything is moving smoothly, with no bumps to cause distress. Hopefully I've convinced you the merger was not responsible for any problems between Norton and Ginny."

"If we eliminate Norton and the merger—well, I'm sure you know my next question. Randolph, do you have any idea who might want to kill Ginny?" Charles asked.

Carrie knew the question was a tough one for Ginny's father. But it was the one question they needed to ask to help Norty.

"Believe me, I've been racking my brain. Ginny was very popular. Everyone—young and old—liked her. I would have said she didn't have an enemy in the world. But then, that's not true, is it? She must have had at least one," Randolph said.

"I know this is a tough day for you. We thank you for taking the time and sharing the information about the merger with us," Carrie said.

"Somehow talking has helped me. I thank both of you. Now I'd better go. I need to meet Helen. You know, funeral arrangements."

Randolph started down the steps and then turned back to the couple. "Regardless of what Chief Engler says, I'm counting on you two to solve this murder."

Carrie watched as Randolph slowly made his way back along the beach, stopping only briefly at the spot where Ginny's body had been found.

15

"Do you think there will be any bad feelings from the attendees about our family coming to the funeral?" Carrie asked Charles while she was dressing for the service.

"I spoke with your father last night. He feels, as a family and as a business partner, there's no option but for him and your mother to attend."

"What about Norty? People will be watching to see if he attends."

"Norton is apparently a little hesitant to attend. But your father is very black-and-white. He knows Norton loved Ginny and isn't guilty of her murder. Therefore, he should be at the funeral. By not going he'd only be fueling the gossip. I think he'll attend."

~

Funerals are always difficult. But Carrie knew they were even more difficult for families at holidays. Most of the world is celebrating and welcoming the joys of a better life, either through faith or secular festivities. For the segment of the population who must face the loss of a life there's always a certain reserve that lingers around that holiday for all future celebrations. And so it was with Ginny's funeral several days after New Year's.

Carrie had never been to the Hanson funeral home before. Located in the heart of the downtown village, it blended in with the decor of the Pear Cove beach atmosphere. The funeral establishment was housed in a large white-clapboard home that had no doubt been the site of many lavish New Year parties of a different type in the past century.

It had been maintained in the same style as the rest of the houses on the street, with a fresh coat of white paint and dark-green shutters. The only thing that distinguished this home as a place of business was the enormous asphalt parking lot that took in several properties, a canvas-sheltered portico, and a conservative wood sign that displayed the name Hanson's Funeral Services. Charles pulled their car into the parking lot, and Carrie saw that most of parking spaces were filling up quickly.

"I hope all these cars mean there's a second funeral being held," Carrie stated.

"I'm afraid that's not the case, my dear Carrie. This is a small town. In a small town, a funeral associated with a murder is an event. Plus, no one wants to be too early or too late for a funeral, so the parking lot fills and empties as if on cue."

To prove Charles's point, the Simpsons, the Watfords, the Smythes, the Schwartzes, Dr. Bessinger, and Otto and Nick all pulled into the lot within a couple of seconds of one another.

"Here's Dad's car now," Carrie said as she was getting out of their car. She and Charles went over to her parents' car. Norton was sitting in the backseat.

"Oh good, I'm glad we arrived together," her father said as he emerged from the car and went around to open Caroline's door. "I do think it's important that we go in as a family."

Carrie greeted her mother and Norton. Then Norton reached into the inside pocket of his suit jacket and removed a sheet of paper, which he handed to Charles.

"Here's that list you asked me to prepare. You know, with the exception of Dr. Bessinger, everyone on the list is a year-rounder, and not everyone is older or married."

"That's okay. It's too early in the investigation to eliminate anyone," Charles said.

Carrie fell in behind the group with Charles as he placed the paper in his pocket. The family proceeded under the canopy up to the front door.

Inside the door Charles was pulled aside by Mr. Edward Hanson, owner of the establishment.

"Such a sad time for both families. Such a lovely girl," Hanson said, shaking his head. "Have you talked with Ginny's parents? Do they have any idea what happened?"

"Carrie and I had a long conversation with Randolph. We are all at a loss why this happened to Ginny."

"I too feel a sense of loss. I knew Ginny. I mean not like my son, Jeff, knew her. They're the same age and run around with the same group of friends. But I saw her often at different social functions. I assume you and Carrie will be doing some sleuthing?"

"Let's just say we'll being doing whatever we can to protect Norton and find the killer. I guess I'd better join the family," Charles said.

⁂

Ginny's body was on view in the largest of the chapels. There was an altar, a podium off to the right, and a set of three pews for the family on the left. The casket sat about twenty feet from the first row of pews. The pews ran in two columns to the back of the chapel and were filling to capacity. At each side of the main chapel were additional viewing rooms. The wide double doors of both rooms were opened to handle the overflow crowd. Around the coffin and along the walls all the way to the back of the room were numerous flower arrangements. Soft sounds of Pachelbel's Canon in D seemed to gently drift from the ceiling, as whispered voices greeted each other. The whispers dropped to a hush when Caroline, Harry, and Norton arrived. Caroline and Harry went right to the Ellwoods and expressed their condolences. Norton held back.

"Charles, is that Fred with Helen and Randolph? He looks so different," Carrie said.

"I think it's his uniform that makes him look different. I'm glad the army gave him time off. He's probably the only person who can bring comfort to Helen and Randolph at this time," Charles said.

"Why is it people in uniform, even when they're at family functions, always stand as if they're at attention?" Carrie asked.

"Probably because when they're in uniform they're still on duty. You stand in a position where the minute someone yells 'attention' you can snap to."

Carrie saw Norton, after a period of time, drift toward the casket. He stared into the coffin and then knelt before it and prayed. Carrie was sure she saw Norton slip a folded note into the casket. He stood, wiped his eyes, and then wandered toward the back of the room. He spoke to several of the young people who were standing at the back.

Charles and Carrie took their turn passing by the casket. Carrie thought the funeral directors did a good job in preparing Ginny's body to look as natural as possible. She was in a high-necked dress, somewhat old-fashioned, but no doubt chosen to hide the bruising around the neck. Carrie thought there was softness about Ginny's demeanor that hadn't always been present in life.

Within a few moments the attendants passed among the crowd and asked everyone to take their seats. The service was going to be conducted by the minister of the local Episcopal church where the both the Kingsfords and Ellwoods were members. They were unable to use the church because of a scheduled wedding. But the chapel room was comfortable and in many ways warmer than the stone church.

"Please Caroline, Harry, Norton, Carrie, and Charles, we would like you to join us," Randolph suggested.

The Kingsfords and Faradays all sat in the three rows designated for the family with Helen, Randolph, Fred, and a sister and brother-in-law of Helen's.

After a brief prayer, Minister Dober read several psalms that he mentioned were the family's favorites. Then he summarized Ginny's brief life, including the upcoming marriage to Norton. He turned the podium over to friends of the family, who told stories about Ginny. Some were humorous, but most expressed great sadness. Carrie was looking for a tissue when Charles handed her his handkerchief. The last segment of the service was reserved for a eulogy by Fred, who represented the family.

"On behalf of my family, I'd like to thank all of you for attending the funeral and helping us during this sad moment. It's very difficult to lose someone. It's more difficult to lose someone so young and just ready to embark on the journey of her life." Fred then summarized special moments he shared with his sister.

Carrie leaned over and whispered to Charles, "What was that you said about people not wanting to be late for a funeral?" Carrie nodded her head slightly toward the back of the chapel where Chief Engler and Detective Hilton had slipped in and were standing quietly.

"Ah, I wondered where they were," Charles said.

"And finally on behalf of my family, I've one more thing to say. We will leave no stone unturned to find her murderer. We will find the truth even if it involves close friends or family," Fred said.

Carrie didn't miss the fact Fred turned his head and looked directly at Norton. Norton's head was bowed so he missed the eye contact with Fred.

"We'll do everything possible, including hiring private investigators if necessary, to bring this person to justice. And now we must accompany Ginny on a different type of journey—a journey that may start at the cemetery, but will last until we're reunited with her."

Carrie's did her best to hold back tears, but most of the women were openly wiping their eyes. Helen cried softly into her handkerchief as she held onto Randolph for support.

Minister Dober, sensing the ceremony needed to move forward, jumped to his feet and offered a final prayer. Then he turned and addressed the mourners, "This ends the service here in the chapel. Ladies and gentlemen, if you're going to the cemetery, the staff from Hanson's will help you get your car in line. And now we'll give the family a few final moments with their daughter."

Reverend Dober started to move slowly down the aisle with his arms outstretched to move the crowd away from the family.

"Whew, that was some speech," Charles whispered in Carrie's ear. "I bet Engler isn't too pleased with the thoughts of having a private investigator poking around his case. What do you think?"

"I think Fred's speech not only made Engler but everyone else a little uncomfortable. People are hurrying to get out of the chapel just so they can get in line for the trip to the cemetery. Charles do you think it would be a bad thing if we don't go to the cemetery?"

"No, I think it will be fine, but we should let your parents and the Ellwoods know."

Carrie stood with Charles by the door of the chapel waiting for her parents. They watched as Chief Engler and Detective Hilton joined the procession going to the cemetery. Carrie was about to make a comment when her attention was diverted by the sound of loud voices coming from within the chapel. Carrie quietly opened the chapel door and entered, with Charles at her side. Just inside the room Fred was yelling at Norton.

"I don't care if the police have released you. You're not off the hook in my book. I know that things weren't the same between you and Ginny. Her last letter to me indicated she was having some doubts about proceeding with the wedding. What happened New Year's Eve? Did Ginny call it off and you couldn't take it?"

Norton didn't say a word. He just stood there looking at the floor. Fred continued, "I'll tell you what I think. Ginny ended the relationship at your parents' New Year's Eve party. She asked for her ring back. You gave her the ring, but then your ego kicked in. You went after her, tracking her down until you finally caught up with her on the beach. You had it out with her, lost your temper, and killed her. She probably threw the ring at you, and that's why the police found it on the beach."

"That's enough, Fred," Randolph said. "We don't know what happened that night, and there's no sense making false accusations. I for one don't believe Norton killed your sister."

"Randolph, perhaps it's better if we don't go to the cemetery. We'll leave you at this time. But if either you or Helen needs anything—please, please call either Caroline or me," Harry said. Carrie's father took his wife's hand and put his other arm around Norton's shoulders and left the chapel.

Carrie wanted to defend her brother, but she didn't know what to say. Instead she kissed Helen on the cheek and turned to leave.

"What Harry said goes for us, too. If you need anything, Carrie and I are here for you." Then Charles turned his attention to Fred. "Fred, I know you're upset and want to find Ginny's murderer. There's one thing with your scenario you might want to check. Norton has never seen the ring you mentioned. And before you think I'm just defending my brother-in-law, you might want to check the ring size. It's way too big for Norton's finger. I can assure you we want to find Ginny's murderer as well so this cloud of doubt is removed from Norton. Perhaps you'll come to realize we're all on the same side."

Carrie took her husband's arm and gave it a squeeze. She did love this man.

16

"There are some interesting names on Norty's list of potential men in Ginny's life. As Norty said, his list is a combination of young, old, married, single. It pretty much includes just about everyone at Mom's party and everyone who was seen at the Barn on New Year's morning. It includes the Hansons—both father and son. There's our friend Engler, plus Otto, Dr. Bessinger, and even Hugh Simpson," Carrie said.

"Any ideas whom you would like to visit first?" Charles asked.

"Let me see." Carrie ran her finger down the list. "Let's start with John Merkoff."

"Which one is he?" Charles asked trying to glance at the list as he maneuvered the car through traffic.

"He's not on the list, but he owns Seaside Jewelry on Main Street. I thought this might be the store where Ginny bought the ring. After all, it's the only quality jewelry store in town."

"You know, Ginny could have traveled into Tri-City or a nearby town to buy that ring."

"She could have. But I think she would have started her search in Pear Cove. If Ginny did buy it from Mr. Merkoff, maybe he'll remember if she said anything about whom the gift was for. If she didn't buy the ring from him, then perhaps he can tell us what other stores might handle that type of ring."

"Then off we go in search of gems of information," Charles said.

"Very clever, Charles. You have such a way with words."

Mr. Merkoff's jewelry store was located at the very end of Main Street, farthest from the beach. The stores along Main Street, like many stores in small towns, were on the first floor of converted town houses. Originally, the shopkeepers and their families lived upstairs. Now most of the upstairs had been renovated and offered as apartments to summer tourists.

The only thing unusual about Main Street in Pear Cove was that the houses were made from brick rather than wood. This gave the resort town a federalist look.

With few tourists in town, Charles was able to find a spot right in front of the store. He headed the car into the curb and parked.

In keeping with the style of the street, the store had a dark-blue door and red shutters on the windows. Carrie and Charles spent a moment looking at the displays in the store's front window. Charles noticed that there was a blue backdrop that kept the casual window-shopper from looking beyond into the store. Perhaps the backdrop was a security precaution, or perhaps it was done to draw the casual onlooker into the store.

The display in the window had a selection of rings, pendants, and some pins, many made from sea shells.

"Maybe I'm wrong about the ring coming from this store. I admit that I didn't see the ring for more than a few seconds, but it certainly looked expensive. The items in this window seem more like vacation souvenirs and costume jewelry. I'd classify this jewelry as trinkets for the tourists."

"Let's go in and see what's inside. Most jewelers don't keep their best items in a breakable glass window. By the way, darling, you can pick anything you want from this trinket window. I'll be more than happy to buy it for you."

Charles took Carrie's hand and swung it like they were two teenagers on a window-shopping date.

Inside, the store was surrounded on three sides by glass display cases. Charles knew the cases were old, but they sparkled with their cleanliness. Beyond the cases were mahogany wood drawers that went halfway up the wall. In the open spaces above the drawers was a series of watercolor paintings of the Pear Cove seaside. The store was so quiet Charles almost missed the man working at a desk to the side and behind the counter. The man had a jeweler's eyepiece attached to one lens of his glasses that were sitting on the end of his nose. He looked up at them with a warm smile that extended from ear to ear on his oval face.

"Be with you in a moment," he said in a soft voice.

"Take your time," Charles responded. "It will give us a chance to look around."

There was a case with diamond rings and matching wedding bands and a case with trays of watches and bracelets. On the other side of the store was a case filled with jade pendants, earrings, and small carvings. Charles pulled Carrie over to this case. Charles had given Carrie a pair of jade earrings for Christmas, but had been unable to find a matching pendant.

"I have some very nice pieces. Jade is one of my specialties, you know. Hello, I'm Mr. Merkoff, the owner of the store."

Charles hadn't heard Mr. Merkoff approach. He was a balding man only about five feet six inches tall. He wore a tan shirt with a sweater vest, over sharply creased brown trousers and a bright green-and-brown-patterned bow tie. "Thank you for waiting. I was at a critical point in my repair."

"I'm Charles Faraday, and this is my wife, Carrie. We're pleased to meet you."

"Do you do repairs right here on the premises?" Carrie asked.

"Many of the older and finer pieces I repair here. Some of the newer pieces, especially these newfangled specialty watches the kids have, I send out. It's better to send them back to the manufacturer with the equipment to figure out which computer Chip isn't working."

"I can relate to that. I believe it's better not to try to repair anything yourself if it's connected with a computer," Carrie said. "I still prefer the look and feel of the older pieces."

"Is there something I can show you?" Merkoff had put his hands together and was tapping the fingertips.

"No, I think we're just looking," Carrie said.

"No, we're not. I…I mean, we would like to see a jade pendant. I bought my wife some jade earrings for Christmas, but I wasn't able to find a matching pendant."

Merkoff reached into the case and pulled a smaller velvet tray from the back. There were six pendants on display. The chains were very fine with a lovely small jade carving attached.

"What do you think, darling?" Charles asked.

"They're very nice," she said unenthusiastically.

Charles knew exactly what Carrie was thinking, so he said it for her. "Actually, I think they're a little small. The designs aren't very distinctive. Do you have something of a better quality?"

Charles saw that Merkoff was unruffled by his negative comments.

"You know, the more intricate the carving, the more expensive the piece. We're talking hundreds of dollars."

"I understand," Charles responded.

Charles was aware that Merkoff was looking them over from head to toe. Charles figured they had passed the jeweler's test because Merkoff removed a ring of keys from his pocket. He turned to the back wall and unlocked one of the mahogany drawers and withdrew another tray of jade pendants. Charles immediately recognized that the difference between this tray and the first one was night and day. The chains, while still fine, were of a higher karat of gold. The jade charms dangling on them were much larger and very distinctive in their designs.

Carrie immediately picked up a pendant that had an intricate and perfectly designed pagoda. "This is lovely."

She started to turn the small price tag over, but Charles stopped her.

"Carrie, you pick the one you like. I'll worry about the price. Well, Mr. Merkoff, is this a piece worth the price?"

"Oh, yes, this is a very fine piece. Notice the purity of the color in the stone. Plus, a great deal of work has gone into the carving of the pagoda design. While it has spent time with me here in the store, it has been one of my favorites."

Charles liked Mr. Merkoff. He treated his jewelry as if he was the caretaker for living creatures. "Would you like this one, Carrie?"

"It's very lovely. But Charles, you already gave me a wonderful present of the jade earrings. There's no need to buy me another gift."

"This present is for the New Year, so we'll continue to have good luck," Charles said. "Mr. Merkoff, why don't you have these better pieces on display? Not everyone will ask if you have other pieces to sell."

Merkoff looked around and then lowered his voice even though there were no other customers in the store. "It's because of the tourists—especially the young people. I think it's the sun. They meet each other on the beach under the sun, and they go for each other. Then they come in here to buy a remembrance."

Charles didn't have the heart to tell Mr. Merkoff that the expression "go for each other" was no longer in vogue, but he let him continue.

"I discovered very quickly that few of them had the money for my better pieces. I brought in a cheaper line of goods just for them. My better customers, like you two, hear about me through word of mouth or the off-season ads I run for the year-rounders."

"Makes sense. Well, this is exactly the type of piece we were looking to purchase. We'll take it," Charles said.

"Thank you, darling, you're more than generous."

"In order to achieve true generosity, one must continually be generous," Charles said, trying to sound like Confucius.

Charles gave Mr. Merkoff his credit card. Mr. Merkoff carefully placed the pendant in a lined jewelry box. He handed it to Charles, who bowed and presented it to Carrie.

"Are you two year-rounders? I ask because as a businessman I always like to know how my customers have heard about me," Mr. Merkoff said.

"We own a home out on the point. Unfortunately we only get down a few weeks in the summer and on holidays. My wife's parents are year-rounders. You may know them, Mr. and Mrs. Harry Kingsford?"

"Kingsford, Kingsford..."

Charles could almost see Merkoff's brain trying to place where he had heard the name. Then it hit him.

"Oh my, are you related to the young man involved with Ginny Ellwood?"

"Yes, Norton Kingsford is my brother. He is...was engaged to Ginny Ellwood. In fact, it was Ginny who recommended your store. I believe she recently bought a ring from you," Carrie said.

Merkoff raised an eyebrow as he handed Charles the charge slip and returned his credit card. "Are you sure it was Ginny who recommended me?"

Charles was surprised by the question but continued with the charade. "Why yes, I'm sure it was Ginny. Remember, Carrie, it was at a family dinner. We were talking about jewelry, and Ginny mentioned Mr. Merkoff's shop and the ring she had recently purchased."

"Yes, you're right. But if you remember, Charles, Ginny never mentioned the ring." Charles caught out of the corner of his eye that Merkoff nodded in agreement with Carrie's account.

"We learned about the ring from the police. Remember the night of the...you know. The police found the ring and showed it to us," Carrie continued.

"I thought so," said Merkoff. "Ms. Ellwood was very secretive when she purchased the ring. You see, your brother purchased the engagement ring for Ginny from me. However, when Ginny purchased her ring she was very clear that I shouldn't mention it to anyone, especially your brother."

"Did you tell anyone?" Charles asked.

"Oh no, I never mentioned it to anyone. The only reason I'm telling you now is because you mentioned the police. Do you think the police will come here?"

"Carrie, I'm not sure we should say anything more. You know how the police are." Charles turned his back to Mr. Merkoff and winked at Carrie. Charles turned back and looked at Mr. Merkoff, who seemed anxious.

"Oh, I don't know, Charles. I believe Mr. Merkoff is trustworthy. I think we can confide in him. Besides, we wanted to learn a little bit more about the ring. Perhaps Mr. Merkoff is willing to share what he knows if we tell him our story."

"Yes, I'm very trustworthy. I've been in business for over thirty years, and I'm willing to share information about the ring with you."

Charles couldn't tell if Mr. Merkoff was a little too anxious to find out information or if he was just expressing a normal curiosity in the case. Carrie looked at Charles, and he nodded approval.

"Okay, it's a deal. I'll go first," Carrie said. "The ring you sold Ginny was found under her body the night of the murder. We think she met the man she was going to give the ring to. We also believe he didn't want the affair to go as far as exchanging rings and the ring was lost in the struggle. The police showed the ring to my brother when they questioned him, but he had never seen it. Unfortunately, the ring was engraved with the words "All my love, G. E." but no other initials to indicate who the recipient might be."

"Oh my, oh my, oh my." Mr. Merkoff had gone quite pale. "It does look like that ring is at the center of things."

Merkoff reached under the counter and pulled out a catalog. He flipped through several pages until he found what he was looking for. He turned the catalog around to show Carrie and Charles. "Is this the ring?" He pointed to a picture midway down the page.

Charles saw the gold ring exactly like the one the police had showed them.

"That's it," Charles said.

"Now it's your turn. What can you tell us about Ginny's purchase?" Carrie asked.

"Not too much more than what I've already said. As I mentioned, when she made the purchase, she asked that I keep it a secret. She made it very clear that it was a gift for someone other than your brother. You know, if the police interview me I can verify that the purchase wasn't for your brother."

"Did she give you any details about the person who was receiving the gift?" Carrie asked.

"Not really. Although I did have the impression it was for an older man."

"Why do you say that?" Charles asked.

"She wanted a conservative ring in gold, with a small diamond. This type of ring is worn on the pinky finger. In general, younger men don't wear rings other than wedding bands. If they do wear a ring, they generally pick something without a stone. They want a ring with an emblem from their college or a sports team logo. Second, it was a rather large ring size. That might mean it was an older man who had put on some weight. Of course, it could be a young man who had fat fingers and liked diamonds."

"When did Ginny make the purchase?" Charles asked.

"She came in just a few weeks before Christmas. I told her I couldn't get a special order at that time of year in such a short period of time. She asked if I could get it by New Year's. She said the New Year would mark new beginnings for everyone."

"New beginnings, huh. Is there anything else you can remember?" Carrie asked.

Mr. Merkoff rubbed his chin. "Wait, there's one more thing. It was when she told me that the ring wasn't for Norton. She said he wouldn't understand who was getting the ring and why her new favorite color was gray. Maybe when she mentioned the color gray I made the assumption it was an older man."

"The color gray. That's interesting. Thank you very much, Mr. Merkoff. You have been very helpful," Carrie said. "I think you can definitely verify the ring wasn't for my brother."

Charles took Carrie by the arm and started for the door.

"Wait, what do you think I should say to the police if they contact me?" Mr. Merkoff asked.

"Tell them exactly what you told us. The truth is always best. However, it might help your experience with the police if you don't mention that you've already shared this with us. The police prefer to learn information before anyone else," Charles said.

"And you can be sure that we'll recommend your store to all of our friends," Carrie added.

Once in their car, Charles turned to Carrie and said, "You know, that last statement about recommending him to all our friends sounded a little bit like a bribe. Don't tell the police we were here, and we'll be sure to recommend you."

"You think? Well, it's important that he doesn't tell the police about us. Engler won't like it. Besides, I do plan on recommending him. This has been a very good day for me. Evidence to help my brother and a lovely present from the man I love. Who could ask for anything more?"

Charles didn't mention that Norton wasn't totally out of the woods concerning the ring. The police could say that Ginny showed Norton the ring she was giving to her new love. That's what caused him to lose his temper. But Carrie was happy with the information and the present, and that made Charles happy.

17

"Hello."

Tom Gaston's voice was hesitant, but it brightened as he realized he had reached the correct person on the other end of the line. "This is Tom. You know, one of the servers at the Barn restaurant."

"Oh, yes, Tom. What can I do for you? Did I leave something behind at the Barn or forget to pay my bill?" the voice laughed slightly at the joke.

"In a way I guess you could say you left something behind," Tom answered, smiling at his own play on words.

"I'm getting ready to go out, Tom. What did I leave behind?"

"You might have said you left a...a witness."

"A witness! What are you talking about?" the voice asked.

Tom wasn't 100 percent sure before he made the call. Now that he heard the voice, he knew he'd identified the right person. This was the person who had called Ginny at the Kingsford party on New Year's Eve.

"I'm a witness to the relationship between you and Ginny Ellwood," Tom said.

"Now, Tom, you're a little too old to be dreaming up these types of fantasies." The voice was still in control.

"Shall I tell you my facts to support this so-called fantasy? Once you hear what I know, you can decide for yourself if it's fact or fantasy." Tom paused, but the voice said nothing. "First, I'm aware of several occasions when you and Ginny seemed to innocently bump into one another the Barn."

The voice started to interrupt, but Tom continued, not wanting to lose control of the conversation. "Of course, by themselves these occasional meetings mean nothing. It's only when I linked these meetings with other information. That's when I began to see a clear picture."

Tom stopped talking. He thought he heard a click on the phone. "What was that?" Tom asked.

"What was what?" the voice answered calmly.

"I thought I heard a click on the line."

"Tom, I hope you're on a secure line. You're not using one of the extension phones at the restaurant, are you?"

"Of course not, I'm on a pay phone in the middle of nowhere."

"Good. Now what were you saying?"

"If you remember, I was also one of the waiters at the Kingsfords' New Year's Eve party. I was the one who took your phone call to Ginny. I know you tried to disguise your voice, but several days later when you were eating at the Barn I recognized you. Second, after Ginny hung up the phone I saw you return to the party from the outside. You made the call on your cell phone. Third, when I returned to the Barn after serving the Kingsfords' party, you were here. You could easily have left the restaurant, gone to the beach, and murdered Ginny."

"Tom, you've simply put together a series of circumstantial events. After all, just because I said hello to someone at the bar or even called her on the phone—so what! It doesn't mean I had anything to do with Ginny's death."

"Of course it doesn't. In fact, I always thought you were a pretty nice guy, and you're a good tipper. It really comes down to whether a man with your prominent position in the Pear Cove community wants it known you were involved with the murdered girl. You know how people talk."

"Tom, for your information, Ginny and I would talk about computer programming. We both had an interest in software development," the voice said.

"It might very well have been just innocent conversation about computers between you two. But people tend to jump to wrong conclusions. And wrong conclusions could ruin a person—his standing in the community and even his marriage. Don't you agree?"

"Perhaps," he answered. "Tom, what do you want? Or should I be blunt? How much blackmail money do you want?"

"I'm no blackmailer!" Tom said. "I'm about to be a college kid who could use a little help with tuition costs. You see, I've been accepted at American University in Washington, DC. But even with a partial scholarship, it's more than my family can afford. I'd really like to go there."

"Have you thought about a student loan? Clearly your family would qualify."

"My father doesn't believe in loans. And I don't want to be in debt for the rest of my life. That's why it's not blackmail. I don't want you to give me a dime. I just want you to pay my tuition. You can send the check directly to the school. You're doing nothing more than helping a promising young student get an education."

"What about your expenses? Don't you need money for food and books?"

"No, no personal expenses. As I said, I personally don't want any money. I'll work part time like I do now for my expenses."

"It seems like you've given this a great deal of thought. Tom, I've no problem with helping out a Pear Cove college kid. That's as long as he understands I had nothing to do with Ginny Ellwood's murder.

"Agreed," Tom said.

"I do have another concern. What assurances do I have that this 'helping out,' as you phrase it, will stop when you finish school?"

"You have my word. As you said, I've nothing more than circumstantial information. Once Norty Kingsford is convicted, interest in the case will end. And once I get my degree, I'm never coming back to Pear Cove. There's nothing here for me."

"All right, Tom, I can certainly afford to give you a scholarship. When do you want to get together? You understand I will want to do this anonymously. I'll need some information about the school and whom to contact. Can we meet somewhere later?"

"I'm scheduled to work tonight at the Barn..." Tom hesitated.

"That's fine. Is there someplace we can meet for a few minutes privately without anyone else being around? Maybe we could meet in the parking lot after work?"

Tom interrupted, "I know a place. How about the Barn's wine cellar? It's downstairs from the dining room. You can slip down to the cellar from the restroom hallway. I'll get the key. Once I lock us in, no one else can get into the cellar. Maybe we could even open a bottle of wine to celebrate. How about nine o'clock?"

"That works. And don't forget to bring the information about the school. I'll see you tonight." The voice was still calm as the call was disconnected.

The voice turned to the person who had been listening on the extension. "What do you think?"

"I think it's time we take care of Tom."

18

Carrie was swimming. It was a beautiful sunny day, and the water was teal blue and cool—very cool and refreshing. As she turned her head toward the beach, she saw Charles on the sand smiling and waving. Everything was perfect. As she started swimming toward him something strange happened. She heard a phone ringing. She looked at Charles, and he was still smiling and waving. She thought, *Why isn't he answering the phone?* The phone kept ringing. She continued swimming until she could stand up in the shallow water. She yelled at Charles, "Why aren't you answering the phone? Can't you hear it?" Then she felt someone tapping her on the shoulder.

"Carrie, wake up and stop yelling. I've got the phone."

Carrie felt Charles reached over top of her and grab the phone.

"Hello, who's this?" Charles asked.

"Charles, it's Nick, Nick from the Barn. I know it's early, but Otto and I are so upset. We didn't know who else to call. Can you and Carrie come right over?"

"Nick, it's three o'clock in the morning. Carrie and I usually save visiting friends until later in the day."

"Aren't we a bit testy when our sleep is disturbed? But this is important. Tom is dead."

"Tom who?" Charles asked.

"Tom, the young kid you interviewed. You know, the one who worked at your mother-in-law's party and took the phone call for Ginny."

"Was it accidental or murder?"

"It looks like suicide, but I'm not so sure. The police aren't saying. Just between you and me, I don't think they believe it's a suicide."

"We'll be right over."

~

"You know, as much as I enjoy the water, I for one will be glad when this restful holiday is over. People in this town don't believe in sleep," Charles said.

"Not getting enough rest, darling? It seems to me that all we're doing is sleeping and eating. Admittedly, we're sleeping at odd times. But once this case is solved our sleeping schedule will return to normal."

The parking lot of the Barn was dark with only a few auxiliary lights to guide the driver. Carrie saw Nick standing at the open door of the restaurant with the interior lights shining brightly behind. Charles pulled their car right up to the door and took a handicapped parking space.

Carrie barely had her door open when Nick was at the car. "I'm so glad you got here quickly."

Carrie let him help her out of the car and guide her toward the door of the restaurant. Once inside, Carrie saw Otto sitting at a table in front of a roaring fire. He was pouring coffee from a glass carafe into four cups. Charles went right for the coffee. Carrie removed her teal-and-navy windbreaker. Then she took Charles's jacket and placed them both over the backs of their chairs.

"Ah, we're glad you have come. Nick and I have so much to think about with this death of Tom. It happened here in our wine cellar."

"I think it would help us understand what happened if you start at the beginning and give us the details step by step," Charles said.

"Yes, that would seem to be best," Otto agreed.

"Otto, I'll start, and then you jump in if I miss something," Nick suggested. "Around nine thirty last night, I became aware that Tom wasn't waiting on his tables. I was getting complaints from the other servers. You know how it is. After a customer waits so long for service from their waiter they call to another server for help."

Carrie reached for the carafe and topped off her coffee. She knew with Nick giving the facts, nothing would be left out. She also knew that Nick would weave the story through a dramatic presentation.

"I started looking for Tom in the kitchen, where I discovered most of his orders were waiting to be served. Of course, the first thing I did was to get the customers' orders out. Once the customers were served, I started to question the staff. Kristen told me that Tom had asked her to watch his tables. He said he needed to leave the floor for a few minutes and that all his orders were current. Then she got busy and assumed Tom had returned. Otto, you tell them what happened next," Nick said.

"Nick calls to me in the office. I too come to the kitchen to help straighten Tom's orders. However, Nick says he'll take care of customers and I should start searching for Tom. First, I went outside. Tom's car was in the parking lot, so I knew he's still in the building. I knew he was not upstairs in office area. I started my search down here. I looked in the bar in case he was meeting someone. Boys sometimes leave floor to meet a girl, but no Tom. Then I checked the restroom in case he not feeling good. Then I go out the back door, where some of the staff takes smoke breaks. Finally, I go down and look in wine cellar. Door is not locked. I find the body of Tom in the wine cellar. I come tell Nick. He goes down to look before he calls police."

Nick pulled out a small notebook. "I wrote a few things down, so I could accurately relay them to you. The body was found three racks over at the back wall where we hold wine tastings. Tom's body looked as if he simply collapsed on the ground. You'll see the police outline of the body when we take you downstairs. There was an open bottle of wine, a merlot, sitting on the table. I assume Tom opened it. I might add it was a very expensive bottle. There was one broken glass near Tom's body. It probably broke when Tom fell. The police took the pieces of glass because they assume the glass contained poison. The bottle of wine didn't break, but the police took that too. On the table was a note. I wrote down what was on the note.

> *I was the other man in Ginny's life. She wanted to end our relationship because of her upcoming wedding. When she asked for her ring back, I lost control. I killed her with her scarf. I'm sorry for the pain I caused. I loved her so much. I hope with my death the pain will stop.*
>
> *Tom*

"What do you think?" Nick asked.

"That sounds like a pretty straightforward confession. Why don't the police think Tom's death is suicide?" Charles asked.

"First, Chief Engler doesn't want to believe anyone other than your brother killed Ginny. The first question out of his mouth was had anyone seen your brother in the restaurant or in the bar tonight. Engler also said they had discovered no information supporting a relationship between Tom and Ginny. He asked me if I knew of their relationship. Of course I had to say no."

"I agree with that. Charles and I have been checking out possible suitors, and Tom wasn't even on the list," Carrie said.

"They also feel the timing is all wrong. A young man doesn't suddenly commit suicide in the middle of serving a dinner crowd. Especially since he told Kristen he would be back in a few minutes. And the final piece of evidence is that Tom didn't take a regular wineglass from the restaurant. He took one of our special crystal glasses that we keep in the cellar just for wine tastings. There are two missing from the rack," Nick said still referring to his notebook.

"The police think Tom go to meet someone down there," Otto added.

"What do you two think?" Carrie said looking first at Otto and then Nick.

"We agree that Tom's death was murder," Otto stated.

"But we disagree with the chief that your brother did it," Nick added quickly. "Plus we have other evidence the police don't know."

"Don't stop now. It's just getting good," Charles said as he also poured more coffee.

"First, remember when Tom told us about taking the phone call for Ginny? He said he thought he almost recognized the voice. Well, Otto and I think that Tom finally figured out who belonged to the voice. We think his meeting tonight was with the voice from the call. Second, we think the purpose of the meeting was blackmail. Tom made a comment earlier to Billy, another server, that he had worked out a solution to pay for his college tuition. Tom told Billy, quote, 'After tonight I won't be waiting tables for my college tuition money. I've come up with a method to have my tuition paid in full.' Sounds like our Tom had a plan," Nick said.

"Did Billy tell the police all of this?" Charles asked.

"Yes. And Engler said this information was very important because it added to the case he was building against his prime suspect."

"Nick, how does this evidence prove that Norton didn't commit Tom's murder? What's to say Tom wasn't trying to blackmail Norton?" Charles asked.

"Charles, do you think my brother is not only a murderer, but a blackmailer, too?" Carrie demanded.

"No, I don't think he's either, but I want to hear what evidence Nick and Otto have that eliminates Norton."

Carrie saw both Nick and Otto smiling. She knew they hadn't told them everything. "What are you holding back, Nick?"

Nick said, "It's really quite simple. First, Tom said his college bills were going to be completely paid. Tom was accepted at a rather expensive college, so the tuition is pricey. Unless something has dramatically changed in the fortunes of your brother, I wasn't aware he was wealthy."

"Nick, the police will just say that Norty never had any intention of paying the money or he would get it from my father," Carrie said.

"Don't despair, Carrie, there's more. Do you agree with us that Tom's death was the result of an attempt to blackmail the murderer? And Tom knew who the murderer was because he recognized the voice from the phone call?"

"Yes, that seems quite logical," Carrie answered.

"Well, I know the caller wasn't Norton. It suddenly all came together for me tonight when I realized Tom identified the caller. You see, I saw Norton in the living room when Ginny went to take the call. He couldn't have made the phone call and therefore didn't murder Tom."

"Of course, of course," Carrie said elated. "You've cleared Norty."

Carrie reached over and hugged Charles.

19

After Carrie's moment of elation it was time to visit the cellar. Charles took his wife's hand, and they followed Nick and Otto down the steps into the restaurant's wine cellar. Charles watched as Otto snapped off the police tape wound through the iron rungs of the locked gate.

"How stupid of the police to use this tape. The locked gate will keep people away. Not this silly piece of tape," Otto stated.

Otto unlocked the gate, and Charles and the others followed him into the room. They turned right between racks of wine bottles toward the back wall. At the end of the racks was a large open area with a long rectangular wooden table used for the wine tastings. On the floor to the right of the table were chalk marks that outlined the final resting place of the young waiter.

"As you can see, this location is at the back of the wine cellar and provides great cover for a private meeting," Nick said.

"Let me see if I understand what happened. Tom brings his assailant back here because it's private and out of sight. Tom decides to open a bottle of wine to celebrate his good fortune. In his mind he didn't feel any danger from the person he was blackmailing. You said two glasses are missing, but only one was broken on the floor," Charles said.

Charles noticed a rack with the glasses suspended upside down above the table. "Did the glasses come from this rack?"

"Yes. One is missing down on the left and another almost in the center of the rack. The police think the murderer took the other glass with him. Don't be surprised if they question Norton about a missing wineglass," Nick said.

"Interesting. I'll call Norton and tell him to destroy any wineglasses he may have in his pockets," Carrie said. "However, I do have a question. How could Tom be sure they would be left alone? Why wouldn't one of the other waiters come down here for a bottle of wine?" Carrie asked.

"To be honest, my dear, we don't get that many requests for the wines that are in our wine cellar," Nick said. "What we keep down here are our most expensive bottles. These wines tend to be requested only on special occasions."

"We sell many bottles over the holidays. But the rest of the year, how do you say? The Pear Cove taste tongue—"

"Taste buds," Nick added.

"Yes, their taste buds don't appreciate a fine wine. Most of the wines down here are for our personal collection," Otto said.

"Our house wine and frequently requested moderately priced wines are kept behind the bar to save time. That's why we keep the wine cellar locked—because we rarely need to come down," Nick said.

"Then how did Tom get the key?" Charles asked.

The men exchanged glances. Then Nick answered, "I normally keep the key on a chain around my neck. With all the holiday catering jobs, I was out of the building more than I was in. All the extra work also tended to keep Otto in the office, staying on top of the orders and the billing. I left the key at the bar."

"That explains why Tom saw the wine cellar as the perfect place for his meeting. He could conduct his business without ever leaving the restaurant," Carrie said.

"And for the murderer the restaurant was a public place where he wouldn't stand out, and the wine cellar would hide him from prying eyes," Charles added.

"Exactly! Tom could lock himself and the murderer in. And way back here, even if someone came down the cellar steps, they wouldn't be seen," Nick said.

"I think we've seen everything here," Charles said.

Charles led the group back toward the gate that protected the wines. The gate had been locked when the group arrived, and Nick used his key.

"Was the gate locked when you found the body?" Charles asked.

"The gate was closed with the key in the lock," Nick said. "The key in the lock is what alerted Otto to search inside. The police took that key as evidence. Of course they didn't ask if we had a duplicate key, and we didn't volunteer," Nick said.

"Why didn't the murderer lock the gate and take the key? It would have given him more time before the body was discovered," Carrie said.

"Perhaps," Charles said. "On the other hand, the key becomes a piece of evidence that has to be disposed of. If he was detained for any reason, he wouldn't want it on him."

"Have you checked with your staff to see if they saw anyone near the wine cellar?" Carrie asked.

"We're way ahead of you," Nick said. "We thought of all those possibilities, but no one saw anything. It was a very busy night. There were lots of people coming and going, but no one stood out to our staff. Besides, if the murderer was one of our regulars, as you suggested, he wouldn't stand out."

"We only really know one thing about this guy. When Ginny bought a ring at the jewelers for him, she implied he was an older man."

"Wait a minute, what ring?" asked Nick. "You haven't told us about a ring."

"The night Ginny was killed a ring was discovered under her body. The police assumed it was Norton's, but Norton never saw it. We tracked down the jeweler, and he validated that Ginny definitely didn't buy it for Norty. The type of ring she bought, the size, and a comment she made indicated it was for an older man," Carrie said.

"Does this not help Norton with the police?" Otto asked.

"Not necessarily. They could always claim Ginny showed Norton the ring, and that's what angered him enough to kill her," Charles said.

Charles watched Carrie's face as he relayed how the police could still use the ring against her brother. He could tell she hadn't thought of that possibility.

"Ah, but you believe when Ginny showed the ring to her new lover it angered him. And that's why he killed her," Nick offered.

"Exactly! That's why I think he's married. Ginny probably asked him to leave his wife. He panicked that the whole affair had gotten out of hand. That's also why he'll be more difficult to find. He kept the affair very low key. I'm sure he and Ginny weren't seen in places where his wife would find out."

"In this day and age it's hard to believe that someone would murder for an affair. Everybody's doing it. Everyone seems more than willing to forgive an indiscretion. Or they quietly divorce." Nick sighed. "And now a second murder. He's getting in deeper and deeper."

"That's why we need to keep the pressure on by asking questions. Hopefully, he remains in a panic state. And he'll make a slip," Charles said.

Charles held the gate in place while Otto locked it. Then the group moved upstairs. They were back at their table, where Charles poured more coffee.

"Need I mention not to tell the police you let us see the murder site? Engler warned us to stay away from his case," Charles said.

"Warned! That's putting it mildly. Knowing Engler, I bet it was a threat. Believe me, we understand. That's exactly why Otto and I waited to call you until after the police had left."

Charles noticed that Otto poked Nick in the ribs as if to urge him to say something. "Was there something else, Nick?"

"When we told you about the police asking if anyone saw Norton, you didn't say anything. You just assumed he wasn't here. In fact Norton was here. He had a sandwich and a soda at the bar," Nick said.

"But earlier, much earlier. Not at murder time," Otto added.

"How much earlier?" Charles asked.

"About six hours. He left before the dinner crowd even started to come in," Otto said.

"Do the police know this?" Carrie asked.

Charles heard the note of panic in her voice as she asked the question.

"Not yet. Josh, the bartender who waited on him, was on early shift. He left before the murder occurred. No one else said they saw Norton. However, the police are coming back to question everyone in more detail today. If they question Josh about Norton, he'll have to confirm he was here. We thought we should tell you."

"Yes, but I can swear," Otto said, raising his right hand. "Norton left long before Tom came on duty. Tom couldn't have spoken to him about a later meeting."

"It doesn't matter. Engler will figure some way of connecting Norty. Believe me, if Engler can find a way to tie my brother to this murder, he will," Carrie declared.

"Personally, I think someone should investigate Engler. He knew Ginny. I understand he has an eye for the ladies, especially young ladies. He certainly wouldn't want an affair revealed. More than angering his wife, it could affect his political aspirations," Nick said.

"An interesting thought. We'll certainly keep it in mind," Charles said looking at Carrie. He knew that Nick's comment would add to her case against Engler as the mystery lover. "Now I think my wife and I will head home. The one thing we're missing with this case is a little shut-eye."

20

"What's our next move? I'm feeling a major disappointment. Tom knew who the killer was, and now he can't tell anyone," Carrie said. She was scrambling eggs for their breakfast. "How are we ever going to find the murderer? Every time we find a clue, something bad happens."

"Don't be too disappointed. How would anyone have known that Tom had the information we needed? Besides we've learned three more pieces of information about our mystery man."

Carrie poured Charles a cup of coffee. She placed the plate of toasted English muffins on the table next to the orange marmalade. When they were both seated, Carrie asked, "What have we learned?"

"First, we know our mystery man is viewed as someone who has money."

"Because of the blackmail theory?"

"Right! You don't think blackmail unless you think the person can pay. Second, we know Tom heard or saw something that our mystery man was willing to commit murder to keep quiet. Where was Tom the night of the murder?" Charles said.

"That's easy. He was catering my mother's party and then returned to the Barn to serve the morning breakfast crowd. Do you suppose he saw our mystery man with Ginny prior to the night of the murder and put it all together?" Carrie suggested.

"It's possible, but let's think. Would you murder just because you had been seen with Ginny? Look at all the men on Norton's list. They had all been seen with Ginny. I think you need more. Is there more coffee?"

"There's plenty. We definitely need more coffee. I'll get it," Carrie said. She gathered up their dishes and placed them in the sink. She grabbed the coffeepot and refilled their cups. "We also know that when Tom was at my mother's party he took the phone call for Ginny. We think Tom eventually recognized the voice. But is this enough evidence for Tom to try blackmail?"

"Maybe not, but the case is building against this guy. Let's put it all together. Tom recognizes the voice from the phone call, he's seen him with Ginny previously, and maybe he sees him at the Barn at the time of the murder," Charles said. "It may not be a smoking gun, but it's enough to attract police attention."

"You know what?" offered Carrie. "We need to check Norty's list of men against who was at the Barn New Year's morning. Then start to narrow that list." She finished her coffee and started loading the dishes into the dishwasher.

"I agree we need to start to eliminate the names on Norton's list, but there's a third piece of information that Nick mentioned last night that I've been thinking about," Charles said.

Carrie had finished cleaning up and came back and sat at the table. She looked perplexed. "What did Nick say?"

"Remember when he said that in this day and age having an affair is no big deal? People do it all the time. They ask for forgiveness, or they part ways. They don't commit murder."

"Yes, I remember."

"That started me thinking. I'm wondering if there's something involved other than a love affair," Charles said.

"There are careers where having an affair can present a problem. Like a man with a political career," Carrie suggested.

"I know you're thinking of Engler. But put our friend Engler aside for a minute and think of other possibilities."

"Well, I guess one of the obvious reasons is money. Our murderer might be married to someone who controls the money. Maybe he didn't personally have the money to pay the blackmail, and the discovery of an affair would cut him off."

"That's the idea. What else?" Charles asked.

"What about the phone call Ginny received? As I said, it was probably made by someone not at the party, right?" Carrie said.

"Carrie, I know you're still thinking Engler. Remember, calls can be made from cell phones. This man could have slipped outside at the party and made the call. That puts a lot of men we would eliminate back on the list."

"You're right, Charles. I need to get past Engler and expand my list of suspects."

"Look, while I run into Tri-City for the monthly editorial meeting, I want you to visit with your father. Check with him and see if there's anyone else who should be on Norton's list.

Remember, our suspect could have been at the party or at the Barn or both or neither."

"Good idea. Maybe I'll find some other clues to check out by going over there."

"Wait a minute. I've an ulterior motive, sending you over to your father's office. I don't want you off sleuthing without me. I know if you're at your father's office, you won't get in any trouble."

21

"Hello, dear," Harry Kingsford said, kissing his daughter on the forehead. "Is Charles parking the car?"

"No, he had to go into Tri-City. I'm on my own. Which reminds me, do you think you could lend me a car or give me a ride home later?"

"You can take my car." Carrie turned to see her brother enter the office. "I can ride home with Dad. Besides, if you take my car, maybe we'll fool the press people who follow me everywhere. What brings you over to our corner of Pear Cove? Have you taken the day off from detecting?" Norty asked.

"Absolutely not! We're not giving up until this thing is solved. Charles and I are working several different angles. However, we haven't had a chance to catch up with you and Dad. I figured with Charles away for the day it would be a great time to fill you in. I was going to come over last night, but time seemed to slip away."

"You should have come over. I had nothing to do. I've been staying at home because of all the adverse publicity. Plus, every time I try to go anywhere I either have a reporter or a nosy neighbor wanting to ask questions," Norty said.

Carrie felt a sigh of relief. She had discovered, without asking any direct questions, if Norty had been home at the time of Tom's murder.

Then Norty added, "I did develop a bit of cabin fever. After dinner I decided to go up on the boards for a walk."

"What time would that have been?" Carrie tried to make her question sound innocent.

"Oh, I don't know. I guess it was about eight thirty."

"I can vouch for Norton being at the dinner table. Your mother made his favorite meal of pot roast, and he certainly ate his share," Harry said.

Carrie could have kicked her father. His comment about vouching for Norton's time made Norton suspect Carrie's question.

"After my walk I dropped into Shenanigans on the lower boards for a beer. I saw a few people I know from a distance, but I drank alone. The bartenders changed shifts while I was there. You would have to check with both of them, but you won't have trouble verifying how long I was there. What's going on? Why are you asking where I was last night?" Norty asked.

"Tom Gaston, one of the waiters from the Barn, was murdered last night."

"And you thought you would ask some clever questions to check my movements. What—every time there's a murder in Pear Cove, someone is going to check to see where I was?" Norton demanded. "Why should I be concerned that this Tom person was murdered? What does he have to do with anything?"

"Of course I don't think you murdered anyone. But you started it by saying you were home last night," Carrie said. She suddenly had a vision of when they were children in trouble with their parents. One of them would always use the excuse "you started it."

"But I do apologize. I should have just told you outright about Tom's murder. Tom is...was one of the waiters from the Barn who also worked Mom's New Year's Eve party. He's the one who took the phone call for Ginny. Then he went back to the restaurant. He served the early morning breakfast during the time when Ginny was murdered. Nick, Otto, Charles, and I believe Tom saw something related to Ginny's death. Because of some comments he made to a fellow worker, we think he might have been trying to blackmail the murderer."

While Carrie was explaining the events of last night, Norty started pacing back and forth across his father's office. When Carrie finished speaking he plopped in a chair.

"Now I understand. You think once our friend Engler figures out that Tom's murder is related to Ginny's he will want to know my movements for last night."

"I'm pretty sure Engler knows the relationship already. He was asking people at the Barn if anyone had seen you last night. I'm surprised he hasn't already been in touch."

"Actually, I may have fooled our good friend Chief Egghead for the moment. Someone did call last night asking if Norton was home. I asked who was calling. He identified himself as an officer from the Pear Cove police department. I said I would call Norton to the phone. Then he said never mind, his superior was calling him. Of course at the time, I was in my study and wasn't aware that Norton had gone out for a walk."

"You know, in the interest of full disclosure, I was at the Barn yesterday. I had a late lunch there. So what happens now?" Norty asked.

"Dad bought us some time with the police. Let's take advantage of it. The police will find out soon enough that you weren't home. Let's get on to my second reason for visiting you guys. Charles and I are still working the list of men Ginny might have known. We're using your list, Norton, as a starting point. I made a copy of the list for each of you."

Carrie handed copies of the list to Norton and her father. "Dad, I want you to put a check mark next to anyone that was at the New Year's Eve party at the house. Norton, I want you to place a check mark next to anyone you saw at the Barn New Year's morning when you were searching for Ginny. If there are any names missing from the list, please add them. And no talking while taking this test."

Carrie wandered around the office looking at pictures on the wall while waiting for them to finish. After a few minutes Carrie's father finished.

"I just can't believe that one of the guys on this list is responsible for Ginny's murder," her father said.

"I'm sure we're dealing with one killer. That means one of these guys is responsible for two murders," Carrie said.

"Are we getting any closer to discovering who it might be?" Norty asked as he handed his updated list to Carrie.

"Some days I feel discovery is just around the corner. Other days we have setbacks like Tom's death. It would be nice if we could find someone who would say, 'Oh yeah, I saw Ginny on several occasions with Mr. X,' but so far that hasn't happened."

"You know, I just thought of something. Lately when Ginny came to visit me she would spend part of her time sitting with Kevin. Sis, you know Kevin, our head programmer."

"I know Kevin," answered Carrie. "He's a good guy. In fact I've spent time talking to him when I've visited."

"He's an excellent programmer," her father added. "I was very lucky when I was able to hire him away from John Watford. Did you add him to your list, Norty?"

"No, I wasn't thinking of him as a suspect. I was thinking he's a good listener and Ginny talked with him...maybe she said something or let something slip to Kevin about who she was seeing."

"Is Kevin working today?"

Carrie asked the question because many of the programmers worked odd hours. They would stay all night if a project was hot. Then maybe come in late or catch up on sleep and not show up for a day. Carrie looked to Norton for confirmation. But Norton shrugged, indicating he didn't know if Kevin was working.

"I'll go find out. If you want me, that's where I'll be."

22

Carrie left her father's office, which was located off a large open circular lobby. From this open area several hallways, like spokes in a wheel, led to other offices and work areas.

Before Carrie wandered down the hallway to look for Kevin, John Watford came through the doors into the lobby. Carrie thought how tan and fit he looked. He was obviously over his New Year's tummy upset.

"Hello, Carrie. Are you joining us for today's marketing and advertising meeting?"

"No, I'm off to visit with Kevin. I haven't seen him in a while."

"Kevin, he's a fine fellow and a good programmer. Did you know he used to work for me?" John said.

"I wasn't aware of that until a few moments ago when Dad mentioned it. But of course"—Carrie lowered her voice and looked around to make sure no one overheard—"his work will benefit all of us now. You know, with the development of the medical software programs."

"Yes, what's being developed is very exciting. But you're right to lower your voice. We don't want to let the secret out until the launch date. That's when I take over and make this medical system a tremendous success. We want to beat any competitors to market and lock in those profits. Lots of profits," John said.

"Well, I better let you get to your meeting. Sounds like big plans are in the wind."

"Good to see you. Be sure to say hello to Charles," John said.

John went down the hallway closest to her father's office, and Carrie took the second hallway, which led to the programmers' section. This was the area of the building where all the software development happened. She passed a conference room with a group of people discussing a project. In the room was a small rectangular table holding papers and computers, but the attendees were all sitting on the floor. The atmosphere was casual at her father's firm, but the design discussions were intense. Everything from games to business programs were under development by these talented people.

Dad was correct to have kept his company in this location where the style of living is different from Tri-City.

It had been a while since Carrie had been in this part of the building, so she needed to check nameplates. She passed several offices before she found Kevin's. He was leaning back in his chair, facing his computer monitor with the keyboard perched on his lap. His feet were propped up on the windowsill, and he was typing and watching his screen for the response.

"Hey, Kevin!" Carrie knocked on the door jamb as she offered her greeting.

A young man in his thirties with an untidy mop of bright-red hair turned to face her. His square face broke into a huge smile when he recognized who she was.

"Carrie, how are you? Geez, it's been a while." He untangled his feet from the windowsill and started to stand.

"Sit down, sit down. No need for formality," she said.

"Charles not with you?" Kevin tried to see beyond where Carrie was standing.

"Not this time. He had to go into Tri-City. Besides I don't drag him along when I come to visit my favorite redhead. He might get jealous."

"Wow, with a line like that, sit down right here next to me." Kevin emptied a chair piled with papers next to his desk.

Carrie caught Kevin staring at her. "What's the matter? Something wrong with my makeup?"

"Heavens no. I was just thinking how lucky you and Charles are to have found each other. I hope it's not too late for me to find someone special," Kevin said.

"In case you forgot, young man, Charles was over fifty, and I was in my late...well...let's just say we found each other later in life. As my mother always says, 'There's someone special for everyone.' Be patient. You'll find her."

"I hope so."

Carrie took the seat and looked across at the computer monitor, which was filled with line after line of code. "Am I interrupting something important?"

"Not really, I'm just checking code before I go on to the next phase of programming. But thank heavens I was actually working when the boss's daughter came to visit."

"Right, like that was ever a reason to work," Carrie said, laughing.

"Norty mentioned that you and Charles were in town for the holidays. Of course, I bet he's really glad you're here now." His tone turned serious. "You know, with the trouble over Ginny's death. I assume you're investigating. I mean, everyone knows your reputation for solving murders."

"Charles and I are quietly looking into the murder."

"Are you here to ask questions about Ginny? Or questions about Norty? I'm not sure I know much. Know even less about the murder. I just can't believe she's gone. So sad. I do know some of the same people. There's a group of us that run around. Of course I'll help. Tell you whatever I know."

Carrie stared at Kevin.

"What?" Kevin asked.

"Kevin, you've got to stop locking yourself up with these computer programs all day. You need to have more human conversation." Carrie saw his dumbfounded look and then watched as a light bulb went off in his facial expression.

"Wow, I guess I was rambling. You're right. I think it comes from working alone. When I see another human being, thousands of words just start pouring from my mouth."

"Believe me, I understand. As a writer and photographer I work alone, too. When Charles gets home from the office I often do a word dump on him. However, you're right. I do have a few questions for you. We know Norty didn't do it, but the police require proof."

"You think I have proof?"

"I'm not up to proof yet. I'm just fact finding." She paused. "Kevin, I'm going to trust you. Charles and I have become aware of—that, well, there's just no delicate way to put this. We think Ginny may have had someone else in her life besides Norty. We think this man was older, married, and probably a seasonal visitor. I'm hoping you noticed someone with Ginny that fits this description."

Kevin rubbed his chin and then scratched his head. "I'm trying to think of men that might fit your description, but it's hard when you're trying to force your brain in one direction. I do know when Ginny became engaged to Norty a lot of guys were disappointed. The problem is most of these guys are my age and year-rounders."

"Then forget my description and tell me about the men who were disappointed."

"I should clarify. As long as the girl is not engaged, the guy hopes he may still have a chance. Once the engagement is announced, he has to accept that he's out of the running. To my knowledge Ginny was only dating Norty."

"Kevin, it sounds like you were one of the disappointed men," Carrie said.

He paused for a moment and swallowed hard. "I guess I was. Ginny and I had gone out on one date before Norty. I really liked her, and I was going to ask her out again. But before I got the chance or maybe the nerve, she met Norty at a party, and that was that. I backed off once Norty and Ginny starting dating. I hope you believe me." Kevin adjusted his glasses.

"Of course I believe you. You're a good friend." Although Carrie made a mental note to add Kevin to the list of men interested in Ginny. "Who else showed interest?" Carrie wanted to get Kevin back on track.

"You need to understand something about Ginny. I can't describe it or explain it. There was simply something about her personality that drew people to her. In fact I remember right after Memorial Day, Junie Watford was having a party at her parents' house. Her parents and several of their friends returned from a dance. Suddenly the two parties were one. The older folks mixing with the younger folks and most of the men, regardless of age, were around Ginny."

"Who were some of the men?"

"I remember there were five men. But they were with their wives. There was Mr. Watford, of course. Although he spent most of his time fixing drinks for his guests. There was Mr. Hanson from the funeral home plus his son, Jeff, who was also there. Mr. Smyth, the president of the country club. You know who else was there?"

Carrie shook her head no.

"Otto, the guy from the Barn. Junie's parents had arranged for him to cater the food for our party. But then I guess he doesn't count because everyone says he and Nick are, well, you know…an item. There was Mr. Buckley. Hey, I just thought of something. Mr. Buckley owns the stationery store in the mall, but he also has two stores in the Tri-City. He spends a lot of time away from Pear Cove."

"You said five guys. Were you counting Otto, or was there another man?"

"No, there were five. The fifth was Mr. Engler, our chief of police."

"Did he show an interest in Ginny?"

"Yup, he was right next to her. You know, all those guys I just mentioned are older guys. Could they all be suspects?"

"I don't know, but keep talking. This is what I meant by fact-finding."

Kevin thought for a moment then said, "Come to think of it there was another gathering one night out at the Seafood Cottage restaurant. Many of the same people from the Watford party were there that night too. Plus there was Engler's sister, Betty, and her husband, Jack Lumley. They were sitting at a table in the bar with John and Sally Watford. Of course the Lumleys would be there because they run the restaurant. You know the Seafood Cottage—out on the point?"

Carrie nodded her head. "Charles and I keep promising that one day we're going to drive out there and have lunch."

"Anyway, there was a huge bunch of us in there hanging out in the bar. They had a band, and we were all dancing. I remember Chief Engler came in. He made a fuss over Ginny and even took a turn with her on the dance floor."

"Was Norty there?"

"Yeah, but he didn't seem to mind. I mean it was one of those situations where everyone was taking turns dancing with different partners. The older men were dancing with the younger women and vice versa," Kevin said.

"That makes two times when you saw Engler on the scene," Carrie said.

"Yeah, but he's our chief of police. You don't think he had something to do with her death?"

Carrie remembered Charles's words not to focus only on Engler. "For now let's assume he was just fond of Ginny. But it might explain why he's going after Norty with such a vengeance. It's personal for him to solve the case."

A silence fell between the two. Carrie could see that Kevin continued to search his memory.

"There's something else that's been bothering me about Ginny. But it's not about potential suspects."

"What's that, Kevin?"

"Ginny wandered into my office one day, just as you did today. She sat where you're sitting and started a conversation. The conversation started with small talk about our friends and recent parties. Then she very quickly changed the conversation to my work. She started asking questions about the software I was programming."

"Is that so unusual? I mean, with the merger her family's company is now part of the business. Maybe she was just interested."

"That's what I thought at first. But her questions were very specific concerning actual lines of code." He looked out the window for a moment and then turned to face Carrie. "When I was talking with Ginny—well, I had the sense she was a spy."

23

"A spy! You're kidding," Carrie said.

"Maybe spy is too strong a word. As you mentioned, what we're working on is all in the family. Did your father tell you what we're developing?"

"Actually, it was Mr. Ellwood who gave us an overview of all the new software. The Kingwood Medical Intel System sounds very cutting edge. Why do you think Ginny was spying?" Carrie asked.

"You see, most people didn't give Ginny credit," Kevin continued. "She was no dummy. She had a degree in computer science and was quite bright. She could have been a first-class programmer if she'd wanted. But she had no desire to work full time."

"Since she was a programmer why do you think her questions were more than just a general interest? I mean, it's the difference between curiosity and industrial espionage."

"Because I really think she was trying to replicate one of the programs. She made several additional visits, supposedly just to chat. But very quickly every visit shifted to specific questions about the program I was working on," Kevin said.

"I'm still not sure that's unusual. I mean, her father was probably letting things slip at the dinner table. Or maybe Norton had discussed some of the programming issues with her. Although I guess I do wonder why she was quizzing you and not Norty or someone at her father's company."

"Because we're doing all of the security to protect the new medical intel system. Tasks were divided between the two firms. Her dad's company is doing the hardware and the interface programming with the different medical databases. You know, things like getting the latest updates on treatments or checking out a particular drug. We're doing the security and original programming for the new system. If you want to break the code for the new system, you need us."

"And you think Ginny was trying to break the code?"

"I do. The questions she asked were those of a programmer encountering problems. In fact, they were the same problems we were attempting to solve. I can tell by the look on your face you don't believe me. Or maybe you think I'm just being paranoid."

"No, not at all. I do believe you. But I'm trying to think why Ginny would want to duplicate a program she could have ready access to by telling her father she wanted to work on the team."

"Unless she didn't want to be part of her father's team but a competitor's team," Kevin suggested.

"Who could be a possible competitor?"

"The world. With all the changes in the medical field, there are hundreds of companies trying to develop new programs. The first company to launch is the winner."

"Wow! Wow! That's all I can say."

"There was something else that added to my paranoia. One day we had a meeting with Dr. Bessinger. Do you know who he is?"

Carrie nodded her head. "Charles and I met him at my parents' New Year's Eve party."

"Anyway, he was here for a discussion about what medical information we needed to integrate his field of biometrics and genetics into the system. Your father, Norty, me, and two other programmers represented our company. Mr. Ellwood was here with his top two programmers. We were just getting started when Ginny arrived. Mr. Ellwood seemed surprised to see her but invited her to join us."

"Did she participate in the meeting?"

"Oh yes, she participated. At every opportunity she asked questions about how we were solving problems with the software integration," Kevin said.

"I'm still not sure that's unusual. Why did you see a red flag?"

"Let me explain it this way. The easy part of what we're doing is the hardware from Mr. Ellwood's company. The tablet device they designed just collects information and transmits it to the servers. It's the server that captures the information and begins to build interfaces with all the possible medical databases. It's our software that manages the servers."

"Kevin, specifically what part of the medical software are you developing? Can you give me an overview?"

"In layman's terms, I'm doing the security program that protects our links. Our software analyzes the input and puts the medical professional in touch with the right database for diagnosis, preventions, prescriptions, treatment options, etc. The program has to be able to go in and out of existing medical databases and gather the right information. Or at the very least, direct the medical professional to the right location to get the information. Then whatever information the doctor downloads or adds to a patient file needs to be secure. We can't have those databases tracking back to a patient or even a medical office."

"When you find a problem with the code, how do you overcome it?"

"When designing software, slowly—very slowly and one step at a time. You see, we're also building in the logic. It not only tracks what's been done, but then it offers assumptions about what could happen next. On top of all the medical pieces, we're building the programming that allows all the information to be easily and securely transmitted between sites," Kevin said, taking a sip from a cup on his desk. "We're also finishing a personal version of the software so an individual can keep track of their own information. If an individual goes on vacation and has a medical emergency, they can quickly provide all of their medical information."

"Very exciting."

"But there's more. It satisfies the needs of what the government requires for medical-record keeping. We have multiple levels of security to eliminate fraud. And last but not least, it's so simple to enter the data that anyone can do it with little or no training."

"Now I totally understand why someone else would want the programming. Have you told anyone else your suspicions about Ginny?"

"You're actually the second person," Kevin said. "I told your brother several weeks ago."

"You told my brother?" Carrie said. She suddenly had a sinking feeling. This was yet another reason for a confrontation between Norty and Ginny.

"What's the matter? He's the team leader of this project and a friend."

"Do you know if he confronted Ginny with your suspicions?" Carrie asked.

"Oh, I get it. You think it gave Norton another reason for killing Ginny. Well, aside from the fact that we both know he didn't kill her, I know for a fact he didn't tell her."

"Are you sure?" Carrie asked.

"I'm sure because Norton and I came up with a plan."

Carrie noticed a slight grin on his face. "Kevin, what were you two up to?"

"Norton and I figured that Ginny was simply playing a game. She was very bright and one of those people who always likes to be right. I think she was trying to prove how smart she was by creating a working program before we did. When the questions got too specific, I simply gave her wrong information. I gave her lines of code that would appear to work but would ultimately crash the program."

"Sounds clever, but what would you have said if she'd come back to you with the problem you created?" Carrie asked.

"I'd have simply told her we were working to overcome the same issue," Kevin said.

"This medical intel system sounds like it could be worth a lot of money when it hits the market. Any possibility Ginny was doing the replication in order to sell it?"

"Ginny's father gave her anything she wanted. That's exactly why she didn't work full time. She did little special projects. For instance, she built the new company's website. It required periodic updating but didn't require her to work every day. Why work when you have everything you need? Although what do they say about people never having enough money? But knowing Ginny, I would bet she was doing it simply for the thrill of proving she could do it. She had a pretty big ego."

"That does sound more like Ginny," Carrie agreed.

They were interrupted by loud talking coming somewhere from the front of the building.

"What's all that noise? Sounds like you're having an employee rally."

"If we're having a rally, no one invited me," Kevin said. "Besides it sounds more like shouting between two people rather than a group party. We should check it out."

24

Carrie and Kevin determined the shouts were coming from the open lobby area near her father's office. Carrie was ready to take off toward the sounds, but Kevin grabbed her arm.

"Wait a minute! Don't go charging up that hallway until we know what's going on," Kevin cautioned. "In this day and age you never know what crazy person might be causing the commotion."

"But my dad might be in trouble!"

"If he is, we don't want his daughter in trouble, too. Come with me this way. We'll go to another hallway and come out on the far side of your dad's office. We can't be seen from that hallway, but we can see what's happening and if we need to call for help."

Carrie knew that Kevin's approach would take longer to reach her father's office. She also knew that Kevin's way was the correct way to proceed. The two virtually ran through the hallways. They slowed once they approached the end of the hallway opening into the lobby. They could still hear the shouting but could now make out the words.

"I don't care what my father or your father says. I don't care about a single word you have to say. I believe you killed my sister. I'm going to make sure you pay for her death."

Carrie turned to Kevin and said, "That's Fred Ellwood doing the shouting."

"Is he drunk?"

"Not sure about the drink, but he sure is mad," Carrie responded.

Carrie and Kevin continued to edge along the wall, until they had a clear view of the area in front of her father's office. Fred Ellwood had his back to Kevin and Carrie and was facing Norty. Norty stood near his father's office.

Kevin had been correct in his approach. Had they taken Carrie's direct route, they would have come out facing Fred.

"Fred, I didn't kill Ginny. I was in love with your sister—very much in love with her."

Carrie noticed that Norton's voice was shaky and barely audible as he answered Fred's accusations. This time when Fred spoke he was no longer screaming, but still loud.

"I'll grant you that you might have been in love with her once, but this wasn't true at the end."

"Fred, how would you even know something like that? You're away in the service. How do you know how Ginny and I felt about each other?"

"My sister and I were very close. She e-mailed me all the time, and we talked on the phone at least once a week. I knew what was happening. The last time we spoke she indicated that she was not going through with the wedding. She said she was no longer in love with you. She also said she hoped this decision wouldn't destroy the business plans between our two families."

Carrie saw her father was now standing at his office door. Fred looked directly at her father when he made this last comment.

Fred continued, "Ginny's biggest concern was how you would take the news, Norty. She didn't want to hurt you. Instead she was the one who got hurt."

"Fred, we've known each other for a long time. You have to believe me when I tell you that I was just beginning to notice a change in Ginny. What do they say about the one closest being the last to know?"

Carrie turned and looked behind her as she became aware of a sound. Coming down the hallway was Ed Grimly, the firm's chief financial officer, and Jim Dancy, another one of the programmers. Both men were over six foot with husky builds. Carrie put a finger to her lips, indicating they should approach quietly.

Grimly whispered, "Your father called us and told us to use this hallway so we would be behind Fred. We're going to grab him if the need arises."

Carrie nodded as she moved out of the way. Kevin edged up with the other two men.

Norton was still talking. "...growing apart. But Ginny never actually said to me that she didn't want to go through with our wedding plans."

"You lie. I think that's what she told you the night you were walking on the beach. You lost your temper and you murdered—"

Carrie never heard Fred finish the sentence. Instead he lunged toward Norty and threw a punch that hit Norty square on the jaw. Kevin, Ed, and John sprang into action and corralled Fred just as he was preparing to throw another punch. Harry and Carrie ran to aid Norty.

"Let me go, let me go," yelled Fred. "I only gave him what he deserved."

"Now, Fred, calm down. We're going to work this out between us. Fellows, bring Fred into my office. Everyone else can get back to what they were doing," Harry said.

For the first time Carrie noticed that the other hallways were filled with workers who had been watching the spectacle. She saw John Watford standing with a small group of people outside a meeting room. *Nothing like airing your dirty laundry in front of everyone.*

As the crowd started to disperse, Randolph Ellwood rushed through the front door and headed toward her father's office.

Once everyone was in Harry's office Randolph turned to his son. "Fred, what has gotten into you? I was in the car on my way here for a meeting when Harry called to say that you were here making accusations. I thought the military would teach you how to assess situations without becoming a hothead."

Fred was subdued as he sat in a chair with Ed Grimly standing next to him. Carrie sat in the sofa opposite him. Her father indicated that Ed Grimly should stay, but Kevin and John could go back to work. The two men left the office.

"Fred, I want you to apologize. This is difficult enough for all of us without you making a scene in such a public forum." Fred made no indications he was about to offer an apology.

Randolph said, "Well, I guess I'll have to apologize for my son. Harry, Norton, I'm sorry for my son's behavior. Come on, Fred, we're leaving."

Carrie had retrieved ice from the small refrigerator in her father's office. She was applying it to her brother's jaw. As the Ellwoods turned to leave, Carrie blocked their way.

"No, don't go. Solving Ginny's murder is vitally important to all of us. As the group who cared the most for Ginny, I think we need to discuss this further. Maybe share some information."

25

Carrie noticed that for someone who wanted to stay and fight, all Fred wanted to do now was leave.

"I'm not telling you people anything, especially if it's going to help him," Fred said, pointing his finger at Norton.

As Fred started to move toward the door, Carrie motioned to Ed Grimly. Grimly blocked the door and stopped Fred from leaving.

"Fred, sit down. It isn't going to hurt to hear what Carrie has to say. Personally I'd like to learn what's going on with the case. The police have told us nothing," Randolph said.

Randolph's plea was successful; Fred reluctantly sat down.

"Thank you, Randolph. Look, Fred, I know Norty appears to be the likely suspect. However, I think once you hear what I've learned over the last several days, you'll see Norty is no longer at the top of the list. Then perhaps you'll share what you know."

Randolph nodded in agreement, but Carrie wasn't getting any response from Fred, so she added, "Our families have been friends for a long time. I think we all want to find who killed your sister. You mentioned that you had received word from Ginny saying she was calling off the wedding?"

Randolph interrupted, "I wish you had mentioned these messages from your sister. Harry, this may put a whole different slant on the conversation you and I had New Year's Eve. It sounds as if Ginny was the one getting cold feet."

"Ed, thanks for your help, but I think we have everything under control now," Carrie's father said. Ed said nothing but nodded at Carrie's father and left the room.

"Fred, did Ginny give you any indication why she changed her mind about the wedding?"

"Yes, she said she had found someone else. I can tell by your reaction that what I'm saying isn't new information," Fred said.

"Well, it wasn't until after her death. Then we began to put things together," Carrie answered.

"She was pretty clear in her e-mails that this new relationship had been going on for some time. I think she first mentioned it to me in one of the messages I got from her at the beginning of summer."

With these words Fred stood up. He didn't move toward the door but instead reached into his back pocket and took out a folded piece of paper. Fred sat back down and started to read.

I really thought I was going to be set for life with Norty. He's a good and kind person, and I did love him. But I guess my love for Norty is more like the love I have for you, Fred. Love for a brother or a good friend. Now, having found true love, I know the real meaning of the word. I'm not going to tell you who it is, or at least not yet. I'm afraid there will be a bit of a stir when I reveal his name. And we're not ready for that just yet. I've been sworn to secrecy. Mom and Dad have always been supportive of what I've done, but I can't see Dad marching down the aisle for this wedding.

Fred interrupted his reading to add, "Now here's the part I was referring to before."

I think initially he'll be mad when I tell him. Especially when he finds out who it is and what we've done. I hope he doesn't overreact. You know he has a bit of a temper. In fact, I may have to leave Pear Cove for a while. Just until things calm down. It won't be much better for my new love when people find out. You see, he's in a relationship, too. He's married, but he's in the process of getting a divorce. We've discussed the fact that it may be better to start our new wonderful life somewhere else. Don't be surprised if you hear from Mom or Dad that I've left town. I'll always keep in touch with you. Remember not to judge me too harshly.

"You see, it's right here in this e-mail. Ginny was worried about Norton's temper when she told him," Fred said, as he refolded the letter and put it in his shirt pocket.

Carrie began, "Fred, I don't know how to put this—"

But Carrie was stopped by Randolph. "It's all right, Carrie, let me. Son, I don't believe Ginny was referring to Norton's temper. I think she was talking about my reaction to the situation."

Fred looked at his father and then a change came over his face. "I just assumed..."

"It's all right, Fred, this entire situation has caused us all to make assumptions," Harry said.

"Do you have any idea who this married man is?" Carrie asked.

"No, in our last phone call she still refused to tell me his name. However, she indicated the man was well known and well respected. That's probably why she thought they would have to leave the area."

"This doesn't narrow the possibilities unless someone knows a well-respected married man who's getting a divorce." No one responded to Harry's remark. Then he asked, "Carrie, haven't you and Charles been following the same theory?"

"We thought it might be a married man based on some of the things we discovered. There are too many on our list right now to start throwing out names. We need more clues." Carrie refrained from mentioning one of the names at the top of her list was Chief Engler. She snapped back to the conversation when she heard Engler's name mentioned.

"From the few pieces of information we did get from Chief Engler, he clearly believes that Norton is the guilty party. Why would he say that?" Fred asked.

"Chief Engler is politically motivated," Randolph said.

"The actual evidence doesn't point to Norty. Engler is trying to stretch it to fit him. Based on what Fred just added I think the evidence clearly points to this married man," Harry added.

"Look, let me share with you what Charles and I've discovered so far. But I must have the promise of everyone in this room that what I say will go no further. We don't have all the pieces of evidence we need to clear Norty. We don't want to tip our hand until we've built a better case. Do I have your promise?" Everyone responded to Carrie's request except Fred. "Fred, I won't say anything until I've got your promise as well."

Fred thought for a moment and then said, "I promise I won't say anything at this time. But should Norton go on trial for my sister's murder, then all promises are off."

"Hopefully you'll hear enough here to know that Norty won't be going to trial," Carrie said. She detailed the time when she and Charles had found the body. She told how she and Charles created a timeline of Norton's movements for the night of the murder. Based on their tracking, Ginny was probably already dead when Norton arrived at the Barn. She then told how she and Charles had discovered the jewelry store where Ginny had purchased the ring that was found under her body.

"Fred, as Charles told you at the funeral, that ring doesn't fit Norty. We think Ginny had it with her to give as a present to this other man, the night she was killed. Didn't you notice the size of the ring when Engler showed it to you?"

"Actually, Engler never showed me the ring. He just told me about it. He said Norty lost the ring in the struggle," Fred said.

"This is what we're talking about. Engler is trying to build a case against Norton where there isn't one. He's telling people, including the media, only bits and pieces of information and making it sound like it all points to Norton," Harry said. "That's why Norton hasn't been charged. The evidence doesn't support Engler's statements."

"Ginny could have shown Norty the ring she was going to give this other man, and that's why Norton got mad," Fred offered.

"Why would Ginny do that? It was a gift for her new love. She would want him to see it first. But I'm not finished. Fred, I'm going to tell you something that Charles and I didn't tell the police the night of the murder." Carrie saw she had Fred's interest.

"We told your father this but made him promise not to say anything. Norty actually discovered Ginny's body. Charles and I were on the beach nearby and watched Norty come on the body first. He was clearly upset at discovering the body. He tried gathering Ginny in his arms. "

"You saw Norty?" asked a surprised Fred. "And you didn't tell the police?"

"I know, I know. Charles and I've been regretting it ever since. It would have helped Norty."

"Wait a minute. If Norton was on the beach, how does that help his case? It puts him at the scene of the murder."

"Fred, when Norty bent over Ginny's body she was already dead. He was discovering her for the first time, just as we did a few minutes later. The murderer wouldn't return after killing her. He would be establishing an alibi."

"Norty, what were you doing on the beach?" his father asked. "And what happened to you after you discovered the body?"

"I had stopped at Carrie's to see if maybe Ginny had stopped by. But Carrie and Charles weren't home. I parked my car in their driveway and walked to the Barn. After I found out that Ginny hadn't been there, I came back to their house by way of the beach. When I discovered her body I was devastated. I ran to Carrie's house to get help. They still weren't home. I'd had a fair amount to drink, and I guess I panicked. I jumped in my car and drove out to the convenience store on the highway and called the police. The police told me it had already been reported. Later, I found out it was Carrie and Charles who'd called the police."

"Then you went home and waited for the police?" asked Randolph.

"Pretty much." Norty was glad that Mr. Ellwood's question kept him from explaining about his drinking before returning home. "I probably should have gone back, but I was shocked and scared. I wasn't thinking very clearly."

"It's understandable, Norton. I can imagine what a shock it was to discover Ginny's body," Randolph said.

Carrie addressed Fred again. "We think Ginny was meeting this man on the beach to give him the ring. Somehow on the beach that night things got out of hand and...well, we know the rest."

There was a long uncomfortable moment of silence. Then Fred said, "Norty, I'm sorry I hit you. I guess I feel like you felt that night. Wanting to do something, but feeling totally helpless. Plus all the evidence that I knew about certainly pointed to you. Again, I'm sorry."

Fred stood and offered his hand to Norty. The two men shook hands.

Carrie saw both fathers nod and smile.

"Good, I'm glad we got this much settled, but we've a long way to go. We need to work together to solve this murder. Right now Charles and I can use all the help we can get," Carrie said. "Is there anything else we can share while we're all together?"

"I do have one other question that no one has been able to answer. I made the assumption along with the police that Norty had driven Ginny to the beach. Now we know they weren't together. The big unanswered question is how she got there. Wouldn't she have driven to the rendezvous?" Fred asked.

"I asked the same thing about her car," Norty said.

"I assumed the police took Ginny's car to check it for evidence," Randolph said.

"No, I called the impound lot to see if her car could be released. They don't have it. So where's Ginny's car?" Fred said.

26

Charles and Baxter were out walking on the beach. Baxter loved the outside and was particularly fond of the sand and liked to roll in it. Unlike most cats, he didn't mind getting a paw slightly wet. A paw or two could be licked or sun dried while he slept in a window. However, he was very unhappy if his coat got wet. He was careful to avoid the big waves.

Charles had spent many hours training Baxter to walk on a leash. He would give Baxter a very long lead. This allowed him to roll in the sand and chase the water out. Then run from the waves as the water came in. The leash was mostly for Baxter's protection. If a dog came along, Charles could quickly reel Baxter to safety.

Carrie had filled Charles in on the events that had occurred in her father's office. He was using this walk to think about what happened with Fred and discuss it with Baxter. Baxter was very attentive to what Charles was saying and occasionally would add a meow. Mostly he just listened.

"This is an unusual case, boy. Carrie and I've done everything possible to prove that the timing is too tight for Norton to have committed the crime. However, there still remains a slight window of opportunity in which Norton could have done the deed. Not that I think he did, mind you. The police say he murdered Ginny before he went to the Barn. Then he went to the restaurant and asked about Ginny in order to establish an alibi. Then we saw him on the beach. I know Norton. He couldn't handle seeing Ginny's body the first time, let alone returning a second time to look. That's why he ran."

Charles was sitting on the sand, and at this point Baxter placed his paws on Charles's knee and stretched out fully.

"What else do we have, you ask? Norton has an alibi for this second murder, but it's weak. Again there's a small window of time while he was walking on the boards alone before he went into the bar. You see our dilemma." Charles stroked the top of Baxter's head, tickling behind the ears.

"And now there's a new wrinkle—this info Kevin gave Carrie about Ginny trying to replicate the new medical program."

Baxter looked up at the mention of the word "wrinkle" and then meowed.

"I don't know if it's important to the murder. The police only have circumstantial evidence against Norton. Unfortunately, we saw what happened to Carrie with only circumstantial evidence in Todd Barrington's murder. Nope, the only hope we have is to find the other man and prove Norton innocent of both murders. We don't want to take a chance on how a grand jury will interpret circumstantial evidence. Thanks for listening. Let's go get some lunch. We need to discuss with Carrie what to do next."

Baxter rolled over in the sand one more time. Then he shook his coat thoroughly and followed Charles to the house. When Charles entered through the kitchen door he noticed there was no lunch on the table.

"Do you want me to start lunch?" he asked. "Or is it too early?"

"No, your timing is perfect. Lunch is ready and waiting. I have it set in the living room in front of the television. Our friend Engler is about to hold a news conference."

Charles sat next to his wife on the sofa, and Baxter curled up on her other side. Charles knew that Baxter wasn't fond of ham and cheese sandwiches with tomato and pickle, but a nap next to Carrie would be nice. Charles grabbed a sandwich just as Engler entered the press room.

"Ladies and gentlemen, thank you for coming. I'll make a brief statement and then take a couple of questions." Engler reached into his jacket pocket, removed a sheet of paper, and unfolded it. "As many of you know, Pear Cove experienced its second murder of the New Year. A young waiter by the name of Thomas Gaston was murdered in the wine cellar of the Barn restaurant. The cause of death has been confirmed as poison. While the investigation of this murder is in its earliest stages, we believe this murder is related to the murder of Ginny Ellwood. Please keep in mind I can't share any specifics of our investigation at this time, but I'll try to answer general questions." Engler looked directly at the camera and smiled.

Charles listened to questions about the discovery of Tom's body—the time of discovery, how the body was discovered, etc. All details Charles and Carrie had already learned from Otto and Nick. The fifth question was direct and to the point. "Is Norton Kingsford a suspect in this second murder?"

"Mr. Kingsford has been questioned in regard to his fiancée's death. We have several witnesses who place him at the Barn near the time of Ms. Ellwood's death, but that investigation is ongoing. The investigation of the second murder has just gotten underway. We urge members of the community who may have seen someone or something the night of either murder to contact the police."

"Can you believe this guy?" Carrie said. "He doesn't say that Norty was questioned and released. Now he's implying that the only reason Norton hasn't been arrested is they're still investigating. Can't Simpson sue him or something?"

"Let's hear what else he has to say before we file suit," Charles said. "I'm sure there will be more reasons to be angry with Engler before he's finished."

"Is it true a ring belonging to Mr. Kingsford was found at the Ellwood murder scene?" A reporter from one of the Tri-City main television stations asked.

"We've several pieces of evidence from the murder scene that we're still analyzing," Engler said, trying to put the reporter off.

The reporter wasn't about to let Engler off the hook that easily. "Chief Engler, since you have verified that a ring was discovered, are you saying you haven't been able to confirm that it belongs to Norton Kingsford?"

"Now, ladies and gentlemen, you know I can't go into the details about a significant piece of evidence and how it relates to our main suspect. However, I will tell you that we continue to gather evidence that we believe will lead to an arrest very shortly. And of course we'll keep you informed. Thank you very much for your time."

The camera followed Engler's departure for just a few seconds and then swung back to focus on the reporter. The reporter, a woman, was in a navy-blue suit with a yellow silk blouse showing at the top of the jacket collar. Her blond hair was perfectly in place. She smiled at the camera and said, "Tim, as you and the folks listening just heard, Chief Engler has indicated that his department is still gathering evidence. However, I don't think there's any doubt from the statements made today that the police consider Norton Kingsford, the fiancé of the murdered woman, the main suspect."

The television switched to the studio where Tim, the anchor, asked, "Marcy, do we know where Norton Kingsford is at this time?"

"After being questioned the morning after the murder, Norton Kingsford was released and told not to leave the area. My understanding is that he's staying at his parents' home. He continues to go to work each day at his father's software company here in Pear Cove."

"Marcy, is there any indication that Norton Kingsford is somehow connected with this second murder of Thomas Gaston?"

"The police are certainly not saying at this time if Mr. Kingsford knew Mr. Gaston. However, as you heard Chief Engler say, he believes the two murders are related. He also indicated Mr. Kingsford is the main suspect in the first murder. I think it's safe to assume that the police are looking very carefully at Mr. Kingsford's movements the night of the second murder."

"Marcy, thank you for staying on top of this breaking story. We'll have more information on the six and eleven o'clock news on the murders in Pear Cove. Of course we'll break in on regular programming if there are any additional developments," Tim said.

Carrie switched off the television. "That pompous ass! He basically convicted Norton in front of the cameras. He sure didn't leave any room for anyone else to be guilty. Can't Simpson do something? Like get a gag order? Norton will never get a fair trial with all this pretrial publicity."

"I don't think Simpson can file anything yet. After all, Norton hasn't been arrested. If Norton is arrested, Engler's press conferences won't help the prosecution. Come and sit down and finish your lunch."

"I can't eat. Oh, Charles, I've never been so frustrated by a case. We don't seem to be making any progress. Even when I was charged with murder, I didn't feel this depressed. In our previous two cases there were lots of leads to follow. With this case we don't have many leads. When we do get a lead—like Tom—it's too late. What are we going to do?"

"Now, Carrie, every case has been the same. There's always that period when we seem to be in the dark, and then that one break will appear. I felt that way about my brother's murder."

"I don't remember a big break. We were constantly gathering pieces."

"No, my darling, the big break was you. After you came along things began to happen." Charles grabbed Carrie from her pacing and gave her a hug and held her. "Just have faith. I guarantee a break will happen." Charles had no sooner said the words than the phone rang.

27

"Should we answer the phone?" Charles asked as he continued to hold Carrie.

The couple hadn't been besieged with phone calls like Carrie's parents. However, the few calls Charles had answered were from people wanting to know about Ginny's death and the latest updates on the police investigation.

"I think we have to answer. This phone doesn't have caller ID. It may be Mom, Dad, Norton, or even Nick and Otto with another startling discovery," Carrie said.

"I hope it's not Nick or Otto," Charles said, getting up from the sofa. "I don't like their discoveries." Charles removed the receiver from its cradle. "Hello, yes, this is Charles. Oh hello, Mr. Phineas. How are you? Did you enjoy your holiday with your family in Tri-City?"

Charles made a face at Carrie. Obviously he was going to be saddled with another neighborly explanation of progress on the case. Mr. Phineas lived two doors down, and he probably deserved an explanation more than anyone. Ginny's body was discovered on the portion of the beach near his home.

Charles was only half listening to Mr. Phineas. He was thinking about how to frame the briefest of explanations without offending their good friend. Suddenly, Charles's facial expression changed.

"Mr. Phineas, could you repeat what you just said? How can you be sure it's Ginny's? I see. Look, I'll be right over. No, don't call the police yet. Wait until I get there, and we'll call them together."

As Charles replaced the receiver, Carrie asked, "What is it?"

"Mr. Phineas wasn't interested in the latest gossip about the case because he has some startling news of his own. Ginny's car is parked in his driveway."

"You're kidding." Then Carrie paused for a moment. "Do you think it's been parked there since the night of her murder?"

"I do. The police assumed Ginny came to the beach with Norton. They weren't looking for her car. Remember, Fred didn't ask the detectives about the car. He called the impound lot. And of course they didn't have it listed."

"But why park in the Phineas driveway?"

"Ginny didn't want her car seen. Especially by Norton. Remember, Mr. Phineas's driveway drops steeply down from the road, hiding any cars that are parked there," Charles said.

"That driveway really does go downhill. Kind of a strange driveway for two older people."

"I asked Phineas one time about the steep drop. He said he and his wife, when they had the house built, wanted the entrance closer to the beach level. That way they wouldn't have so many steps to navigate. The trade-off was to have the steep driveway."

Charles was zipping up his jacket when Carrie jumped up from her seat. "Hey, wait for me. I'm going too."

"Hold on. I've something else I want you to do before you join us. How about calling that nice reporter, Marcy Whittaker, who was on television a few minutes ago? Invite her and her camera crew to visit Mr. Phineas. I think it's time we give Chief Engler a taste of his own medicine. You call the reporter, and I'll go down and look around for a few minutes. Then, like a good citizen, Mr. Phineas will call the police."

"Hopefully, the television cameras will get there before Engler. Oh, and try not to sound like Carrie Faraday. I think an anonymous call to the television station would be better," Charles said.

Charles turned and went out the door as Carrie went to make the phone call.

28

Mr. Phineas's house was a brick rambling rancher that stretched across most of his half-acre lot. With the house below the street level it offered a great deal of privacy. The only thing visible to the occasional passerby was the roof line of the house and thick shrubbery that adorned the front of the property.

The house design turned out to be the right choice when Gloria Phineas developed both arthritis and heart problems. Mr. Phineas could drive down into the garage. Gloria could walk from the car into the house without having to deal with any steps. After Gloria's death, Mr. Phineas sold their house in Tri-City. He retired and became a permanent resident of Pear Cove.

When Charles arrived he didn't even have to ring the bell. Mr. Phineas was standing at the door waiting for him.

"Do you see it? When I came home it was sitting right there, blocking my garage door. I had to park next to Ginny's car. I'll tell you, I was pretty mad. But come, come in. We don't need to talk out here."

Charles entered the house. With the exception of a couple of suitcases sitting in the entrance hallway, the house was immaculate. The rooms were neat and clean with everything in its place. Mr. Phineas led Charles into the living room, and they sat in chairs facing each other.

"We don't have a lot of time, because we do need to call the police," Charles said. "The police will check how quickly you called them once you discovered it was Ginny's car. However, I do want to ask you a couple of questions. It looks like Ginny's car, but I assume you have checked to be sure it's hers?"

"Yes, there's no doubt it's Ginny's. As I said, I was pretty mad when I saw the car. I marched right over and found that the driver's door wasn't locked. I opened it right up and checked for the registration in the glove box. I must say I calmed down very quickly when I saw whose car it was."

"Now think carefully. Did you touch only the door handle and the glove box?"

"Yes, yes, that's right. No wait! I touched the steering wheel as I pulled myself across to the glove box, and my other hand touched the seat. The seats are leather, so my prints will probably show there too."

"Why didn't you call the police right away?" Charles could tell that his neighbor was wondering why he was being drilled. "I'm asking because the police will ask you these same questions."

"Yes, of course. Good idea to practice before they come," Mr. Phineas agreed. "You see, I started to think about why Ginny would park her car in my driveway. Then I thought about the murder and her murderer. I won't tell the police this, but I figured I owed it to you and Carrie to tell you first what I had found. I still remember the way Carrie came to our home in Tri-City and cooked for me and Gloria. Carrie made sure we had everything we needed during Gloria's final days."

Charles smiled and nodded. "That's what neighbors are for, and you've returned the favor. Now I need to ask my neighbor for another favor. Did you happen to see the news conference Chief Engler held today around lunch?"

"No, I missed it. That was the time when I was arriving home. But I've been watching the news coverage all week in Tri-City. I know Mr. Engler hasn't been kind to Norton."

"You got that right. In fact today, Engler all but announced that Norton was the murderer and it will be just a matter of time before he's arrested," Charles said.

"Oh my, I bet that was very upsetting to Carrie."

"You can say that again. Carrie wanted to sue Engler, but our hands are tied. He never really accuses Norton. He just implies the guilt. That's why I want to ask for your help. While I'm over here talking with you, Carrie is placing a call to the local television station. Hopefully she can talk with the same reporter who covered the earlier news conference. We're hoping that if this reporter interviews you, there'll be a different slant for the public to hear."

~

Carrie looked briefly at the red sports car as she headed to the door of Mr. Phineas's house. Carrie rang the bell and was greeted by Charles.

"Come in, darling. Mr. Phineas is calling the police to report the discovery of Ginny's car." Under his breath Charles quietly asked, "Did you make your call?"

"Good news. Turns out Marcy and her camera crew were on their way to the Barn for an interview with Nick and should be here momentarily."

"Then we better help prepare Mr. Phineas for his fifteen minutes of fame."

"Hey, before we go through with all this, are we sure it's Ginny's car?" Carrie asked.

"Oh yes, it's hers. Mr. Phineas checked the registration."

"Carrie, I'm so sorry about all this trouble your family is experiencing. Especially with this being the New Year," Mr. Phineas said, returning to the room. "You know I'll do anything I can to help."

"You can help right away. Did Charles tell you that I called the local media?"

"Yes, he mentioned that it's important that I tell my story to the press before the chief puts out his modified version," Mr. Phineas said.

"Correct. Chief Engler is putting a totally different spin on the facts to suit his own personal motives. I got in touch with the camera crew who will be here before the police. I think it would help Norty's case to have the press hear from you first," Carrie said.

"I was kind of hoping it would be a print reporter. I've never been on television, but I'll do my best."

Carrie barely had time to assure Mr. Phineas that he would do fine when there was a loud rapping at the door.

29

Carrie was amazed how quickly the television crew was set up and ready to film. The crew seemed to know that they were only moments ahead of the police. Mr. Phineas and Marcy sat next to each other in matching chairs. Marcy spent a couple of seconds chatting with Mr. Phineas to put him at ease, and then the cameras began to roll.

Mr. Phineas recounted how he had been away in Tri-City for the holiday. He returned home to find a strange car parked in his driveway. "And you can imagine my surprise when I discovered the car belonged to Ginny Ellwood. Such a tragedy. It's tough to lose someone so young and then to find out it was due to murder." Mr. Phineas shook his head.

"Even though you were away, you were aware of the murder?"

"Oh yes, Marcy. I've been following you and your station's coverage of the story," Mr. Phineas replied.

Carrie knew this statement totally endeared him to Marcy. She smiled broadly as the camera focused on her.

"Did you personally know Ms. Ellwood?" Marcy asked.

"Yes, Pear Cove is a small community. I had met her several times over the years. And of course my good friends and neighbors are the Faradays. Mrs. Faraday is the sister of Norton Kingsford, Ms. Ellwood's fiancé. I've been at the Faraday home when Norton and Ginny were there."

Carrie could tell that Marcy was surprised that Mr. Phineas knew several of the players in this drama. Carrie was impressed by how quickly Marcy jumped on this new information with her next question.

"Mr. Phineas, I know this next question will be difficult for you, especially considering your friendship with the Faradays. Do you think Norton Kingsford is responsible for the murder of Ginny Ellwood?"

Mr. Phineas looked directly into the camera and said, "No, I don't. I've known Norton for many years, and he's a very fine lad. I've also seen with my own eyes the love this young man had for Ginny. I know he couldn't have murdered Ginny, regardless of what circumstantial evidence the police have."

"One final question: Do you think the police are doing a good job of handling this case?"

"Oh, I don't know much about police work." Mr. Phineas paused for the briefest moment and then added, "Marcy, don't you think Chief Engler seems to be concentrating only on Mr. Kingsford? Perhaps there are other possibilities and people he should investigate."

"Could you elaborate on what you mean?" Marcy asked.

"I heard on one of your earlier broadcasts when you reported that the police believed Norton drove Ginny to the beach. But now we discover her car parked just a few hundred yards from where she was murdered. It looks like Norton had nothing to do with driving Ginny here. Perhaps Chief Engler needs to rethink other statements he made about what he thinks Mr. Kingsford did or didn't do."

Carrie could barely believe what she was seeing and hearing. Mr. Phineas looked as if he was in deep thought as the cameras swung back to Marcy. Somehow, between his words and gestures, Mr. Phineas had presented a totally different viewpoint. He had said what Carrie wanted the press to hear.

"Some very interesting points, Mr. Phineas. I guess we do have to wonder how the police missed finding Ginny Ellwood's car. Especially when it was parked so close to the murder scene. We will certainly have some more questions for Chief Engler. This is Marcy Whittaker with an exclusive interview with the man who discovered Ginny Ellwood's missing car. We'll have more details as they become available. And now back to the studio."

Carrie was absolutely overjoyed with Mr. Phineas. The minute he was clear of his microphone and Marcy had moved away, she ran to him. She hugged him and whispered, "You have single-handedly improved the balance of coverage for Norton! We owe you a great deal," she said.

"Great job!" Charles said, shaking Mr. Phineas's hand. "We would like to thank you. Will you join us for dinner tonight?"

"Actually, that would be very nice. I haven't had a chance to get to the grocery store."

"I'll call you later with the details. Oh my, I think you're about to get some more company," Carrie said. She had noticed during the interview that a police patrol car had drawn up to the house. The two policemen had immediately placed yellow police tape around Ginny's car but hadn't approached the house. Instead they stood next to their cruiser and waited.

Now as the television crew was taking equipment out, Chief Engler and Detective Hilton arrived. Carrie tried to get Charles's attention so they could leave. But Marcy was thanking Mr. Phineas and blocking the exit. Marcy turned to ask Carrie about an interview when Chief Engler came storming into the house.

"What's going on here?" Engler demanded as he spotted Carrie, Charles, and Marcy. "How did all these people and a television crew get in here? This is a crime scene. Why hasn't this area been sealed?"

"The crime scene isn't inside my house, Chief Engler. It's in the driveway outside. If you're going to shout orders, please go outside. If you wish to talk with me about my discovery of Ginny's car, then you may stay. As to these people, they're my neighbors. I asked them to advise me what to do when I found the car."

"And I guess they advised you to call the television station?"

"I never called the television station," Mr. Phineas answered honestly.

Carrie looked at Mr. Phineas in amazement. Carrie saw that he was not the least bit intimidated by Engler. Engler had lost his temper when he arrived, but Carrie saw how quickly he got himself under control.

"Marcy, as you know, I'm always willing to cooperate with the press. However, the discovery of this car is an important piece of evidence. My apologies if I seem upset. But it's important for a good police investigation not to have the evidence compromised in any way. Especially by interfering amateurs."

Carrie felt Engler's eyes on her.

"As soon as my team and I have had time to evaluate this new evidence, I'll be glad to address the press," Engler said.

"What you have here is the evidence that throws your theory about my brother's involvement in this murder right out the window," Carrie said.

Carrie felt Charles taking her hand and pulling her in the opposite direction from Engler. She turned back to Mr. Phineas and said, "I'll call you later about dinner."

30

Carrie had thought about preparing a home-cooked dinner for Mr. Phineas. However, she thought better of it for two reasons. Since this was a quick holiday stay at the beach house, she hadn't replenished the pantry the way she would for the summer months. She also thought that after three weeks of home-cooked meals with his family, Mr. Phineas might enjoy a dinner at a restaurant. She decided to call him and see what he wanted to do.

"Charles and I were just discussing dinner. We thought we would call and give you your choice. Would you like to celebrate your television debut with dinner here on our deck or would you like to go out to a restaurant as our guest?"

"If you don't mind, I'd just as soon go out. It's been a while since I've been out to eat. That is, unless you've already started preparations for a deck dinner."

"I haven't prepared a thing. How about Charles and I pick you up in about fifteen minutes?"

"Oh yes, I'm ready. You know, we don't have to go somewhere far or somewhere fancy. I'm happy to eat down the road at the Barn."

"Then the Barn it is. It's certainly where the action has been for this murder case. We'll see you in a few minutes."

~

Nick greeted the trio as they walked into the restaurant, "Ah, our local television celebrity. Boy, you sure nailed Chief Engler with the facts." Then he added, "I think everyone in this town has wanted to do that since Engler became head cop."

Mr. Phineas beamed, now sure he had done the right thing with his interview with Marcy. This conclusion was reinforced as the trio was being seated. The senior Mr. and Mrs. Hanson stopped them as they passed by their table.

"That was a nice job you did with the press this afternoon, Jay. We all want to find who killed Ginny. I think you brought some perspective back to the case," Edward Hanson said.

John and Sally Watford waved from the other side of the room. They also gave him a thumbs-up. Others stood and shook his hand or patted him on the back as he passed.

Mr. Phineas seemed glad Nick placed them at a table that provided the trio some privacy but allowed them to see the other tables on the main floor of the restaurant.

After a quick look at the menu, Mr. Phineas and the couple ordered. His drink arrived, but his first sip was interrupted by a toast from Charles.

"To Mr. Phineas, on his discovery of Ginny's car and his magnificent handling of the press."

"Hear, hear! And don't forget," added Carrie, "his ability to bring truth and balance to a botched police investigation."

A broad smiled covered Mr. Phineas's face as he accepted the toasts. "Always glad to be a good neighbor. And I have to admit it was kind of fun. But you two must do one thing for me."

"Anything," Carrie answered.

"You two have to stop calling me Mr. Phineas and call me Jay. Mr. Phineas is much too formal for people sharing a murder investigation."

"I agree, Jay," Charles said.

As the various dishes of food arrived, Jay spent time talking about his holiday visit to the family in Tri-City. But by the time they reached the end of the meal, the conversation was back to the topic of murder.

Mr. Phineas listened while the couple gave details of discovering the body, Tom taking the phone call at the party, Tom's possible blackmail attempt, his murder, and what they saw in the wine cellar. They outlined Norton's movements during the times of both murders and even the implications of Ginny trying to replicate the computer program, and they ended with their discoveries about the ring.

"We know the ring purchased by Ginny wasn't for Norton. Mr. Merkoff, the jeweler, had the impression she was buying it for an older man," Carrie said.

"And we think the ring may have caused her death, if her lover wasn't ready for the relationship to get that serious. We suspect our mystery man is married, and perhaps Ginny threatened to reveal their affair. Anyway, he panicked and strangled her with a scarf," Charles said.

Jay listened carefully. He took his final forkful of lemon meringue pie. Then he asked his first question. "Where did the scarf come from? You said she was at your parents' party. Did Ginny have the scarf on at the party?"

Mr. Phineas clearly saw the look of surprise on Carrie's and Charles's faces.

Carrie answered, "We hadn't given the scarf any thought. We should have, especially since it was the murder weapon. Somehow we got all wrapped up concentrating on the ring."

"I can't remember whether Ginny wore a scarf at your parents' New Year's Eve party," Charles said.

"I'm surprised you can remember anything from that party," Carrie said.

Mr. Phineas grinned at the marital exchange.

"But you're correct, darling. I'm positive she didn't. I remember thinking how Ginny looked so nice and chic in a basic black dress with no accessories. Which takes us back to the question of where the scarf came from."

"Perhaps the scarf was a gift from the man she was meeting," Jay suggested. "I mean, you're assuming she went with the ring as a gift for him. Wouldn't he come with a gift for her?"

Charles and Carrie had a look of people traveling through a dark tunnel when someone suddenly switched on the light.

"I think that's a most logical conclusion. How stupid of us not to have thought of that possibility before," Charles said.

"If we missed this clue, I bet our man Engler didn't do any checking on the scarf either," Carrie added.

"I doubt it. He probably assumed, as we did, that Ginny was wearing the scarf and it became a weapon of convenience. It makes much more sense that the murderer brought the scarf with him. He's in the process of placing it around her neck when the mood starts to change and well...we know what happened next," Charles said.

"If it was a gift, maybe it came from some sort of a specialty shop, and we can track the purchaser. Of course it might have been purchased out of the Pear Cove area, but at least we've got a new lead," Carrie said.

"I'm so glad you joined us for dinner tonight," Charles said.

Mr. Phineas accepted the compliment by raising his glass and taking a sip of wine. He savored the taste of the liquid and then added, "You know, there's one other item. It's one of those things that when it happens, you don't give it a second thought. However, Carrie, when I heard you give your profile of the killer, I remembered something. Although I hope I'm not jumping to a conclusion, since this is someone we don't particularly like."

"I think we make a good team. We balance each other out. So let's hear it," Carrie said.

"Well, here goes. As I mentioned earlier this evening, I eat here frequently. Since I come alone I usually sit at the bar." Mr. Phineas stopped, as if he was still wrestling with his inner voice about revealing the information. "I guess it won't hurt to share this. On two occasions, I saw Chief Engler and Ginny Ellwood sitting together."

Mr. Phineas stopped speaking to wait for the couple's reaction. When they sat silently, he continued. "On the first occasion, Ginny was already sitting at the bar. We had exchanged pleasantries, then I went down to the far end of the bar to order my dinner. Within a few minutes Engler arrived, looked surprised to see her, and then sat next to her. The second time when I saw them, they were both already sitting at the bar."

"Interesting," Carrie said. "How did they act toward each other?"

"The first time, it seemed like it was a chance meeting, although I noticed that Engler picked up the tab. The second time, they were already engaged in conversation. However, it didn't seem to be serious or even flirtatious. There was some laughter, but they weren't sitting too close or touching each other or looking into each other's eyes. You know, the way I saw Norton and Ginny act with each other. What do you think?"

"On the one hand, it explains Engler wanting to solve the case quickly. He knew her and feels a personal responsibility for bringing her killer to justice. On the other hand, he's an older married man who fits the profile. Maybe he was the one that Ginny was seeing. Either scenario could explain his relentless pursuit of Norton," Charles said.

"He definitely fits my profile. He's a man in a position of power who stood to lose a lot if his affair was revealed," Carrie added.

Mr. Phineas was listening to Carrie, but he was also distracted by something behind her. "Speak of the devil, here's Chief Engler now," he said.

Mr. Phineas and the couple watched as Chief Engler went to the front desk and spoke with Nick. The chief was followed by Detective Hilton and two uniformed policemen, who were escorting a handcuffed Norton.

Charles jumped up. "Carrie, call Simpson and let him know that Norton has been brought to the scene of Tom's murder without legal representation."

31

The policemen and Norton had barely reached the bottom of the steps leading to the wine cellar when Charles was on them.

"Hello, gentlemen. May I join the party?" Charles asked.

Instinctively the policemen turned and blocked Charles. Charles smiled as Engler turned to see what was going. When Engler recognized Charles, his facial expression changed.

"What is it with you people? Do you live at this place?" Engler snarled.

"It's close, it's convenient, the food is good, and I usually like the people who come here," Charles answered.

"Good for you. Now this is official police business. So leave," Engler said.

Charles didn't move. Instead he looked straight at Engler and said, "If this is official police business, then Norton shouldn't be here without his lawyer. Norton, don't say a word, regardless of how innocent the questions may seem."

"We allowed him to call his lawyer," Engler said.

"Is that right, Norton?"

"I called Simpson before I left the house. But I had to leave a message with his answering service. Plus, when Simpson gets the message he'll think I've been taken to the police station. That's where I thought they were taking me. I think I'd rather leave with you, Charles."

"Let's go," Charles said. Charles made a half turn, placing his back toward the policemen and making an opening for Norton.

"You aren't going anywhere, Mr. Kingsford," Engler said. "But you are, Mr. Faraday. Officers, escort Mr. Faraday away from this area."

Charles held his ground as the officers touched his sleeve. "Engler, you're breaking the law. Norton is here without his lawyer and has indicated a desire to leave. This won't be good for your career when this little mistake is revealed."

Charles moved aside as Detective Hilton, who had been standing quietly behind Charles, spoke. "Chief, he's right. You really shouldn't have this young man here without his attorney."

Charles saw that the red that had started creeping up from Engler's neck had reached his face. But before Engler could say another word, Carrie, Mr. Phineas, and a man Charles didn't recognize came down the steps.

The unknown man stepped forward. "Chief Engler, my name is Justin Halloway. I'm a consulting attorney who works with Hugh Simpson." Halloway held out a business card. Chief Engler took the card gingerly, as if the ink were still wet, and then flipped it back and forth between the tips of his fingers.

Halloway continued, "It's a violation of my client's rights to bring him to a murder scene without legal representation."

"We allowed him to call his lawyer. I assume that's how you arrived."

"Actually, I arrived based on a phone call Mrs. Faraday made. Luckily, I was eating here in the restaurant. But that doesn't matter. Exactly what's going on here?"

Charles moved back next to Carrie and whispered, "How did you find this guy?"

"I called Simpson. He had just picked up a message from Norton. This is where luck was on our side. Halloway is a criminal attorney whom Simpson brought down from Tri-City to discuss Norton's defense should he be officially charged. Simpson was unable to meet with him until tomorrow and had recommended the Barn for his dinner. Simpson described Halloway, and Jay and I found him."

"Is Simpson coming over?" Charles asked.

"No, he's going to go to the police station and wait for Norton and Halloway to arrive. Halloway is going to insist that they take Norty to the police station without any theatrics here in the wine cellar," Carrie whispered.

Charles had no sooner heard Carrie's explanation of events than they heard Halloway say, "My client isn't going on a tour of a murder scene. If you think he murdered the waiter, then charge him. If not, we're leaving."

Charles stood quietly during an uncomfortable moment of silence that was finally broken by Detective Hilton. "Chief, don't be pressured into doing anything foolish. Remember what the district attorney said."

Engler had turned a deaf ear to his detective. "That works for me," Engler responded to Halloway. "Norton Kingsford, I arrest you for the murders of Ginny Ellwood and Thomas Gaston. Detective Hilton, read him his rights. Does that satisfy you, Mr. Halloway?"

32

Carrie, Charles, and Halloway arrived only minutes behind the police car that brought Norton to the station. However, the minute they arrived they were blocked from getting near Norton. Engler had an officer waiting at the door who immediately redirected them into a large room with rectangular tables and chairs. In the far corner of the room there were several vending machines. At first Carrie thought they might be in a break room. Then she realized they were in the daily briefing room for the officers.

Halloway went off to find Simpson and left Carrie and Charles sitting at a table.

"Do you want some coffee?" Charles asked.

"Coffee out of a machine? I think I'll wait until I'm really desperate for a cup," Carrie said.

"I only offered the coffee because I know you're tense."

"And you're not."

"I'm concerned, but I'm not sure this is going anywhere. I don't believe Engler has any more evidence concerning Ginny's murder than he had when he first questioned Norton. With the murder of Tom he has absolutely nothing that links Norton to the crime. I imagine Detective Hilton is having real difficulty filling in the paper work to process Norton," Charles said.

Before Carrie could comment further her parents were escorted into the room. Based on their appearance Carrie wondered if they had already been in bed when they received the call from Simpson to come to the station. Her mother and father looked as though they had just grabbed the nearest items of clothing and thrown them on.

"Oh, Carrie, Charles, I'm so glad you're here. Your father wanted me to stay home, but I said not this time. But once we got here we were told we couldn't see Norton until after he was processed," Caroline said.

"Have either of you seen Simpson?" Harry asked.

"Simpson and Halloway are somewhere in the back hopefully helping to free Norty," Carrie said.

"Oh good, I'm glad Halloway came in from the city," Harry said.

The group sat quietly until they heard a commotion at the door.

"Don't be ridiculous. Of course we have something to do with the case. We're the bail people."

Carrie was sure she recognized Nick's voice. A moment later, Nick walked into the room carrying an oversized canvas bag accompanied by a very, very large man. Charles was tall, but this man's height and bulk made Charles seem tiny. His short buzzed haircut did nothing to reduce his height.

"Hi everybody! The restaurant wasn't much fun after you left, so Otto took over for me. I thought you might need a friendly face. Besides, I want you to meet my friend, Bruno Rappold. Bruno is a bail bondsman," Nick said.

Bruno nodded to the group. "Prior to Mr. Kingsford going before the magistrate I need to talk to someone about collateral for his bail," Bruno said in a deep voice.

"I can help with that," Charles said.

"Thanks, Charles, but I got this covered. When Simpson called, he said we might need to arrange bail. I brought our house title with me," Harry said. He stood and shook hands with Bruno. Then the two went to a table in the far corner of the room. Nick took Harry's place at the table.

"Is his name really Bruno?" Carrie whispered.

"Not sure he was born with that name. But as long as I've known him, he's been Bruno."

"And why do you know a bail guy?"

"Wouldn't you like to know," Nick said with an arched eyebrow. "But I do have something you will like. I have fresh coffee. Who wants a cup?"

Nick reached into a canvas bag and removed a huge thermos. Then he took out cups, sugar, and real cream. Everyone, including Harry and Bruno, was soon enjoying Nick's coffee. So much so, they never noticed that Helen, Randolph, and Fred had entered the room.

"This looks more like a party instead of waiting for an accused murderer to stand before a magistrate," Fred said.

"That's enough, Fred. Don't make a scene," Randolph said.

"Don't make a scene? I should have punched Norton's lights out when I had the chance. Now the police have arrested him for a second murder."

Harry pulled Fred out of the room. Caroline and Carrie went to sit with Helen.

"Helen, I'm so sorry about Fred. I know he's upset," Caroline said.

"Caroline, I'm not sure Fred is wrong. I can't believe Norton is involved with a second murder."

"Helen, Norty had nothing to do with either murder. We've been through this before with Engler. He continues to focus only on Norty. Norty didn't even know the murdered waiter."

"I don't know what to think," Helen said.

Randolph returned to the room with Fred. While Randolph sat with his wife, Fred sat alone at the table near the vending machines.

"It's not a party by any means, but I do have coffee that tastes a lot better than those machines," Nick said.

"No, none for us. We just want to see Engler and go home," Randolph said.

"Did Engler call you? Is that why you're here?" Charles asked.

"He called and said he made an arrest in Ginny's murder and wanted us here for the announcement," Helen said.

An officer entered the room. "Mr. and Mrs. Ellwood, Chief Engler apologizes for the delay. It will be a little longer before he's ready for the press conference. He thanks you for your patience." He turned and left the room.

"There's your answer. This isn't about getting information concerning your daughter's murder. It's another news opportunity for Engler. It will look good to have the victim's parents next to him when he makes the announcement," Nick said.

"If that's what Engler wants, we're going home," Randolph said. "Helen, Fred, let's go. I'm not participating in any media show of Engler's."

"But, Dad, don't we want to know if Norty gets charged?" Fred said.

"We'll know soon enough if that happens. Harry, Caroline, I hope...I hope it's only good news for you tonight," Randolph said.

Helen, Fred, and Randolph departed. Then Bruno left to check if a magistrate was being summoned to hold night court. The family and Nick sat and waited and waited.

Finally Harry said, "That Bruno seems like a very capable fellow."

"Oh, yes, he's the best in his field," Nick said. "I keep telling everyone that the Barn is the heartbeat of Pear Cove. If you want to know something or you need a service, just ask me."

The door opened, and another couple came in. Carrie didn't recognize them, but Nick went over to greet them. Nick only had time for a few words before the same officer who had asked the Ellwoods to be patient returned to the room and escorted them out.

"What's that all about?" Charles asked.

"It seems our good friend Engler is interviewing people who ate at the Barn around the time that Tom was murdered."

"I bet I know the number one question: Did you see Norton Kingsford on the premises," Carrie said.

The door opened again, and this time Sally and John Watford walked in.

John looked surprised. "Hello, everyone, what's going on?"

Unlike her parents, John and Sally looked like they had just come from a social event. John wore a beautifully tailored dark-blue suit, a light-blue shirt, and a pastel colored tie. Sally had on a lovely pastel flowered dress that picked up some of the same colors as John's tie.

"Engler has Norton in the back," Charles said. "I guess you're potential witnesses for the prosecution. Were you at the Barn the night Tom Gaston was murdered?"

"We were. We had dinner with the Schwartzes. I don't know why they're interviewing any of us. I understand Tom's murder was around nine. We finished our dinner around eight thirty and left. Isn't that about right, Sally?"

"Yes, that's correct. We said good-bye in the parking lot and drove off long before nine. The Schwartzes came in yesterday for their police interview. They called to tell us about their experience and said one of the questions was if anyone saw Norton."

The officer once again appeared at the door and asked the Watfords to follow him.

As John was leaving he turned to Harry and said, "Harry, if you need anything, please call on me. Especially concerning what we're working on at the company. I can certainly help to keep things moving toward the launch date if you get involved with...with helping Norton."

After another half hour, with more of Nick's good coffee and no more witnesses for the prosecution, Simpson arrived in the room.

"We're getting him processed now," Simpson said.

Caroline gasped and grabbed Harry's arm.

"Sorry, Caroline, I didn't phrase that correctly. We're getting him processed out. Norton and Halloway will be here in a moment."

"What's been happening?" Charles asked.

"There was no doubt Engler had every intention of locking Norton up for a double murder. The first thing I did was place a call to District Attorney Bennett. I reminded him about his promise. We had agreed earlier that if Norton was charged, he would call me, and I would have Norton surrender himself. He was furious when he found out that Engler had taken Norton to the site of the second murder without his attorney and then made a public spectacle of the arrest."

"I take it he dropped the arrest," Harry said.

"He did, but not before he drove over here to speak in person with Engler. That's what was taking so long. He wanted to see for himself what evidence Engler had against Norton. He discovered that Engler had no additional evidence linking Norton to Ginny's murder. Then, when he discovered that Engler had absolutely no links between Norton and Tom's murder, he ordered that Norton be released."

Carrie nodded at Charles. What happened was exactly what Charles had said would happen.

"Then why this parade of potential witnesses?" Caroline asked.

"The key word is potential. Not one of those witnesses saw Norton the night of Tom's murder. Engler has nothing. That's another reason why Bennett was so angry. He said that Engler's behavior would cause the case to be thrown out before he ever got to make an opening statement."

All eyes turned as the door opened. This time it was Norton and Halloway. Caroline jumped up, ran to her son, and hugged him.

When Norton was released from her arms he turned to everyone and said, "Thanks, you guys, for coming and sitting here. And Nick, you too."

"We owe Nick a big thank-you. He brought a bail bondsman. And he provided Barn coffee, which made the wait almost bearable. He's been a true friend to us," Carrie said.

Harry, who was closest to Nick, patted him on the back while everyone else voiced a thank-you.

"No need. I'm always glad to help," Nick said as he placed the coffee items back in his canvas bag. "I'll leave you folks for now. See you at the Barn."

Carrie was sure she saw tears welling up in Nick's eyes as he passed her.

"Let's get out of here. If I'm in the unenviable position of waiting to see what happens next, I'm glad to be waiting at home."

33

Even though they were up late, Carrie woke Charles early the next morning. She decided they should get started on the search for the shop that sold the scarf. Maybe the scarf was unusual enough that the shopkeeper would remember who had made the purchase.

Carrie had Simpson e-mail her a copy of the scarf from a police photo. She made color copies for Charles and her to show to shopkeepers. Before leaving the house, she and Charles spent time going through the local phone book and making a list of stores that potentially carried accessories.

Carrie was surprised how many stores were on the list. She decided it would take too long if they went together, so she split the list between them. Carrie had Charles drive her to her parents' house so she could borrow her brother's car. She knew her brother would be staying at home. The Pear Cove rumor mill had been at work all night.

Carrie decided they should start in the center of Pear Cove and work outward toward the county line. She would meet Charles at noon for lunch, and they could compare notes. She could keep in touch with Charles by mobile phone should anything develop.

Although the process was tedious, it went fairly quickly. She would pop into a shop. Ask for the manager or a senior salesclerk. Show the picture and ask if they carried the scarf. When they said they didn't carry the item she would leave quickly and head for the next stop. Occasionally her progress was slowed by a clerk questioning why she was asking about one particular scarf. In other cases the manager liked the scarf and wanted to know how they could add it to their inventory. Carrie did run into one other problem. A couple of shops had closed for the season and wouldn't reopen until late March. She made a note of the emergency phone number that hung on the door. If none of the other shops panned out, she could call these stores later. However, Carrie firmly believed the scarf was purchased as a holiday gift by Ginny's mystery man, and he would have bought it from a shop that was open.

"Any luck?" was the first question from Carrie when she met Charles for lunch.

"No. Everyone thought I was trying to find the scarf as a gift for a special lady in my life. They were right about a special lady in my life, but unfortunately no one carried the scarf," Charles reported as he gave Carrie a kiss.

"Thank you for the kiss. You just lifted my spirits from my lack of success."

They ordered a quick lunch of sandwich and soup. As they were finishing their lunch Carrie asked, "I'm down to four stores. How many do you have?"

"I've got three left, but we'll probably finish around the same time because I've got the store out in Petersville, which will take longer to reach. Where do you want to meet when we're done?"

"How about we meet back at my parents' house? I have to return Norton's car. Plus I made my last store the one in the mall over near Mom's house."

"That works for me. When we picked the car up this morning, your mother was getting ready to bake. She said it was the only thing that calmed her nerves. Hopefully there will be some coffee and a snack when we arrive," Charles said.

"Do you need to eat baked goods to calm your nerves?"

"Oh yes, baked goods always calm my nerves."

Carrie got a big smile, a farewell kiss, and money to pay for lunch from Charles. Carrie paid the bill and started on her afternoon of scarf searching.

At the first three stops Carrie encountered the same negative responses she had received all morning. However, at her final store in the mall the clerk seemed to recognize the scarf.

"Look, it's really important to me to find this scarf. If you think you recognize the scarf, I could sure use your help. Do you think your store carried it?" Carrie tried to sound pleasant.

"I'm trying to remember," the clerk responded.

Carrie knew the clerk was annoyed that her afternoon magazine reading had been interrupted.

"It looks familiar, but I don't think it's an item we carried in this store."

Carrie watched as she closed her eyes as if trying to extract the information from deep inside her brain. The clerk was young, with dyed-blond hair in a style that left uneven points of hair sticking out in different directions. She had long—very long—nails painted a deep magenta with little white flowers painted on top. Carrie wondered how this girl could punch the keys on the register without nicking her nails. However, this wasn't the question Carrie needed to ask. She needed to get this clerk to help her.

"Oh my, I love your nails. How very stylish! Where do you get them done?" Carrie asked.

The atmosphere immediately changed between Carrie and the salesclerk. A broad smile broke across her face as she stretched her fingers out and admired the design.

"They're nice, aren't they? I get them done right here in the mall at Nail Care." Suddenly, the clerk looked up, and Carrie could almost see brain activity taking place. "That's it, that's where I saw the scarf! The girl who does my nails was wearing one just like it."

"Are you sure?" Carrie asked.

"I'm sure. It takes about an hour to get my nails done. I stared at that scarf the entire time."

"What's the girl's name who does your nails?"

"Donna. Donna does my nails. She's the best nail tech they have. Most of the other girls at Nail Care can't handle the more complicated designs. Doing nail designs like this is a real art form." She held her hands out and admired the work once more. "Yes, a real art form," she repeated.

"Do you think Donna is working today?"

"What? Oh yes, she should be. She normally comes in at one, except on Saturdays. She doesn't work Saturdays and Sundays. That's strange, when you think about it. You would think that Saturday would be her busiest day. But I think she has a sideline of some kind of clothing business. I guess that provides enough money to miss weekends."

"A clothing business?" Carrie could feel her excitement mounting.

"Yeah, I think the business is actually her sister's, but Donna helps her on weekends."

"Do you think the scarf may have come from her sister's clothing business?"

"Probably—that would make sense, wouldn't it?" the clerk said.

Carrie didn't want to seem rude to the girl who had provided the first real scarf lead, but she needed to get to Nail Care. "You've been a great help. I think I'm going to see if Donna can do my nails. Thanks a lot."

She turned quickly to leave the store. She was practically running out the door when she heard the clerk yell after her.

"Hey, be sure to come back and let me see how your nails turn out."

34

Carrie thought about her conversation with the young salesperson as she walked toward the Nail Care salon. *It's all a matter of finding a subject the person finds interesting and is willing to talk about. Then the next thing you know, the person is talking about what you want to know.*

Nail Care was about midway down the mall. It was one of the smaller stores in width, but even the smallest stores had great depth.

Carrie entered the store and was greeted by a young woman with a tag indicating her name was Pippa. Based on age and looks she could have been the sister of the clerk Carrie just left at the accessory shop. But there was one difference. This young woman was furiously chewing a piece of gum. She looked up as Carrie approached the desk.

"I was wondering. Does Donna have time to do my nails?" Carrie asked.

"This is so cool," Pippa said.

Carrie was bewildered by her response.

Pippa continued, "I mean, like I just hung up the phone with someone who cancelled her appointment with Donna. Ya know, people aren't supposed to call that way. I mean, she called at the exact time of her appointment. But she's like one of our best customers, so I can't say nothing." She continued to chomp away on her gum. "I was just feeling awful about having to tell Donna about the cancellation. She would have to sit for an hour before her next appointment. Then you walked in. Now everything is fine. Just follow me, and I'll let Donna know about the switch in appointments."

Wow, Carrie thought. *Luck is on my side.*

As Carrie followed Pippa toward the back of the store, she saw Sally Watford approaching. When Sally saw Carrie, a big smile came across her face.

"Hello, Carrie. How are you doing? Is everything okay with Norton?"

"Unfortunately for Norton, Chief Engler seems determined to charge him with a crime, even though Norton had nothing to do with either murder and has perfectly good alibis."

"Good to hear. About the alibis, I mean. Everyone except Engler believes Norton is innocent. Please let Norton know that John and I support him. On a lighter subject, I didn't know you came here for your nails."

"Normally I don't. But I'm giving myself a little holiday treat. And Donna was highly recommended."

"She's the best," Sally said this as she raised her hands and wiggled her fingers.

Carrie noticed that Pippa was growing impatient. "I guess I'd better let Donna work some magic on these nails. Thanks for your kind words. I'll be sure to pass them on to Norton."

Carrie continued following Pippa toward the back of the salon.

There were five other nail technicians working with clients, and the women barely looked up as Carrie and her escort passed by. They were too engrossed in their own conversations and nail preparations. Pippa stopped at the last light-gray table; it was laden with various nail-care supplies. Carrie found herself sitting in a soft, comfortable, black leather chair across the table from a matching chair with wheels for Donna.

While Carrie was getting comfortable in her chair, she noticed that the entire decor of the shop was black-and-white with shades of gray. However, the technicians in the shop were wearing the brightest and most shocking colors available. Each technician seemed to be in competition with the others for who could wear the most outrageous outfits. *I wonder if the nail designs reflect all these bizarre color schemes. Oh well, it won't matter, if I can find out information about the scarf.*

Carrie was lost in her own thoughts about the scarf when she became aware of a woman approaching her table. The woman was in her early forties. Her blond hair was professionally styled. She was wearing a conservative cream-colored pantsuit similar to one Carrie owned. The woman didn't sit down but instead offered Carrie her hand along with a broad smile.

Carrie couldn't help herself as she stared at the brightly colored orange-and-pink scarf the woman wore around the collar of her suit. It wasn't the one that had been used to murder Ginny, but it was of a similar design.

"I'm so glad you chose this time to stop by and have your nails done. Hello, I'm Donna, but of course you know that. And you are—?"

"Oh hello, I'm Carrie Faraday."

"What nail color were you thinking of having today?" With her question, Donna took Carrie's hand and turned it over to look at her nails.

Carrie withheld the urge to snap her hand back out of fear that her nails wouldn't live up to expectations. "As you can probably tell I haven't had my nails done professionally in several months. I was at the Accessory Boutique here in the mall. I was admiring the clerk's nails, and she highly recommended you."

"Oh, that would be Sylvia. She comes in once a week to have her nails done and sends me lots of business. Now, don't worry about how your nails look. If they were perfect, you wouldn't be coming to me. Did you want your nails done like Sylvia?" Donna asked.

"Oh no!" Carrie hesitated. "I mean...something a little—" Carrie wanted to say conservative, but didn't want to offend Donna's sense of design.

Donna simply smiled and said, "I know exactly what you want. I'll do a french manicure. I'll shape and polish your own nails. The tips are done in a soft white polish and the nails are painted in a natural-color polish."

"That sounds perfect," Carrie said. She hoped the relief in her voice didn't show.

Donna started by filing and shaping Carrie's nails. The nails on her right hand were quickly squared with rounded corners. While Donna worked with her left hand, her right hand was soaking in a special bath to loosen the cuticle. Then her right hand had the cuticle trimmed while her left hand was in the bath. Then the nails were cleaned in an acetone solution. While Donna worked they exchanged small talk.

"Carrie, are you new to the area?"

"I'm not a year-rounder. My husband and I have a summer home in Pear Cove. This year we decided to come down for the New Year holiday. And I must say it has been very enjoyable. Do you do any other women from Pear Cove?"

"Oh my, yes, quite a few. Let me see, there's Doris Engler. Her husband is chief of police, and also Chief Engler's sister, Betty. Did you see Sally Watford? I just finished her nails. Then there's Jenny Benson, Harriet Smyth, and Martha Hanson. Her family runs the funeral home in Pear Cove. Let me think. I do Helen Ellwood, and I used to do Ginny Ellwood's nails. Wasn't that just terrible what happened to Ginny? And of course I do poor Mrs. Kingsford. You know, according to Chief Engler's wife, Mrs. Kingsford's son is the prime suspect for Ginny's murder. What a terrible sadness for both families. Not to mention having all this happen at this time of year when everyone else is celebrating." Donna made a clicking sound with her tongue.

Carrie couldn't believe her ears. Her mother came to Donna. Carrie debated whether to tell Donna who she was and why she was there. She knew she had come to the right place, and she did like Donna. She almost blurted out she was Caroline Kingsford's daughter but decided to wait until she had time to ask a few more questions.

"That's a lovely scarf you're wearing. Did you purchase it here in the mall?"

Donna's face brightened at the comment. "Isn't it nice? My sister, Paula, has a line of clothing accessories. Paula sells scarves along with other items, like belts, gloves, hats, jewelry, and even men's items like ties. Many of my customers compliment me about the accessories I'm wearing. I keep one her catalogs right here at my table. Would you like to see it? Of course, we'll have to wait until we get one hand dry enough so you can turn the pages."

Donna knew what she was doing and was very efficient. Carrie realized her hour appointment was quickly passing. As soon as Carrie had one hand free from the nail dryer, she began gingerly turning the pages in the catalog. Carrie was only a few pages into the catalog when Ginny's scarf leaped out at her from the page.

"Do many of the women from Pear Cove buy from your sister's catalog?" Carrie caught the questioning look from Donna and quickly added, "I've seen many of the women you mentioned earlier with very attractive accessories. I was just wondering if they were purchased from your sister's line."

"I'll bet many of their accessories are from my sister. I think all of those women have purchased at least one item over the years."

Carrie turned the catalog toward Donna. "This is a beautiful scarf. I'm sure I've seen it on at least one of the women in Pear Cove."

Before Donna had a chance to answer, Pippa arrived. Between snaps of her gum she announced that Donna's next appointment had arrived. Carrie realized Donna was finishing the topcoat on her second hand. Carrie couldn't waste any more time. She had to take a chance on Donna.

"Look, Donna, I can tell you're a good person and...well, to be honest, I haven't been one hundred percent straight with you."

Carrie saw Donna raise an eyebrow as if she couldn't imagine what was coming next.

"You see, my married name is Carrie Faraday, but my maiden name is Kingsford." Carrie waited for the information to sink in.

"Then you're related to Caroline Kingsford, of course. You're Carrie—Caroline."

"Yes, I'm Caroline's daughter, but that also makes me Norton's sister. And I know my brother didn't kill Ginny Ellwood. My husband, Charles, and I are unofficially investigating Ginny's murder."

"I appreciate your honesty, but I also assume there's more to this discussion than a confession of who you're related to." Donna calmly checked the hand that was still under the nail dryer to see if the topcoat was dry.

"Yes, there's more. But first I must ask for a favor. I need to ask you to keep confidential what we discuss."

"This is a bit of an intrigue, isn't it?"

"I'm serious, Donna. Even if the police come and ask questions, I'd appreciate it if you could avoid telling them I was here. This includes Chief Engler, his wife, or his sister."

"Believe me, if Chief Engler asks me anything, I won't tell him a thing. I've heard enough stories from his wife about his wandering eye. Apparently he uses his position as chief of police to pick up women. I've no time for a man like that. His wife is a nice woman. You said you need two favors. What's the second?"

"I need your help in tracking down an item. When I was asking questions about the scarves that your sister sells, I was looking for a particular scarf. I found it here in your sister's catalog." Carrie showed the catalog picture of the scarf to Donna. "I need to know if anyone recently purchased this scarf from your sister. Especially any of the women from Pear Cove."

"Does the scarf have something to do with the death of Ginny Ellwood?" Donna lowered her voice as she asked the question.

"She was wearing the scarf at the time of her death." Carrie didn't want to say that the scarf was the murder weapon. But the look on Donna's face made Carrie believe she knew how the scarf was used. "Now you know why it's so important I find out the names of who purchased that scarf."

"I'm sorry, Carrie. I've no way of knowing. Most of the women look in the catalog and fill in the order form after I finish their nails. They leave the form, and I send the orders over to my sister. Paula ships the products directly to the clients. Occasionally she gives an item to me to give the customer at her next appointment. But the items she gives me are sealed in boxes or bags. Unless the women tell me about a particular item or they wear the item to an appointment, I never see what they order."

"Oh, I was so hoping you could help." Carrie couldn't hide the disappointment in her voice.

"Now, don't give up hope. I may not know what the women order, but I'm sure my sister does. Paula has a very sophisticated computer program that tracks all the orders. If I'm not mistaken, I think she can punch in an item number and get a printout of everyone who made that purchase."

"Do you think you could call her now and ask?" Carrie asked excitedly.

"Carrie, I'll certainly call her for you, but it won't help to call her now. She's on a buying trip in Tri-City. I know she's attending a fashion show and won't be picking up calls. However, she always takes her laptop with her, so I'll call her tonight. I'll tell her what we want, and maybe she can create the report and send it from her hotel room."

"That's wonderful!" Carrie said and stood up, ready to leave.

"Wait a minute, Carrie. We have one more step to perform on those nails." Donna sprayed her nails with a quick-drying conditioning spray. "A little extra protection for those nails while the polish sets."

"Donna, I can't thank you enough. I'll wait for your call."

Carrie left the mall pleased with her freshly polished nails, disappointed that she didn't immediately have the information she needed, but elated at the prospect she had tracked down the murder weapon. She couldn't wait to tell Charles.

It was nearly noon, and Carrie had been pacing the floor for the last twenty minutes, wondering why Donna hadn't called.

"Carrie, pacing isn't going to help," Charles said.

"I know, but pacing fools me into thinking that I'm doing something. Besides, it helps me to think."

"And what are you thinking?"

"I was wondering what our next steps will be if we don't hear from Donna," Carrie said.

"If she doesn't call, we need to know why. Is it because she wasn't able to get in touch with her sister? Or her sister wasn't able to track the sale? Did her computer crash? Maybe Donna and Paula are part of the conspiracy and have decided to run away to the circus to avoid prosecution. In fact, that's not a bad idea. Maybe your brother, mother, father, you, and I should consider joining a circus as an alternative solution to this case."

Charles's comments had the right effect on Carrie. She laughed out loud as she pictured her family in the circus. "And you would be in charge of the clowns in your new role at the circus?"

"Of course," Charles replied.

Carrie watched as Charles did a little dance. As he was going backward, his feet got tangled, and he fell onto the sofa.

"Really, Carrie, just relax. It's a little too early to be concerned about what the next steps should be. Remember, Donna said Paula was staying overnight in Tri-City to attend a fashion show. She was probably out late with her hosts. Let's assume Donna only reached her this morning. She needs time to pull the report and send it to her sister. How about if we eat some lunch while we wait?"

"How can you think about eating?"

"Because I'm hungry. Besides, I'm not suggesting we go out to lunch. You can fix something from our kitchen," Charles said.

"And why do you think I should fix you lunch?"

"You need to have an activity to keep your mind off the waiting. What better activity than feeding your husband?"

"Since you put it that way, I'll be happy to fix you something."

Carrie started for the kitchen when the phone began to ring. Carrie ran for the receiver. "Hello. Donna, I'm so glad you called. Was your sister able to track who purchased the scarf?"

Carrie grabbed the pen and paper they kept near the phone. Carrie listened and wrote on the paper. Then she said, "Yes, I see. Donna, I can't thank you enough. And please thank your sister for me. Now that I've found someone who does such terrific nails, I'll be back."

Carrie replaced the receiver and removed the page of notes from the tablet.

"Well?" Charles asked. "I couldn't tell by your responses whether the news was good or bad."

"I guess in some ways it's a little of both."

Carrie came and sat next to Charles on the sofa, holding the paper with the list of names.

"Oh, Charles one of the people who purchased the scarf was my mother. That's means Norton had access to the murder weapon," Carrie said.

"Was your mother the only purchaser?"

"No. Donna and her sister sold quite a few of this particular scarf prior to the holiday to people in the area. Aside from Mom, there was one to a Mrs. Wilshire, who is a widow and lives on the far side of Pear Cove, two for Sally Watford, two to Jennifer Hanson, two for Doris Engler, and one for Engler's sister, Betty Lumley. And get this, Nick and Otto bought a dozen."

"A dozen to Nick and Otto! That's interesting."

"Apparently, every year Nick and Otto give gifts to their employees. This year they contacted Paula and selected a scarf for their female employees and a tie for their male employees. They give the gifts with the employees' bonus checks at the holidays. The point is Norty was at the Barn numerous times. Could he have gotten ahold of one of their scarves?"

"That's a long shot to assume your brother went into the Barn's offices and took a scarf just in case he needed a murder weapon. Overall this information still helps Norton's case. The defense team will show how many other people had access to the murder weapon."

"Of course, there are two other interesting people who bought the scarf: Doris Engler and her sister-in-law," Carrie said.

"Let's not jump to any conclusions about the Engler family. We've a lot of work ahead of us to track down all these scarves. Then, just maybe, we'll know where the scarf around Ginny's... who belonged to the murder weapon."

"Let's start with the easiest. Call your mother and see if she can locate the scarf she purchased. Put the phone on speaker, in case I think of a question to ask her," Charles said.

Carrie punched the speaker button on the phone and dialed the familiar number. After exchanging a few pleasantries Carrie said, "Mom, I had my nails done by Donna over at Nail Care. While she was doing my nails she mentioned that you purchased a real pretty scarf from her sister. It's navy, red, and gold."

"Yes, I did. In fact, I buy quite a few items from Paula's catalog. They never have the right accessories in the department stores anymore, and it's very convenient to select items when Donna does my nails. Are you looking for a recommendation about the quality of the merchandise?"

"No, Mom. I specifically want to know about the scarf I mentioned. Do you know which scarf I'm talking about?"

"Yes, I know exactly the scarf you're talking about. Why?"

"Do you still have the scarf?"

"Of course I do. But, Carrie, why are you asking questions about my scarf?"

"I'll tell you in a minute, but I need you to answer this question very carefully. Are you sure you still have that scarf? Could you check and be sure it's in the house?"

"I'm absolutely sure. I don't have to check. The scarf is around my neck. I'm wearing it today."

Carrie gasped when she heard her mother use the term "around her neck."

"Carrie, what's this all about? Charles, are you there? It sounds like I'm on speaker."

"Hi, Caroline, sorry for all the questions. With the help of Donna we're tracking down anyone who purchased that scarf. Caroline, that style of scarf was the murder weapon," Charles said.

"Oh my." Caroline paused. "But I see the reason for all the questions. If I wasn't able to produce my scarf, it would mean Norton had access to the murder weapon. Don't you worry! I assure you I have my scarf. As soon as we hang up, I'm locking it in the safe in your father's study in case I need to produce it for the police."

"That's a good idea, Mom."

"You know it's funny about that scarf. I was wearing it one night when Ginny was here at the house with Norton. She made a big fuss about how nice it looked with my suit. I told her where I purchased it. Also that the items were stylish and reasonably priced. Donna did her nails too, but she had never purchased anything from the catalog. Are there other people on your list?"

"Yes quite a few. We're checking with Nick and Otto next. They bought twelve scarves as gifts for their female employees.

We need to get a list of the women they gave the scarves to," Charles said. "Is Norton over there with you?"

"Yes, he's been here all morning. There are quite a few reporters camped outside. He definitely doesn't want to deal with them."

"Good! I think once we have the names from Nick and Otto, we'll drive over and see if Norton can make a connection between any of the names and Ginny."

"Good, he could use some visitors to cheer him up. I'll see you two later."

"Feel better?" Charles asked Carrie as she hung up the phone.

"I do feel better. But we still have a major hurdle to check out all these other people who had access to a murder weapon."

"The only way to get over the hurdle is to get started. I'll call the Barn."

"Wait a minute, Charles. Do you think there's any possibility that either Nick or Otto could be involved in Ginny's death? I mean, Ginny was killed on the beach between here and the Barn. Tom worked for them. He took Ginny's mysterious call at a party catered by Nick and Otto. Tom was killed in the restaurant. Maybe Nick was having an affair with Ginny, and Otto was jealous—or vice versa."

"My instincts tell me no. However, at this point I don't think we've a choice. We have to keep asking questions. If Nick and Otto are involved, maybe they'll slip up when they find out we know about the scarf. I think we have to take the chance. You want me to use the speaker phone?"

"No, you call them. I'll sit here and think for a moment."

Charles made the phone call from the kitchen phone, and Carrie heard only pieces of the conversation. She was too engrossed in her own gloomy thoughts.

When Charles returned to the room he said, "Guess what."

"Now what?" Carrie responded.

"Nick and Otto just accounted for all twelve of their scarves, and we don't even need a list," Charles announced.

"How's that possible?"

"It turns out that Nick and Otto give the gifts out after New Year's, not at Christmas. The gifts are given with a year-end bonus. With all of the holiday parties, they waited until after the New Year. They only gave out the twelve scarves yesterday, long after Ginny was murdered."

Carrie looked at her husband. "That just eliminated the majority of our list. We accounted for Mom's scarf, and the twelve from Otto and Nick."

"And I think we can eliminate Mrs. Wilshire. No one knows her, and she lives alone. Did you think of anything else while sitting here?" Charles asked.

"Actually I did have one thought. I think the scarf might have been responsible for the murder."

"It was. It was the murder weapon."

"No, I mean it might have been the cause of the confrontation. Think about it. Ginny arrives with an expensive gold ring as a gift. Her lover arrives with a scarf she knows is an inexpensive item purchased from a catalog. Since most men don't go to nail salons, Ginny probably also realized it was bought by his wife. She brings a serious gift to mark the start of their life together, and he brings a cheap token."

"I think that's a real possibility. Good sleuthing, darling."

"So who's next?" Carrie asked.

"It's not who, it's what. It's definitely time for lunch. I've changed my mind. Let's go out and get something to eat. Grab your camera and let's get rolling."

36

"Aren't we going to the Barn?" Carrie asked as Charles turned the car left and headed out toward the highway in the opposite direction from the restaurant. "Charles, we need to be investigating the other names on the list. We should grab something quick and get back to work."

"We'll keep working, I promise. But I want to get away from the people we know. I thought we would take a quiet drive and then find a place for lunch. We can discuss the names on our list quietly while we eat and decide what to do next."

"Why am I bringing my camera?"

"As I said, we need to clear our heads. It's a beautiful day, and I thought we would take the scenic route out by the inlet. You might see something you want to snap. Plus, when you're taking pictures you're concentrating on the photos and not other things. If we think about something other than this case for an hour or so, we might see things in a new light."

Carrie thought it was unusual that Charles said he wanted to get away from the case. When he was in the middle of working on something it wasn't like him to stop, even temporarily. However, Charles was right when he said it was an absolutely gorgeous day. The sky was clear and bright with an intense blue hue and billowing white clouds. There was just enough of a chill to remind her it was winter, but it was not too damp or too cold to make it unpleasant. The farther away from Pear Cove they got, the more Carrie knew Charles was correct about clearing their heads.

Out on Route 216 Carrie was surprised when Charles pulled into a convenience store. He went in and reappeared in a few minutes. He then went over and looked at the pay phone and made an entry in his notebook. When he returned to the car Carrie saw he had purchased a financial magazine and a pack of gum.

"Can I borrow your camera for a minute?" Charles asked.

He took the camera and took a shot of the front of the convenience store that included the pay phone. She said nothing as he got back into the car.

They made another stop at a bar, because Charles said he had to use the men's room. Carrie noticed he still had the camera in his pocket. He jumped back into the car, and they continued north. Then Charles made a right turn onto a narrow, heavily wooded country road. After a short distance there was a break in the dense wood to reveal the water. They were traveling slightly above and about a quarter of a mile back from the water's edge. After another couple of miles, they were riding even with the water, and the water was only a few hundred feet to their right.

There was a wide section of the road with an enlarged shoulder, and Charles pulled the car over so Carrie could get a shot of a sailboat passing through the inlet.

"This is quite lovely. How come we haven't been out this way before?" Carrie asked.

"Because like most people, we're creatures of habit. We don't come to the beach house that often. When we do, we always come out of our road and turn toward the town or the Barn. I've decided that in the New Year, we should go exploring more."

"I see. And how did you find this road?"

"This road? I looked at a map of Pear Cove to see what other opportunities were available for a lovely drive. Piece of gum?" Charles offered his recently purchased gum pack to her.

"All right, that's enough! What's going on?" Carrie demanded.

"Why, whatever do you mean? Can't we go for a drive in a different direction? You're always saying I should be more spontaneous."

"It's true I do say that, but in fact, you're not spontaneous. Here are the facts, my fellow detective. When you're hungry you want a meal, not a drive in the country. You never look at maps to find where we're going, you never have to go to the men's room within an hour of leaving home, you know more about finances than any person I know, so you don't need a financial magazine. And don't say you bought the gum for me."

"You're wrong. The gum is mine, and I'm rescinding my generous offer to share it with you." Charles put the gum in his pocket.

"What else do you have in that pocket? What's in that little notebook you have? Let's have it, Charlie Boy. Fess up."

"I never could keep anything from you. That's what I told Norton," Charles said.

"Ah, so you two were in cahoots. I thought you both got kind of quiet when I appeared on the deck. What's going on?" Carrie asked.

"Before you joined us on the deck Norton was reviewing his movements the night of the murder. Before midnight he was out this way looking for Ginny. After Norton discovered the body on the beach, he drove out this way a second time. He made his 911 call from the pay phone at that convenience store so as not to use his cell phone. I bought the gum and the magazine so I could ask the clerk if she remembered him. But the two clerks there today weren't on duty New Year's Eve."

"Then we'll have to come back at night for more gum. Sorry, I don't mean to be sarcastic. It's a good thing to follow his trail," Carrie said.

"The trail but more important, the timing of his trips," Charles said.

"And the pictures?"

"Don't react negatively, but I'm taking those just in case the defense should ever need them. And before you ask, I didn't tell you what I was doing because I didn't want to get your hopes up in case we didn't find anything."

Carrie said nothing for a moment and then asked, "And the men's room stop?"

"Norton stopped for a drink at that bar. I went in to talk to the bartender. The bartender remembered Norton.

He was drinking heavily. When the bartender thought he'd had enough, he stopped serving him. The bartender also remembers seeing Norton asleep in his car after he closed the bar. He didn't wake him because he thought it was better for him to sleep it off and not be out on the roads. So, my fellow detective, it looks like good news. Norton's story is checking out."

"I guess that's a positive, but of course all this occurred after the murder. There's nothing in these facts to prove Norton didn't do it. My dad finds out from Randolph the kids are having problems. Ginny leaves the party alone. Norton follows her. He arrives at the murder scene within minutes of her death. He doesn't call the cops from the scene of the crime. Instead he calls the police from a convenience store. He's been drinking and ends up sleeping in a bar parking lot. This behavior will not help him when presented to a jury," Carrie said.

"Is this coming from the woman who believes in her brother's innocence? Besides, I'm hoping this case never goes to the jury. We have to concentrate on the timing factor rather than the behavior. The timing for all the people involved needs to be gathered. Where there's a gap in the time is where we will find the murderer."

"You're saying we map where everyone was and hope someone will have a hole in their story," Carrie summarized. "Of course, having a motive would also help."

"You got it. But I think we have motives. I think your idea of a married man who didn't want his relationship with Ginny known is one. Then there's the mystery of Ginny trying to steal computer code."

"But in order to get the police to leave Norton alone, we're going to have to produce this married man or Ginny's partner in the software scheme," Carrie said.

"All in good time. For now, as you so accurately pointed out, when I'm hungry I want a meal."

37

Charles pulled into the parking lot of the Seafood Cottage restaurant.

"Here's our next step," Charles announced. "This one is different from the other locations. Norton stopped here prior to the murder."

Before they entered the restaurant Carrie snapped a few photos of the restaurant and the boats, pier, and water below. The view was fantastic. It was the type of scene you would find on vacation postcards. Carrie had spent most of her life as a professional photographer shooting layouts for national magazines. However, her previous job required a great deal of travel. Now she preferred to spend her time with Charles. She was content to do the occasional photo for a marketing piece, and she still enjoyed adding to her portfolio with shots like the ones she was getting today.

The Seafood Cottage restaurant was a rambling white-shingled building that sat atop a grassy knoll overlooking the water. The main building resembled an English cottage with blue shutters, blue scalloped awnings, and blue window boxes adorning the front windows. The land to the right was grassy, with benches placed around various garden displays. The gardens led to wide wooden steps that descended to the pier and the water. Stone walkways with small shrubs edging each side led to the front door. Inside, the visitor was greater by a long oak-paneled hallway with benches lining each side.

"This place must really get busy in the summer. Between the benches in here and the benches all around the outside, I bet there must be quite a wait," Carrie observed as they entered the main hallway.

"Seashore restaurants in the summer that serve even slightly decent seafood draw a huge crowd. I'm glad it's winter. I'm too hungry to wait," Charles said.

At the end of the hallway was a hostess counter. Standing at the counter was a very tall distinguished-looking woman. As she looked up to greet the couple, Carrie gave Charles a slight nudge. Carrie noticed that this woman had the infamous scarf draped over her shoulders, accenting her navy dress.

"Hello, welcome to the Seafood Cottage. Are you here for lunch?"

"Oh yes, we're definitely here for lunch. We've heard so many good things about this restaurant. But we've never had the pleasure of eating here," Charles said.

Carrie loved it when Charles laid on his charm.

"Are you from the area?"

"Yes, we have a place over near the beach. I'm Charles Faraday, and this is my wife, Carrie," he said.

"Welcome. I'm Betty Lumley, and I'm one of the owners of the Seafood Cottage. I'm so glad you have decided to try us. I hope this is the first of many visits."

She led the couple down one of two hallways that split off from the waiting area, passing several dining rooms. Most of these front dining rooms were in darkness and not serving customers in this slower off-season. The individual rooms had no doubt been added one at a time over the years. The separate rooms provided a cozy effect and probably provided soundproofing when the restaurant was packed with people.

Carrie and Charles were escorted toward the back into a larger dining room. The room had been designed with large windows that offered the diner great views of the water. They were about to be seated when Carrie noticed Dr. Bessinger seated at a window table near the front of the room.

"Excuse me a moment. I see someone I know." Carrie veered over toward the doctor's table while Charles and Betty Lumley waited.

"Dr. Bessinger, hello," Carrie said. Dr. Bessinger started to stand, but Carrie stopped him. "Please stay seated, I just wanted to say hello. Do you eat here often?"

"Actually Ginny Ellwood recommended this restaurant. And I've enjoyed both lunch and dinners here."

"This is our first time. If we decide to eat out, we usually go to the Barn because it's so close," Carrie said.

"I've eaten there as well, and the food is excellent. But I enjoy looking at the water while eating, so I come here."

"Is the food good?" Carrie asked.

"Quite good, especially any of the seafood dishes. But as they say, all good things must come to an end. I'm heading back to Tri-City tomorrow. There's nothing to keep me here now. However, anytime I come back to Pear Cove, I would certainly eat here."

"Your work with Dad is done."

"Yes. The programming phase is nearing completion. Of course, I'm still on call should they need my input on anything else. Before I go, I do want to say it was a pleasure meeting you and your husband." With that comment Dr. Bessinger waved at Charles. "And I hope everything with Norton works out. He's a very nice and bright young man."

"Thank you for those kind words. Well, I mustn't keep you from your last lunch. Enjoy, and I hope we meet again."

Carrie rejoined Charles and Betty Lumley. She noticed to the left of this dining area and down a few steps was a large open room that resembled a club room with light-oak paneling. In the center was a massive horseshoe bar. This room was nearly full, with a large crowd of people dressed in jeans and work boots. Obviously this room was for the local fishermen and workers who could enter directly from the piers through a lower door and eat their lunches without waiting with the tourists.

"That's very ingenious to have an area where the locals can access the restaurant from the docks," Carrie said.

"Actually, when my husband's family opened the business many years ago the bar area was the entire restaurant. We served mostly fishermen and dock workers as they came off their boats. As the area became more of a resort destination, we needed to accommodate the beach communities and the tourists. That's when we added our first dining room and then another and another until we built the restaurant you see today," Betty said proudly.

"I'm sure you're the envy of all the other restaurants, having a steady worker population that keeps the place going in off-season," Carrie said.

Betty smiled at Carrie's compliment and said, "Jessica will be your waitress. I hope you enjoy your meal," Betty said and headed back to her post at the front desk.

"I guess we've just met Engler's sister as well as eliminated another scarf from our list," Carrie said.

"And what about the good doctor?" Charles asked.

"A couple of things. Ginny is the one who recommended this place to him. That may mean he knew Ginny on a social level. Perhaps her recommendation occurred when she came here with him."

"You said there were a couple of things. What else?"

"The doctor is leaving the area. He says his work with Dad is done, and to quote him, 'there's nothing to keep him here.'" Carrie looked toward his table and saw that Dr. Bessinger was leaving. He waved good-bye, and Carrie returned the wave. "Dr. Bessinger is the right age, and he's certainly gray enough to represent Ginny's favorite new color."

"I'm sure you realize there are a couple of problems with Bessinger being Ginny's older man. First, he's not married. He's a widower. And he's neither a year-rounder nor a summer settler," Charles said.

"Maybe we need to adjust our thinking. Maybe the affair with Ginny wasn't about his wife finding out but Randolph and Dad finding out. After all, they were paying him as a consultant. He's working on the program, knows its value, and enlists Ginny to help him develop a copy."

"I hate to disappoint, but there's one more thing. Where did he get it?" Charles asked.

"You mean the scarf? That little item keeps showing its ugly head, doesn't it," Carrie said.

"Don't worry. Let's order something to eat. Then I've another bartender to talk to."

Carrie had just begun to look at the menu when Jessica arrived with a warm loaf of round bread and a dish of whipped butter. She gave them a few minutes and then was back to take their order.

"What are you having, Carrie?"

"I'll start with the New England clam chowder. Then I'll have the sautéed scallops with fresh tomatoes and basil over angel hair pasta. And blue cheese dressing on my salad, please," Carrie said.

"Sounds good. I'll have the same soup, but instead of the scallops I'll have the fried oyster platter with potatoes and slaw."

38

The food arrived quickly and was remarkably good, considering the large variety of items available on the menu. They talked very little while they ate their lunch, but at the end of the meal Charles excused himself. Carrie knew he was having a chat with the restaurant's bartender.

When Charles returned to the table Carrie asked, "Did you verify that Norton was here?"

"All good. The bartender on duty today was the same bartender on duty the night of the murder. He verified that Norton was in here about one fifteen. He's sure of the time, because at one o'clock the restaurant started to offer a breakfast buffet. He said the staff had just finished putting the buffet out, which took about fifteen minutes. Norton arrived and ordered a beer. Norton discovered that Ginny had been here earlier and then asked around if anyone knew where she might have headed next. The bartender added that Norton wasn't upset or annoyed. Norton said that he and Ginny got separated at a party and he was trying to catch up with her.

"And there's more good news. There were quite a few people here that Ginny and Norton know. Therefore, there are even more witnesses to verify Norton's time. The bartender also verified that Norton left at one twenty-five. If you allow for the time to drive to our house and walk to the Barn, and then the time Sally Watford said she saw Norton, it's getting harder and harder for Norton to have been on the beach with Ginny."

Carrie's face lit up. "Oh, Charles, this is good news."

"You folks ready for dessert?" Their waitress reappeared. "We have some of the best desserts made right here on the premises."

"I think a dessert would be in order, to celebrate our progress," Carrie said.

"I couldn't agree more. What would satisfy your sweet tooth, Carrie?"

"I'll have the crème brûlée and coffee," she said.

"Make it two."

Carrie was sipping her coffee and licking her spoon with the last remnants of the dessert when a familiar face appeared at their table. Without asking permission, Chief Engler grabbed a chair from a nearby table and sat down with them.

"Hello, Chief Engler, won't you join us? What brings you to the Seafood Cottage? If you're looking for a lunch recommendation, I highly recommend the scallops, and I know we both recommend the crème brûlée," Carrie suggested.

"I'm not here for a food recommendation. I know the food quite well. The restaurant is owned by members of my family," Engler snapped.

"How interesting! This is the first time we've eaten at the Seafood Cottage. I must say the food was quite good. We'll certainly recommend it to others."

Engler's demeanor softened a little. "I'll convey your kind words to my sister, who manages the restaurant. It has certainly flourished under her guidance. However, let's not play games with each other. I asked Pete what he discussed with you."

"Pete?" Carrie asked.

"The bartender. The one your husband just questioned about Norton's movements the morning of the murder. I warned you two that I didn't want any interference from amateur sleuths. In case you didn't hear me the first time, I don't allow amateurs to get involved in my cases."

"Whether we're amateurs or not, you must realize that Pete the bartender is confirming everything my brother said. Second, Pear Cove is part of the United States, and in the United States people have the right to drive anywhere they want, eat in any restaurant, and have conversations with anyone they choose," Carrie said.

"I'm quite aware of what Pete has confirmed, but that still doesn't let your brother off the hook. He has no witnesses for the time of the murder. And for your information, Mrs. Faraday, interference with a police case is also protected by the laws of the United States."

"Engler, we've been asked by Norton's defense team to look into the case on his behalf. While we respect your role as police chief, you must respect ours as representatives of

Norton. Surely it doesn't hurt to have others looking at the facts from different angles," Charles said.

"But you're not representatives. You're not private detectives or attorneys. You're simply amateur meddlers."

"That's not a problem. If you would prefer, I can make several phone calls. I can afford to have the best private detectives down here within a couple of hours. And believe me, I won't hire just one. I'll hire two or three along with sending investigative reporters from my various publications to help. Between the detective Fred Ellwood said he was planning on hiring and my team, you'll be dealing with a half-dozen professional snoops. Instead of, as you put it, two amateurs asking a couple of innocent questions," Charles said.

"You think you're pretty clever, don't you," Engler said, adjusting the sleeves of his shirt.

"Clever has nothing to do with it. We believe my brother Norton is innocent, and we don't feel you do. This was proved the other night when you took him to the station and tried to charge him without sufficient evidence. We're just trying to balance the picture a little. We promise not to do anything more than ask a few questions. And we're more than willing to share. If we find something of interest, we'll bring it to you. We're not trying to outdo you," Carrie said.

"You want to share, then let's start sharing right now. What do you know? I mean the facts, not just your feelings that Norton is innocent," Engler said.

Carrie looked at Charles, and he nodded. "You see, we know now the man we saw on the beach New Year's Eve was Norton.

It proves he didn't kill Ginny. She was already dead on the beach when he arrived."

"Why didn't you tell me on the night of the murder you thought it was Norton?"

"Because we didn't know for sure it was him until after we verified it with him the next day," Charles said.

"You mean you wanted to protect your brother from the beginning."

"Don't you think we regret now that we didn't call out to him? But unfortunately we didn't," Carrie said.

"All right, let's leave that for now. What else have you discovered?"

"Not much. We've been trying to verify how Norton spent his time after leaving our parents' party. Both Sally Watford and Otto talked with Norton at the Barn during the time you believe Ginny was murdered. You know Otto, correct?"

"Yes, yes, I know who he is. We all belong to the Pear Cove Restaurant Association."

"Then today, Pete verified the time my brother left here. As a result of what we've learned, we know there was not enough time for Norton to have left here, been seen at the Barn, and gone to meet Ginny on the beach."

"That's it?"

Carrie was sure she detected a slight smile from Engler.

"Is that it?" Engler asked a second time.

"Afraid so. I told you we were just verifying the time," Charles said.

Engler sat for a moment looking at the floor. When he looked up he stared straight at Carrie. "What about the pictures? Are you going to share them?"

"What pictures?" Carrie asked, surprised.

"Mrs. Faraday, you're known for your photography. Are you telling me you didn't take any pictures between finding the body and calling the police?"

"You may find this hard to believe, Chief Engler, but I didn't have a camera with me New Year's Eve. My cameras were all in the house. We called the police, and there was simply no time for me to run back down and take pictures. Besides, pictures of a dead person aren't anything I want to add to my portfolio."

Engler continued to stare at Carrie, and her eyes met his gaze. "All right for now, but there had better not be any pictures that turn up later. If they do, you'll find out how the law applies to interference in a police case."

"What about your investigation? Do you have anything to share with us?" Charles asked.

Chef Engler stood and placed his chair back at the adjoining table. "I'll share everything with your brother's official representatives prior to his trial." Carrie noticed his smile this time was from the corner of his mouth, which gave him a sinister look. He walked away.

"I bet this restaurant does a big business in antacid tablets if they allow him to sit and visit with the customers," Carrie said. "I'm glad we didn't mention the scarf."

"Look at the bright side, Carrie. After he heard our information he didn't order us to stop investigating."

"Why was that?"

"Based on that sneaky little smile he has, I suspect it's because we convinced him that we've absolutely nothing."

"I think I'm beginning to feel depressed again. Let's get out of here. The food might be good, but I'm not putting it on one of my favorite places to visit," Carrie said.

"I don't want to eliminate the Seafood Cottage from our food choices. However, next time I'll call ahead for a reservation. Except I'll make the reservation using an alias, and I'll make sure Engler isn't on the premises."

Carrie lifted her wineglass in a toast to Charles's suggestion.

based on that cheeky little smile he has. I must remain [illegible] because we convinced him that we absolutely must [illegible]

"I should be heading to the [illegible] places [illegible] here. The food is quite good. [illegible] on my travels, places to visit. [illegible]

[illegible]

[illegible]

39

"I certainly enjoyed yesterday. I even enjoyed the lunch at the Seafood Cottage," Charles said. He and Carrie were sitting at the kitchen table, sipping coffee and watching the rolling waves beyond their deck.

"I enjoyed the food and also taking some pictures. You were right. It always helps me when I do my photography. Plus, I think the shots of the afternoon sun over the water on coast highway will make a nice addition to my portfolio. There's something about the color of a January sky that's so different from a summer sunset. Since yesterday helped to clear our heads, where do you want to start today?"

In response to Carrie's question, Charles rolled out a long piece of paper across the end of the kitchen counter. It was the end of a roll of paper that was used to print the publications at Faraday Press. Charles always kept a couple of these paper ends at the summer house. They were great for spreading out on the picnic table when they were eating steamed hard-shell crabs or shrimp.

"What's with the crab paper?" Carrie asked.

"Well, in addition to its value at a crab feast, I decided the paper would be great for creating a timeline. Last night after you went to bed, I started to map out the time between the phone call that Ginny received at your mom's party and the rest of the early morning events."

"What a great idea. Let me look."

Charles moved the kitchen stools out of the way. Then he taped each end of the paper to the counter so it wouldn't roll back up. "Across the top I've listed the time in fifteen-minute increments starting at midnight, and down the left-hand side I've listed all the players who were at the party or at the Barn, or who saw Norty while he was wandering around looking for Ginny. I started by filling in the time for you and me and Norty. Then I added the other people at your parents' party or at the Barn. I also put a star next to anyone who bought a scarf from Donna."

"Charles, this is wonderful. By figuring out where everyone was at a certain time we can determine who has a gap in their story. Whom do you want to begin with? I'd like to begin with Chief Engler."

"Okay, let's get Engler out of the way. We know he was doing the rounds at several parties and ended up at the Barn. We also know he was there at the same time Norty was there." Charles found his name on the chart and circled the time when Norty saw him. He wrote the word Barn under 2:15 a.m.

"I knew it, and this chart places him at the scene of the murder at the right time."

"Carrie, I don't know how to tell you this, but Norty has given Engler his alibi. Since he was already in the restaurant when Norty saw him seated at a table, laughing with a group of friends, he couldn't have been on the beach with Ginny. Remember, we've narrowed the murder down to between two and two forty-five, when Norty found the body."

"I hear what you're saying, but I'm going to think about how Engler could have managed it. In the meantime, let's go on to the next person."

"Norty said he saw the Buckleys. He also spoke to Otto."

"Do we eliminate both of those people?"

"Actually, we can eliminate the Buckleys. No scarf and no motive. But Otto—"

"You think Otto is a suspect?" Carrie said with disbelief.

"Remember what Norty said. Otto came down from upstairs when it got busy. What's to say he didn't come in from the beach?"

"But we accounted for his scarves," Carrie said.

"Haven't you ever heard of a baker's dozen? Buy twelve get another one free," Charles answered.

"But what's the motive? You're suggesting Otto was in love with Ginny, and she threatened to tell Nick? I don't buy it."

"I don't buy it either. All I'm saying is that according to the timeline, there's a gap for Otto."

"All right let's keep going. Who's next?"

"The Hansons," Charles said.

"Okay, Norty said he talked to the younger Hansons for a few minutes. According to Donna, Jennifer bought a scarf. Could Jeff have gone to the beach?"

"Jeff is too young to be the older man. Plus they were eating at the time of the murder," Charles said.

"All right, cross them off. Next is Josh the bartender. He served Norty a beer. No motive, no scarf. And he couldn't have left the bar for any length of time without being noticed."

Charles drew a line through the bartender's name.

"Norty also mentioned that the party was breaking up at the Habers' while he was walking to the Barn. I guess Mr. Haber could have run across to the beach for a few minutes," Carrie suggested.

"I don't think so. Not enough time if he was standing on his front porch saying good-bye to folks. You know how it is at parties. Once people start to leave, they tend to go in groups, so it's unlikely he could have slipped away at that point," Charles said.

"True, plus Mrs. Haber isn't on the list of women who bought a scarf," Carrie said.

From his chart, Charles read several more names that they were able to eliminate.

"Okay, who's left?" Carrie said.

"Only the Silvas and the Watfords," Charles said. "The Silvas are a total blank. Sally said they were having breakfast with them, but they hadn't arrived when Norty was there. I'll put a question mark next to their name, even though we know Mrs. Silva isn't on the scarf list."

"That's the whole group because the Watfords, like Engler, were sitting in the Barn at the designated time," Carrie said.

Carrie had no sooner spoken the words that Charles turned and looked at her in disbelief. He knew they both had the reached same revelation.

"Are you thinking what I'm thinking? We can really only account for one Watford," Charles said.

"Wait a minute. Let's think about this. Norty said he saw John coming out of the men's room. So even though Sally was sitting alone, John was there."

"Actually, Norty said he saw John coming down the hallway from the men's room. If I remember correctly, there's another door to the outside from that hallway that leads to the back parking lot. And look at the timeline from when Norty arrived, talked to Otto, said hello to Sally, ordered, and drank a beer at the bar. More than twenty minutes in a men's room because you're feeling sick? If you're that sick you would want to get home and go to bed. Not eat a meal."

"Let me look at that." Charles moved to one side so Carrie could look at the chart more closely. "Is it possible John Watford is our killer?" Carrie asked.

"I don't know. Other than Otto, he's the one person with a gap in his timeline. He was at the Barn but not on the floor. Instead he's supposedly in the men's room located next to a door that leads outside."

"He knows his wife, Sally, is probably table-hopping and chatting with everyone. I'll bet she wasn't even aware how long John was gone."

"He certainly fits the profile. Gray hair, older, married," Charles added.

"John also had access to a scarf since his wife bought two. He probably asked his wife to get something for a secret Santa gift at his office. Now what do we do?" Carrie asked.

"Call Norty at your mom's and tell him we're coming over," Charles said, rolling up the crab paper. "Let's take our chart and see what they think about our discovery."

40

"Hello, Norton?"

"Yes, this is Norton."

"Norton, I got your cell phone number from John. I thought this was the best way to reach you. This is Mrs. Watford, Sally Watford—Junie's mother."

"Oh yes, Mrs. Watford. What can I do for you?"

"Norton, John and I are very sorry about Ginny's death. Of course even more disturbed to learn of the trouble you're having with the police. We think that you being treated as a prime suspect is just ridiculous."

"Thank you, Mrs. Watford."

"Please, Norton, call me Sally. Everyone does."

"How can I help you…Sally?" *Just another nosy neighbor calling to get details of my arrest,* Norty thought. He tried to remain polite as he answered, "Unfortunately, because I'm under suspicion of Ginny's murder, I'm not able to discuss any details of the case with you."

"What? Oh, of course you can't. I didn't call to get details about the case. I called because I've something to help you with your defense."

"You do? How do you—I mean, I don't understand how you could help."

"Let me explain. I don't know whether you remember. John and I were eating at the Barn the night that Ginny was killed."

"Yes, I remember. I briefly spoke with you."

"That's right, you did. Anyway, I saw something. It didn't seem so unusual at the time. But the more I thought about it, the more I realized what I saw could be linked to the murder."

"What did you see?" Norton couldn't hide his excitement.

"It's not so much what I saw, but whom I saw."

"Whom did you see?" Norton kept his voice even as he tried to pry meaningful sentences from Sally.

"Norton, I don't want you to get your hopes up until we talk. I don't want to say anything more on the phone. If I'm right, this person has killed twice. I need to be careful."

"I understand your concerns. However, the more you share, the more it minimizes your personal danger. Won't you tell me what you know?"

"Of course I will. But not by phone," Sally said.

"I understand. Sally, where can we meet? Should I drive over to your house?"

"A face-to-face meeting would be best. Let's see, I want a place that's private and secure, but not my home. I don't want a trail of reporters following you here. Somewhere out of the public eye—"

Norton could tell she was trying to think of a place. "How about the high school parking lot or one at the back of a shopping center," Norton suggested.

"Now, wait. Let me think." She paused. "I know. How about under the boardwalk at Tenth Avenue? That's the section of the street where we can park our cars under the boards. We can't be seen from the cars passing by or any people strolling on the boardwalk above us."

"That's fine. I know where that is. What time?"

"How about four o'clock? That's in thirty minutes. Can you make it that fast?"

"Yes, but I'll have to hurry. If I'm a minute or two late, please don't leave. I'm definitely coming," Norton said.

"Oh, and Norton, please don't tell anyone else. And please make sure you're not followed by a trail of reporters. I'm very nervous about all this. If I see other cars approaching, I'll leave."

"I understand. I won't tell anyone," Norton said. Norton thought for a minute about ignoring Sally and leaving a note for his father. But there really wasn't time. If he got there ahead of Sally, he would call Carrie and Charles and tell them.

He grabbed his jacket and went out through the basement door. He had the foresight to park his car on the street behind his parents' house. He could leave through the back without tipping off the reporters who were camped in their front yard. He slipped along the garage wall and then through an opening in the hedge into the neighbor's backyard. Within moments he was in his car and heading to the Pear Cove boardwalk. His constant checks in the rearview mirror revealed he wasn't followed.

He wondered who Sally Watford had seen the night of Ginny's murder. There were so many possibilities.

41

"Everything seems so crystal clear now and makes such perfect sense. Why didn't we see that John Watford was a prime suspect before?" Carrie asked.

"Now, don't be too critical. There's always that one last puzzle piece that solves the case and puts everything into perspective," Charles said as he made the turn onto the main road. "Besides, you should be pleased with your original profile of the murderer. You were right on the money! As I remember, you said it would be a married man who wouldn't want his affair known."

"True, but I also said I thought he was a summer settler and John is a year-rounder. You were correct when you said we should expand our pool of suspects."

"That's why we make such a great detective team. It's working together and playing off each other that led to the solution of our previous two cases." Charles reached over and patted his wife's hand.

"I bet if we went back and tracked Ginny's pattern of behavior, we would find John nearby. It also explains our theory about the murder. Ginny saw the new medical system programs as a way to have a new life with John. John may have viewed it as only a business partnership," Carrie said.

"Exactly! John gives Ginny the scarf. She knows it's an inexpensive gift from a catalog from talking to your mother. She loses her temper. She starts to yell. Maybe even hits John. He panics, knowing his wife is sitting at a table in the Barn, waiting for him to come back from the men's room. He certainly didn't want a scene on the beach that would attract attention," Charles said.

"What about Tom? What do you think Tom had on John? Maybe he saw him come in from the beach after the murder?"

"Possibly," Charles answered her. "But I think it started with that New Year's Eve phone call to Ginny. Tom eventually figured out it was John's voice. He may have even seen John go outside and use his cell phone."

"I'm glad you reminded me about cell phones. In my mind I was eliminating anyone who attended my parents' party. Why didn't John just go up and whisper in Ginny's ear to meet him somewhere?" Carrie said.

"Maybe it was the fear of being seen or overheard." Charles eased the car to a halt at a red light and then said, "It's a shame John killed Tom. He might have found a sympathetic jury that felt Ginny's death was provoked. But with the premeditated murder of Tom, I'm afraid John is going to prison for a long time. And poor Sally. I wonder how she's going to handle all this." Charles realized Carrie hadn't responded to his comment.

"Carrie, I've lost you to your own thoughts again. You have to share."

"Charles, I was just thinking about Sally. Maybe that's what has been bothering me. John and Sally have always seemed so inseparable. In fact I'd classify Sally as the stronger personality of the two. I can't imagine John was able to slip away and meet Ginny without Sally becoming suspicious."

"Maybe because of Sally's strong personality John needed an outside diversion. Maybe his concern about Ginny getting too serious was growing because of his fear of getting caught," Charles said. Carrie didn't get a chance to answer. "Hey isn't that your brother going the other way?"

Carrie spun quickly and looked at the car passing on the other side of the highway. "It's him. Only Norty has that funny blue stripe on his car. When I called Mom she thought Norty was at the house."

"Maybe Caroline didn't get a chance to tell Norton we were coming over. He shouldn't be speeding like that. If the police stop him, Engler will probably arrest him for trying to leave town. Where do you think he's going?"

"It looks like he's heading for the beach area. He's making a right on Wildwood," Carrie said, straining her neck to follow the car. "Charles, don't ask me why, but I think we should follow him. Call it sister's intuition, but I've a funny feeling that something important caused Norty to leave the safety of our parents' house."

As the light changed, Charles waited for the car on his left to move forward. Then he swung into the left lane and made a wide U-turn across the highway. Charles's sharp turn and the speed caused Carrie to slide into the passenger door.

"Hey!" Carrie yelled.

"Sorry, darling, but you said not to lose him." Charles also made a right on Wildwood, but Norton was already several blocks in front of them. Charles looked in his rearview mirror and saw a police cruiser two cars behind him. The light on the corner changed to yellow, and Charles slowed to a stop.

"Why didn't you run the light? You could have made it. Now we're going to lose Norton."

"We've got to cool it. There's a lovely blue-and-white car behind me that would run the light with me. Then stop me for the presentation of a ticket. As much as the red light will delay us, getting stopped for a ticket would delay us more."

"Do you think the policeman saw that U-turn you made?" Carrie asked.

"No, he missed my exotic turn. He wasn't behind us until after Lighthouse Drive."

The light changed, and Charles proceeded through the intersection. Two streets later, Charles made another right turn. Charles checked his rearview mirror and saw that the police car continued on Wildwood.

"Did you turn onto Ocean Highway to lose the copper, or did you spot Norty?"

"Neither. I turned here to head to the beach. I assume that's where Norton was going, since there's not much else down this way," Charles said.

Charles saw Carrie lean forward in her seat, straining to spot Norty's car, and said "I hope we can find him before—"

42

At the far end of the Pear Cove boardwalk, the biggest attraction was fishing. The boardwalk had been extended, and a long fishing pier was added perpendicular to the boards, jutting out several hundred yards over the water. In the middle of the pier was a locked gate. It restricted everyone but members of the private Angler's Club from fishing off the end of the pier. Few visitors traveled this far down the boards. There were no shops or fancy eateries to attract them.

The extended boardwalk had been built atop a large retaining wall that created spaces for cars to park underneath. Steps and ramps located at the beginning of each street allowed the fishermen to get their favorite fishing spot along the boardwalk. Access to this section of the beach was by way of a narrow road referred to as Boardwalk Alley. During peak season, parking under the boards was by permit only. However, off-season parking permits weren't required.

Norton turned onto Division Street, the smaller of the two roads that led to the water. At this time of year, Division Street was the less traveled road and attracted fewer police cars.

At the end of the inlet, the motels and tourist attractions began to thin. When Norton reached Third Avenue he made a right off Division Street down Boardwalk Alley. He drove six blocks and then slowed down at Ninth Street. Norton pulled his car into a space near one of the steps leading up to the boards at Tenth Avenue. Between the pilings and the retaining walls, it was difficult to see if any other cars were parked in the area.

Norton bounded up the steps to the top of the walk. He saw no one. He walked several blocks beyond Tenth Avenue toward the fishing pier. There was a small cottage that marked the beginning of the private pier for the Angler's Club. There were no signs of Sally or anyone else. It was too cold and windy on this late January afternoon for anyone to be out on the pier fishing.

Norton walked back toward the block where he had parked. He looked at his watch. It was just four o'clock. He decided to call Carrie and let her know what he was doing. He had just dialed the number when he heard a faint voice. Sally Watford was standing by the steps two blocks away near Seventh Street. She was waving her arms and motioning for him to join her.

Without thinking, Norton placed his phone with the open line back in his pocket as he headed down the boards to Sally.

~

Charles slowed the car to almost a stop, as he scoured the streets looking for Norton's car.

"Where could he have gone? He wasn't that far in front of us," Carrie said.

"I guess there are two possibilities. One, he was simply out for a ride. As we were coming down Ocean Highway, he was on Division Street heading home. Two, he stopped and parked."

"I don't think he was out for a ride. He hasn't been leaving the house since the second murder. Let's assumed he stopped, but where? At this time of year almost nothing is open," Carrie said.

"If anything is open, it will be for the fishermen. Let's go to the very end where the fishing boats are docked and come back using Boardwalk Alley," Charles said.

"Sounds like the only logical choice."

Charles headed the car along Division Street. When he reached the end, he spotted an open tavern called the Last Pier. Charles entered the parking lot and cruised around. They looked for Norton's car, but it wasn't there. A couple of fishermen smoking outside the building eyed the couple as they drove past.

"I don't see Norty's car," Charles said.

As Charles left the parking lot, Carrie's phone rang. She took her phone from her handbag and looked at the display.

"Charles, it's Norty. "Hello, Norty, where are you? We passed you on the highway. Norty...Norty?"

"What's the matter?" Charles asked.

"The line is open, but he's not answering. Should I call him back?"

"No, don't hang up! Place the phone in the dashboard holder and put the phone on mute so we can't be heard. If Norton called you, there may be something he wants us to hear."

It was only a moment before Carrie and Charles were able to hear conversation through the phone.

"Norton, I'm so glad you came. Let's go down to my car, where no one will see us," Sally said.

"Look, there's no one around up here. I'd just as soon make this quick. Then we both can get back to our cars."

"I agree, but I'm cold. I was thinking we could sit and talk in my car, where it's warm."

Norton followed along obediently as Sally descended the steps. They were almost to the bottom step when Norton felt something sharp in his back. Then he heard John Watford's voice.

"No need to turn around, Norty boy. What you're feeling in your back is a gun. Keep walking."

"Hey, what's going on, John? What's this all about?"

~

"Charles, what are we going to do? Norton is with the Watfords!"

Charles turned onto Boardwalk Alley and slowed to the car to a crawl.

"Why are you slowing down? Go faster."

"Carrie, we need to find Norton's car so we have an idea where he is."

Charles was just passing Tenth Avenue when Carrie yelled, "There, there's his car."

Charles stopped the car, backed up, and pulled in next to Norton's car under the boardwalk.

"I wonder where he is. There are no stores or shops, and all of the houses we passed appear to be closed for the season," Charles said.

"Maybe they're up on the boardwalk. Let's go!" Carrie said.

They left the car and ran up the steps to the boards. They looked in both directions but saw no one.

"I know it's cold, but let's walk down a few blocks," Charles said.

Charles pulled Carrie close to him, and they moved quickly down the boardwalk toward Seventh Street. They heard only the sounds of the waves. Even with the sound of the waves, the loneliness of the walk made for an eerie silence. As they approached Seventh Street, Charles stopped and stood still.

"What is it, Charles?"

"I thought I heard something. Listen!"

Carrie listened and then said, "It sounds like voices. But I can't make out the words or the direction."

"Let's move up the boardwalk a little farther, but let's move over toward the water away from the street side," Charles whispered. "Whatever we're hearing must be below us, because there's no one up here." The couple was just a few steps from the ramp that led down to Seventh Street.

"Charles, that's Norton's voice," Carrie whispered as she started to move toward the down ramp. Charles grabbed her coat and pulled her back toward him. At the same time with his finger to his lips, he indicated she should be quiet.

It took only a moment of listening to the conversation to understand what was going on beneath them. Charles moved Carrie away from the ramp to the other side of the boards.

"Did you grab your cell phone? Mine is at home, charging."

"No, I left it sitting on the dashboard."

"You need to get to the phone and call the police. Call Detective Hilton at the Pear Cove station. Then also call the state police in case Engler tries to stop Hilton from coming." Charles reached into his pocket and gave Carrie his keys and some change.

"What's the coin for?"

"It's in case you see a pay phone before you get to the car. After you make the call, stay in the car and wait for me," Charles said.

"What are you going to do?"

"I hope nothing before the police come. But if things turn serious, I'll create a diversion to buy some time. Now hurry, but don't run. I don't want them to hear your footsteps hitting the boards."

Charles watched as Carrie took off, walking as fast as she could. He maintained his position above the Watfords and Norton, listening to the conversation. The next time he looked up, Carrie was no longer on the boardwalk.

43

"Sally and I have decided to tie up some loose ends. You, Norty, are the last little thread."

"Look, there's no need for the gun, John. I understand. You two think that I might be a murderer and you have to protect yourselves. Believe me, I had nothing to do with Ginny's death."

Sally joined the men under the pier. "Oh, we do believe you. We know you're not the murderer, because we know who is. You see, John killed Ginny!"

"John!" Even though he had been told not to, Norton turned and faced John. "What possible reason did you have to kill Ginny?"

Charles knew what John meant by tying up loose ends. John meant to murder Norton, too. He hoped Norton would stall for time while he thought up a contingency plan.

"My sister thinks Ginny was having an affair with the man who murdered her. Were you having an affair with Ginny?" Norton asked.

"John, let's get this over with. No more talk," urged Sally.

"It doesn't hurt at this point for the boy to know the facts before he departs. I mean, I know it's a shock to hear that his girlfriend preferred me over him. Ginny did love me, you know."

"Then how could...why would you kill her?" Norton asked.

"As I said, Ginny loved me. I'm afraid I didn't feel the same about her. I love my wife. I wanted to establish a working partnership with Ginny, not marry her. You see, my interest in Ginny was strictly survival."

"Survival? I don't understand."

"John, let's get going. The longer we're here, the greater the chance someone will spot us," Sally said.

Charles knew Sally was nervous about being seen, but unfortunately there was no one else around.

"Don't worry. We can't be seen under the boards, and no one will tie the car we rented to us even if it's seen. Now, as I was saying, my interest in Ginny was strictly survival. Your newly formed company is working on the same medical software that I planned on developing. I don't have to tell you that the company that gets to market first with this new system is the winner in terms of monetary rewards," John said.

"But, John, you're part of what we're doing. You have the contract for all the marketing and advertising, which would be very lucrative for you," Norton said.

"You're comparing thousands to millions. I can't tell you how upset I was to discover Kevin was the designer. When he worked for me he produced nothing other than a program to track our jobs. We were just starting to discuss doing a medical program in light of all the changes in that field. Suddenly he ups and leaves. The next thing I hear, he's in charge of designing a whole medical system. You can't tell me he didn't take the idea for the medical program with him. My program!"

"I can absolutely guarantee you that Kevin didn't bring your software idea with him. I'm the one who developed the concept for our company. But I'm not good with difficult code. That's why we hired Kevin. He's an expert in this area. I gave Kevin all the parameters of what I wanted, and he's managing the team that's writing the specific code. When he came to us he said there was nothing new on the horizon at your company," Norty said.

"I briefly mentioned the program. I just hadn't shared all my plans with him."

"All right, let's assume you had the same idea. How did Ginny get involved with you?" Norty asked.

"Ginny and I just happened to meet one night in the bar at the Barn months ago. We started chatting. You know, about life, people we know, and what we have in common. She said that you were working a lot of late hours with Kevin. I mentioned that Kevin used to work for me and asked what he was doing at the new company. She told me he was working on programs for the new medical system. The medical system would introduce the new company. That's when I realized that my program idea had been stolen by Kevin. He probably thought it would impress his new bosses to come up with a new idea the minute he arrived," John said.

"Kevin never mentioned anything about your concept."

Good, Charles thought. *Keep John talking.*

John continued, "Just because Kevin didn't say anything, it doesn't mean it wasn't my idea. I needed to find out more about what Kevin was developing. I called Ginny and asked her to meet me for a drink. Then we started seeing each other regularly. It turned out she was enjoying our little meetings more than I realized. To impress me, she found out more and more about the programming code. Then I challenged her to see if she could replicate a smaller program that could hit the streets quickly to launch our new company. It's a shame she got so serious about our personal relationship. In another couple of weeks, our software version will be ready."

"I doubt if you're going to be able to launch your program. You see, Kevin became aware that Ginny was asking some very specific questions about program code. He suspected she might be trying to create her own version, so he started feeding her information that wasn't quite correct. If she ever got the program up and running, after several entries the program would go into an endless loop and crash," Norty said.

"What! You're lying! Why would Kevin do that to the boss's daughter?"

"Kevin has known Ginny for years. He figured she was trying to prove how capable she was in duplicating the program. We figured that as we neared the end of the project, Ginny would go to her father and show how she got the program working first. Even though she was family, I thought for security reasons someone outside the team shouldn't be given access. I approved

Kevin feeding her incorrect information. Now I see that decision was correct."

"John, enough is enough. Let's end this," Sally said. "Shoot him."

Charles was waiting patiently until he heard Sally Watford say, "Let's end this." He looked around for something to create a diversion. He thought of starting a fire in a trash can, but the one nearest to him was empty. Then he heard John start to talk again. He waited, hoping that Carrie and the police would arrive before it was necessary for him to do anything.

"Wait a minute! I have to think. What are we going to do about the possibility that the program is corrupted?"

"That's not the issue. What are we going to do about Norton? We certainly can't let him go, regardless of an error in the program."

"Sally, we did all this to save our company. If the new medical program doesn't work, the awful things we've done become meaningless. What information did Kevin feed Ginny?"

"Right, John. You think I'm going to tell you? Although maybe we can work something out. That is, of course, if you don't kill me," Norty said.

"John, now that you know there's a bug in the program, your team can work it out. Give me the gun, John," Sally demanded.

When Sally said, "Give me the gun," Charles knew it was time to act.

Charles picked up the trash can drum and raised it above his head, starting down the ramp at full speed. Sally's back was turned to him, and she didn't see him approach nor hear him until it was too late. Charles lowered the drum to cover his chest and ran past Sally, knocking her to the ground. John got off a shot, but Charles didn't stop.

Charles heard the sound of a bullet hitting the edge of the metal drum and then the thud as the drum smacked into John. Charles saw the gun fly into the air as he fell forward onto John with the drum.

"What the hell—" were the only words John was able to utter.

Charles rolled quickly off John to find the gun. As if in slow motion, the group watched as the gun slowly descended.

"John, get the gun. Don't let Charles get it," Sally screamed as she got back on her feet.

But Sally's request was too late. Charles watched as the gun landed in Norton's outstretched hand. Norton turned the gun on the couple.

Charles moved next to Norton. He heard the sound of approaching sirens. He saw Carrie barreling down the alley in their car behind the flashing lights of the police cars.

Sally started to rush toward Norton and the gun, but Charles grabbed her and spun her around, pinning her arms behind her.

"Sally, no more! It's over!"

44

It was two days since the Watfords had been arrested and John was charged with the murders of Ginny and Tom. The Faraday and Kingsford families had gathered for the last time this holiday season for a family dinner. Tomorrow Carrie and Charles returned to Tri-City and their normal lives.

They were enjoying after-dinner coffee while watching the evening news. Carrie snuggled against Charles. Their favorite police chief was once again in front of the news cameras. He was trying one more time to elevate his role, as he explained the resolution to the Ginny Ellwood murder case. However, Carrie knew this time the news media wasn't buying it. They were barely allowing Engler to respond to one question before they threw another one at him.

"Chief Engler, aren't you concerned that it took two private citizens—not the police department—to figure out the solution to this case?"

"It was a mere coincidence that we had two citizens at the final confrontation with the murderers. They just happened to be in the right place, or perhaps I should say the wrong place, at that moment in time," Engler said, maintaining his smile for the camera. "Again, I want to emphasize that I had already determined the Watfords were the most likely suspects, and my men were closing in on them."

He was interrupted by another question. "Chief Engler wasn't your investigation focusing on Norton Kingsford? And it was only through the investigative efforts of Mr. Kingsford's sister and brother-in-law, the Faradays, that John Watford was uncovered as the murderer?"

"Please remember that Norton Kingsford was not in custody. Most of you are not aware that the Faradays and this department were in close contact throughout the investigation. In fact, only this week I had a luncheon meeting with the Faradays. We met at my family's restaurant, the Seafood Cottage, where we shared information about the case."

Carrie jumped up from her chair. "I can't believe this guy! Sharing information, my foot!"

"Sit down, dear, or you'll miss the rest of this fantasy," Charles said.

"Can you verify it was the Faradays who placed the emergency call to the police alerting them to the capture of the murderer?" another reporter asked.

"As I mentioned, it was a lucky break that the Faradays ran into the Watfords as we were closing in. I'm sorry, that will have to be the last question for now. I'm scheduled to meet with the district attorney to lay out our case. I'll schedule additional news conferences as more details become available."

Carrie grabbed the remote control and silenced Engler and the television. "You gotta love this guy. He's using our brief encounter at his restaurant—where, I might add, he reminded us to stay out of his investigation—as an example of our working together."

"Love isn't the word I would use," Charles said.

"It was also rather clever the way he got in a plug for his family's restaurant," Caroline added.

"But you know, in many ways we were just as bad as Engler," Carrie suggested.

"You could never be as bad as that pompous politician," her father said. "Besides, you don't have a restaurant to plug."

Carrie kissed the top of her father's head and said, "Thank you, Daddy, for the compliment, I think. But I'm afraid in some ways we were as blind as Engler. He was so sure that Norton had committed the crime that he was blinded to any other evidence. On the other hand, I think I wanted Engler to be the culprit. That's why it took us longer to zero in on John."

"I think you're being a little too critical, Carrie. We really didn't have all the puzzle pieces until the end. Plus, I think initially we were thrown off by your New Year's Eve party, Caroline," Charles said.

"Our party?" Caroline replied.

"Yes, your party. You see, for a long time we held on to the belief that anyone at the party couldn't have called Ginny. We should have realized sooner that in this day and age the call could have been made from a cell phone. We initially eliminated people at the party."

"I see, but there must have been more clues than the phone call. What else did you discover?" Harry asked.

"I guess the first clue was from Norton," Charles said.

"Me?" Norton said, surprised. "I actually had a clue to this case?"

"Yes, you did. You gave me a clue when you and I were talking on the deck. You told me you saw Sally in the bar at the Barn, but not John."

"That's right," Norton said. "I'm having a pleasant conversation with Sally in the Barn and extending my wishes that her husband feels better. In the meantime, he's on the beach killing Ginny."

"Go on, you two. It's fascinating how you take little pieces and put everything together," Caroline said.

"Another clue we picked up at your office, Dad. However, we really didn't relate it to John until the very end. It was Ginny's unusual interest in the development of the new Kingwood Medical Intel System. Why was she so interested in Kevin's computer programming? Kevin felt that for someone who never cared about the company, she was showing this inexplicable interest."

"You know, I still can't believe the motivation behind the killings was a computer program," Harry said.

"When I was under the boardwalk and John told me he was certain that Kevin had stolen the idea, I mean, there was a look in his eyes I can't explain," Norton added.

"It's such foolishness. John's company implements software programs and gets them to the marketplace. They aren't known for program development. And what's really sad, the deal Randolph and I struck with John's firm for the marketing launch would have made him a fortune. Of course, that's assuming the program takes off. We were even going to give him a percentage of the profits based on the sales he generated," Harry said.

"I think money was a problem. Sally spent a lot of money refurbishing the house here in Pear Cove. They have a condo in Tri-City, a couple of the latest cars, and a daughter in college, just to mention a few items. I'm sure when the police dig deeper into their financial affairs, they'll find more debt. As money became tighter, the more John imagined all the money the new company would make from the program. He wanted it all, not just a percentage," Charles said.

They all sat in silence for a moment, and then Caroline asked, "What else?"

"We already told you about the ring. However, the break in the case was due to the brilliance of my husband and his crab paper," Carrie said. "I'll be back in a minute."

Carrie left and went out to the car to grab the crab paper, which was still in the backseat.

She was just returning when she heard her father ask, "Charles, what's crab paper?"

"I'll explain," Carrie said as she returned with the roll of paper. "Charles used some of the roll of paper we put on the table when we're eating crabs—thus the name crab paper. Charles created a timeline of everyone's movements the night of Ginny's murder. Once we listed all the people involved, it didn't take long to spot that John was missing for about twenty minutes during the time of the murder."

Everyone gathered around as Carrie unrolled the paper on the cocktail table. She pointed out the different names and where everyone was on New Year's Eve. Carrie finished the demonstration by circling the missing block of time for John.

"At the Barn, Sally told Norton that John wasn't feeling well and had gone to the men's room. It wasn't until Norton was ready to leave that he saw John coming down the hallway from the men's room. Between your arrival and the time when you actually saw John, he was away for at least twenty minutes. That was more than enough time to meet and kill Ginny," Charles said.

"But you know, Charles, that's not conclusive. John could have been in the men's room," Norty said.

"True, but think about it. A man who's so sick that he spends that much time in the men's room wouldn't return and eat more food with his wife and friends. He'd want to go home and curl up in bed."

"You're right, Charles. When Harry is sick, even mildly sick, he wants to get right home and let me take care of him," Caroline said with a smile and a wink.

"All right, Caroline. They don't want to hear about me."

Carrie enjoyed the friendly teasing between her mother and father. It meant life was returning to normal.

"I'm still not sure I understand when Sally Watford knew about her husband's affair with Ginny and how it went so wrong," Norton said.

"I think Sally knew about the affair from the beginning," Carrie said.

"Really, Carrie? I find it hard to believe that any wife would let her husband have an affair. I certainly wouldn't let Harry go off with another woman with my blessings."

"Caroline, darling, you won't let me even go to the golf course without your blessings. And I love you for it," Harry said.

"For Sally, it wasn't supposed to be an affair. It was supposed to be a plot to get the new system design away from your company," Charles said. "John convinced her that without the software...well, it would be the end of his business and of the lifestyle they enjoyed."

"The two of them figured out the best way to find out company secrets was to use Ginny. John already knew Ginny from casual meetings at various social functions. Early in the summer he started to talk with Ginny and convinced her to help," Carrie added.

"John probably challenged Ginny that she couldn't replicate the program. I'm sure she rose to the challenge to prove she could do it," Norton said.

"Or he might have convinced her that Kevin had stolen the program when he left his company and all he wanted to do was check it out. In any case, Ginny was John's spy. His plan was working just as he'd anticipated. However, there was one thing John didn't expect," Charles said, looking at Norton.

"It's all right, Charles. I knew something had gone wrong with our relationship. I just didn't know what or who it was," Norton said.

Carrie reached over and touched her brother's arm.

"Go ahead, Charles, go ahead," Harry said impatiently.

"Ginny fell in love with John…or thought she had. Perhaps John also encouraged the relationship to get more information. However, what he couldn't handle was Ginny's gift," Charles said.

"How could a ring cause a murder?" Caroline asked.

"It's not the ring, but what the ring stood for. Ginny thought this was a serious relationship. Based on Fred's information, she expected to marry John. John goes to the meeting to make sure Ginny is progressing with the program development. Ginny goes hoping that after she gives John the ring he'll finally tell his wife about them. When he doesn't agree, Ginny may have realized John's true motive."

"I can guess what happened next," Norton said. "Knowing Ginny, I think she became emotional and started to yell. When she got emotional, no one could reason with her. You needed to just walk away."

"And John didn't walk away," Caroline whispered. "What will happen to John and Sally now?"

"Simpson found out from one of his contacts in the DA's office that John completely broke down. Apparently the gravity of what he did finally hit him. He's feeling remorse," Charles said.

"Yeah, he's showing remorse now that he's been caught," Norton said. "He certainly showed no remorse when he was about to murder me."

"I agree. Not to mention he's been busy working a deal. He admitted to both murders in exchange for lesser charges against Sally. He claims Sally knew nothing about the murders until after they happened. He will enter a guilty plea with no jury trial in the hopes of getting a lighter sentence," Charles said.

"I don't know about that," Carrie said.

"You don't know about what, dear? You don't think he should plead guilty?" Harry asked.

"No, I'm talking about Sally's role in all this. We're treating Sally like the loyal wife who was simply helping her husband. She overspends the family budget and likes vodka in her lemonade, but she's a good person at heart," Carrie said.

"And you disagree?" Caroline asked.

"Yes. You see, I think she's a murderer!" Carrie was aware everyone was staring at her. "And before you ask, I don't have any hard evidence. But I think Sally murdered Tom. After all, poison is a woman's method of murder."

"Now that you mention it, sis, I think I agree with you. When we were under the boards it was Sally who kept urging John to shoot. She was the cold-blooded one."

"Exactly. John murdered Ginny on the spur of the moment because of the situation. On the other hand, Tom's murder was carefully planned. Also remember it was Sally who lured Norton to the boardwalk," Carrie said.

"Unfortunately, without evidence—and as long as John maintains his version—Sally will face the lesser charge," Charles said.

Carrie then directed her attention to her father. "So what happens now with you, Dad? Can you and Randolph put the years of friendship back together?"

"I don't think that was ever in doubt. We decided early on we'd leave the kids alone to work out their own future.

The business was always separate. And things are working out, right, Norton?"

"Yes, they are. Fred Ellwood came over this morning, and we talked. He hoped we could be friends. I told him to hurry and finish his army service so he could come back and help the firm."

"Well then, that takes care of everything," Carrie said.

"Not exactly," Charles said. "I'm still in desperate need of a quiet holiday rest."